THE RUNAWAY

Also by Randy Rawls

Tom Jeffries Series
Thorns on Roses
The Runaway

Beth Bowman Series
Hot Rocks
Best Defense

Ace Edwards Series
Jake's Burn
Joseph's Kidnapping
Jade's Photos
Jingle's Christmas
Jasmine's Fate
Jeb's Deception

THE RUNAWAY

by

Randy Rawls

THE RUNAWAY

Rawls, Randy
The Runaway / Mystery-Thriller / Randy Rawls

ISBN: 978-0-9899904-2-4

DEDICATION

Especially for Tracy and David, my children, with my love.
And for Ronnie, always My Honey. For those who tolerate me and
critique my writing: Sylvia, Earl, Ann, Gregg, Richard, Stephanie,
and Vicki.
For Joanne at *Murder on the Beach Mystery Bookstore*, a friend
to every author.
AND, especially for readers everywhere.

.

THE RUNAWAY

CHAPTER ONE

Tom Jeffries parked his Chrysler convertible well away from the entrance to the Publix Super Market. Door dings, or the lack thereof, were more important to him than a few extra steps. Besides, as he told Abby when she complained, the exercise was good for them.

He flipped his phone open and dialed as he stepped from the car. A smile creased his face when he heard Abby's voice. It happened every time, not something he could control. How could a beautiful, intelligent woman like her be engaged to an old soldier like him?

"Tom. Are you on the way home?"

"Sure am, Sunshine. I'm going into Publix now for the milk. Do we need anything else?"

"No, can't think of anything—unless, of course, you need more crazy stuff to pile on top of your pizza. You're still planning heartburn-city for dinner, aren't you?"

"Sure am, created to the Jeffries' standard. I'll be there soon. Love you."

"Me, you, too," Abby said and clicked off.

As Tom walked along the front of the strip mall, the lights began blinking on in the lessening light. He marveled at the number of storefronts for lease. What had once been a thriving shopping center was now dying—the result of the recession that had gripped the area for years. With few active shops, other than Publix, it would only be a matter of time before grime and crime moved in. By then, recovery would be far more difficult as merchants had to fight to reclaim the turf.

Even the sign towering over the turnoff from Route 441 looked dingy, a sure sign of lack of investment—and interest—by the owners. It was a vicious circle. Stores went out of business, the mall owners lost revenue, the area suffered from poorer upkeep, and new stores were hesitant to move in. The result was a degradation that drew crime, further degrading the area.

The Canberry Mall wasn't a normal stop on Tom's route, but he had seen the Publix and decided to swing in. As good a place as any to pick up milk, although Tom wondered how long the Publix would remain the anchor for a failing mall.

A few minutes later, he exited Publix, swinging a plastic bag holding a gallon of milk, and turned toward his car.

A noise penetrated his thoughts of Abby. He stopped, wondering what he'd heard. Silence. *Probably a cat calling for a mate.*

"Please, please don't hurt me. I'll do it. Just . . . please, not here. It's so dirty." The muddled words sounded like the plea of a desperate female.

Tom looked around, trying to pinpoint the direction of the voice, and saw an alley a few buildings away. Did the voice come from there?

A second voice floated on the evening air, the words too indistinct to understand. But they were male—definitely male—and they were gruff, angry sounding.

Checking the parking lot in both directions, he saw no one. It had to be the alley. Shifting the bag to his left hand, he headed that way.

When he turned the corner, a musty stench assaulted him. Discarded boxes, trashcans, and other debris lay about, leaving a narrow path down the middle. At the end of the alley, two figures moved, back lighted against a rear parking area. He started toward them, and the smell grew worse.

"C'mon girlie. You ain't no virgin, and even if you is, we don't care. Why should we? Shit, you shore ain't got nothing you want to die for. Same as all girls got. Ain't special. All you gotta do is spread for a few minutes, and we'll give you a thrill."

"Yeah, prob'ly ain't never had a real man before," another voice said. "After we finish it'll be as good as it was before. Can't wear 'em out, you know." A sinister cackle echoed along the alley.

Tom heard laughter, two separate tones—one high-pitched, the other guttural. Under that, the faint sounds of sobbing. He listened, separating the voices. Two males, one female. Not a fair match—not fair at all.

He walked toward the sounds, not bothering to be quiet. Seeing a pile of beer cans, he kicked, sending them clanging off a metal trashcan. Rats scurried. Tom never varied his pace—not fast, not slow, just casual.

"Who the hell— Hey, Rocky, looks like we got company. Who you, mister? You want sloppy thirds? Cost you that nice hat you wearing."

"Yeah," Rocky said in a high-pitched voice. "I been wantin' a cowboy hat. That looks like a good'un. Trade you for a piece of this girl."

Tom maintained a steady stride, saying nothing.

The first speaker was big, well over six feet. He also carried a lot of extra bulk. At that distance, Tom couldn't tell if it was blubber or muscle. His cohort was short and thin, underweight even.

"Hey, you dumb or somethin'? You don't say somethin' fast, I'm gonna gut you." The distinctive click of a switchblade accompanied his words as Rocky stepped forward.

Tom smiled. The punk had played true to character.

The lighting in the narrow alley was sufficient for Tom to see the knife waving in a small circle, but not enough to cast shadows. That worked. Less chance of an innocent bystander interfering.

Tom stopped about five feet from the duo. They looked to be in their early twenties, which gave him at least fifteen years on them, and many more years of experience. His years in Special Forces had brought him bigger challenges—much bigger. He risked a glance toward the girl who struggled to become part of the wall.

Jumbo's hand slid into his pocket and a moment later, he waved a switchblade. "This honky ain't smart enough to live. Maybe we ought to whack his dick and leave him here."

"Five inch blades?" Tom said in a quiet voice. "You know they're illegal, don't you? Get you arrested if a cop sees them."

"Huh? Man, you crazy?" Rocky said. "Ain't no po-lice nowhere near here. This is our turf. They don't come here. There's us and there's you—and that nice white thing we 'bout to sample."

Tom glanced at the girl. Her head was down, her hands covering her face. He thought she might be peeking at him.

"Let me see your knives," Tom said. "From here, they look cheap, like something you'd get in a dollar store. Are they real? Will they cut?"

"He's nuts, ain't he, Jumbo?" Rocky said. "You want mine, I'll lend it to you—the whole thing—right through your belly button."

Tom gave them the once-over. Not much. Street trash that should have been swept up a long time ago. They looked more like a Laurel and Hardy than a Rocky and Jumbo. Tom decided the bulk on Jumbo was fat, probably not a muscle anywhere except between his ears.

Jumbo stepped forward, looked Tom up and down, and then examined his blade. "Ain't enough man for me to git my knife dirty on. You take care of him, Rocky. I'll git this nice tasty piece ready." He turned toward the girl, whose hands sprang into a defensive position as she pushed harder against the wall.

Tom shook his head. There was no way to avoid a fight. He'd been in worse, many times over—shootouts with death as the guest of honor. A combination of luck and skill had allowed Tom to walk away each time.

"Okay, fun's over." Tom jerked up his right pants leg and pulled a knife from a calf sheath. It was black with a nine-inch stainless steel blade and a hollow, leather-covered handle capped with a thick metal plate. The front edge was hair-splitting sharp. The back swept upward from the point with a cutting edge, Bowie knife style, for three inches before straightening. The next three inches were a standard saw blade that changed into a hacksaw the rest of the length. "If you boys are interested in knives, you should take a look at mine. I designed it myself. I'll be happy to show it to you. Step on up."

Rocky's eyes locked on Tom's blade, then his. With less confidence, he said, "Ain't important the size of the knife, it's how you use it." He lunged at Tom, who sidestepped, sweeping Rocky's arm away.

As he flew by, Tom slapped him behind the head, and then pirouetted in a fighter's stance, turning sideways to keep both punks in view. Rocky's momentum, with Tom's help, took him several steps away.

"Hot damn, a knife fight," Tom said, forcing excitement into his voice. "It's been two or three weeks since I had a good one. Now, Skinny, you proved you're no competition, so I suggest you get Fatso in here to help. Two on one's still not fair, but there're only the two of you, so seems that's the best odds I can get."

"Bullshit," Rocky said and lunged again.

Tom stepped aside and cracked Rocky's wrist with the haft of his knife. "Not good, not good. Your style is really poor. Best you give up knife fighting before you get hurt." Without taking his eyes off Rocky, Tom said, "Fatso, you'd better get in here. Skinny needs you."

"You mighta broke my arm, you dam' fool," Rocky screamed. "You gonna pay for that." He switched his knife to his left hand, then circled to the right. "Jumbo, you git on that side. This muther's gonna die."

"Nice talk," Tom said, sliding his feet to maintain fighting space between him and Rocky. "You should study more, get a better vocabulary. They say a man's words are a mark of his character. Guess your character is pretty low. Now, do you want to get out of here before your pain is bigger than your mouth?"

Tom feinted toward Rocky, then laughed when Rocky stumbled, jumping back. "You seem a little nervous, Rocky. You sure you're a knife fighter?"

"Jumbo, git over here and git this bastard. I could take him easy if he hadn't hurt my arm."

Tom threw his head back and guffawed. "Sure, fat ass. Get over here and help him. If you don't, when I'm finished carving him up, I'll give you liposuction the hard way, a slice at a time."

"That did it, you som'bitch. Nobody calls me fat and lives." He jumped at Tom, his knife outthrust.

"Bad move," Tom said, knocking the knife aside and slamming the gallon of milk into Jumbo's head.

The plastic jug burst, sending milk cascading over Jumbo's upper body. His blade flew from his hand as he fell on his face, not moving.

Tom toed him with his boot, then shook his head. "Your buddy must have a glass jaw." He took a step toward Rocky, whose eyes had tripled in size. "Down to you and me. Here, I'll fight left-handed." He shifted his knife. "There. Does that make you feel better? We're even now."

Rocky glanced behind him, inching backward. "Man, you double-crazy. You don't know enough to be scared. You—"

His words stopped as Tom grabbed his arm and spun him into the wall. His head made a satisfying crack as it whipped into the concrete block. His eyes rolled up, and he twisted and slid down, settling on his butt before toppling sideways. Blood trickled from the back of his head.

CHAPTER TWO

Tom stood for a moment, looking first at Rocky, then at Jumbo. Satisfied the fight had disappeared from the two, he walked over and picked up their switchblades. He stuck the blades into a crack between two concrete blocks and snapped them off. Throwing the handles down beside Jumbo and Rocky, he said, "Little boys shouldn't play with knives. They might injure themselves."

He turned to the girl, who attempted to scoot farther away. "Easy, miss. I mean you no harm. And," he glanced at the two thugs, "they seem to have lost interest. Nice to see them sleeping so peacefully, isn't it?"

Tom retreated a step, hoping to ease some of the girl's fear. He knelt, taking himself down to her level as she sat against the wall. It worked with children, maybe it would work with her. "I'm one of the good guys—the one on the white horse."

He paused, hoping to see a semblance of a smile. Didn't happen.

"What's your name? Mine's Tom Jeffries. Do you live around here?" As he spoke, he re-sheathed his knife.

Her hands gradually came down from the defensive posture they had assumed. "Uh, Renée. My name's Renée and . . . No, I don't live near here. I was walking by. They grabbed me and dragged me into this alley. They were . . ." She took a deep breath. "They were going to. . ." Her hands went to her face again, and she began to sob.

"I understand," Tom said. "You're safe now. I'll call the police and—"

"No," she exclaimed. "Please don't call the cops. They, uh, uh. Please don't."

7

Tom watched as she struggled to her feet, her back pressed against the wall. She wore a dirty T-shirt and dirtier jeans. From what he could see, filth covered her hands, face, and arms. Her hair looked like it hadn't seen a comb in days. In the shadows, he couldn't judge whether the grime came from the alley, or she'd brought it with her. Her body odor added to the stench of the alley.

"Okay, calm down. I won't call if you don't want me to." He made a point of looking at Jumbo and Rocky. "I suggest we get out of here before they wake up. They'll be in pretty foul moods when they find out I broke their toys. Tell me where you live, and I'll take you home. Of course, I have to get another gallon of milk. Fatso soaked up most of the first one."

Renée stared at him, fear coating her face as she edged away.

Uh-oh, wrong approach, Tom thought. Slow things down. "I understand. With what you've been through, I'd be leery of a strange man myself. Take it easy a moment while I think of something." He walked away and leaned against the opposite wall, rubbing his chin.

A moment later, his head popped up. "I know, how about I call my fiancée? She'll tell you I'm not a bad person." He took out his cell phone and took a couple of steps toward her, holding out the phone.

She flinched and inched away.

"Okay, okay, I'm backing off." He returned to the wall. "I promise. I'm only calling my honey. You'll like her. Her name's Abby. I'll let you talk to her." He made a couple of punches at the keypad and a ringing noise echoed in the alley. "I set it on speaker so you can hear." He held it out in her direction.

The phone rang a second time.

"Tom. Where are you? I thought you'd be home when I got here." The voice showed a bit of exasperation.

Turning the speaker toward him, but keeping the phone at arm's-length, he said in a loud voice, "Sorry, Sunshine, but I got sidetracked. I picked up the milk, but it got spilt."

"Why don't I like the sound of that? What happened? Are you in trouble again?"

Tom held his hand over the microphone and whispered toward Renée, "She's always so protective of me." Into the phone, he said, "Nothing serious. A couple of punks had the bad luck to cross my path. But that's not why I called?"

"Oh, yeah?" Suspicion almost dripped from the phone.

"There's a young lady here—says her name is Renée—who needs someone to comfort her. I'd like to bring her to your house, but she doesn't trust me. She can hear us, so I'd like for you to assure her I'm just a harmless teddy bear."

"Uh-huh, and I'm a rock star. Let me talk to her."

"She's all yours." Tom held the phone out to Renée, but didn't move from the wall.

She studied it and him as if both might be radioactive. Seconds ticked by.

"Hello, hello," Abby said. "Tom, are you still there? Where's the girl?"

"One minute," Tom said toward the phone. "She's still thinking about it."

Abby said, "Renée, talk to me. Tom's no threat to anyone. Well, almost no one."

Renée took the phone, staying as far from Tom as she could. "Hello."

"Oh, there you are. My name is Abby Archer. You've met my boyfriend, Tom Jeffries. He looks scary, but he's really a nice guy, a real cream puff—but don't tell him I said that. He likes to act tough. What happened to you?"

Renée looked at Tom, who smiled, then at Rocky and Jumbo. "They tried to rape me." Tears started as she broke. She acted more like a little girl than someone capable of being raped. "He, he stopped them. He hurt them bad. They're both unconscious. I don't know what to do. I'm scared."

She looked so pathetic Tom wanted to fold her into his arms, but knew he had to stay put. One wrong move and she'd bolt.

"Yeah, that'd be my Tom," Abby said. "He tends to overreact when nasty people do what they do best. I understand how you feel. I'm sorry you got mixed up with such trash. I'm glad Tom happened along, though. How old are you?"

9

Renée sniffled and wiped a dirty wrist under her nose. "Uh . . . eighteen. I'm eighteen, old enough for everything except drinking." She said it as if she'd practiced the line exactly that way. She squared her shoulders and looked at Tom.

Tom was careful to show no reaction, but he figured that age was a stretch.

"No problem. If you say you're eighteen, I believe you. Look, I have an idea. When Tom gets home, we're going to have a simple dinner. A salad and pizza. It sounds like you need to get away from where you are. Why don't you eat with us? I don't promise you a four-star meal, but we enjoy what we have—and we laugh a lot."

Renée's eyes darted around the alley. "I can't. I mean . . . Uh, I have to be somewhere. What time is it?"

"Honey, it's seven-thirty," Abby said in a soothing voice. "Why don't you come with Tom? Do you have a place to stay tonight? I have an extra room. You can camp in with me, then go wherever you need tomorrow."

"I . . . uh . . . You won't make me go home, will you?"

"No," Abby said. "I promise dinner, a bed, and breakfast—that's all. After that, you're on your own."

"Uh . . . well . . . I guess I could go to your house. Do you have a shower? I feel so dirty."

"Yes, and lots of soap," Tom said, "and a washer to clean your clothes."

CHAPTER THREE

Abby laid the cordless phone on the kitchen counter, her forehead creased in a frown. She opened the refrigerator, grabbed a package of mixed lettuce, and set it beside a carton of cherry tomatoes and a cucumber. After taking off her engagement ring, she pulled shreds out of the bag and mumbled, "What did he mean, two punks crossed his path?"

She sighed, hoping for the best, but knowing how violent Tom could be, she worried. He had no patience with the vermin who walked upright and threatened women. She'd met him through such a situation. He eliminated a gang who violated and murdered the stepdaughter of his best friend, Charlie Rogers. She looked at the phone as if it held the answer to the questions swirling through her mind. If only she didn't love him so much. But she did, so that was that. The problem now was the girl he was bringing home.

She perked up. *I can call Lonnie.* Lonnie was Charlie's widow, and Abby's and Tom's closest friend. *She has a calming influence on Tom. And she can help me with Renée.* She dialed. *I wonder how old that girl really is. Didn't sound eighteen. Younger, maybe much younger.* "Lonnie, this is Abby. Can I ask a favor for tonight?"

"Of course," Lonnie said. "Anything for you."

Abby explained what Tom told her and asked if Lonnie could come for dinner and help her with Renée.

"I'll be there as soon as I change into jeans. I'm lounging around in my exercise clothes. Shouldn't take more than— Hey, I'll grab a couple of things from Mary Lou's closet. From what you said, I'm betting this Renée isn't packing any clothes."

"I don't know, but you don't want to do that," Abby said. "You need to keep—"

"No, I don't," Lonnie said, firmness in her voice. "Mary Lou will live forever in my heart. I've been telling myself to clean out her closet. This will give me an excuse to get started."

"Okay. Get here as soon as you can. I expect Tom any minute, and you know he won't be any help."

"On the way."

Abby placed the phone down, feeling guilty. She hoped she hadn't peeled the scab from Lonnie's wound that would never completely heal. Lonnie had lost her daughter and her husband, all in the period of a few weeks—both to brutal situations. Abby thought of Tom. Having him die would devastate her. She couldn't fathom losing him and a child, but knew she wouldn't handle it as well as Lonnie had.

* * *

Tom wheeled his red Chrysler convertible north on US 441 past the almost continuous strip malls of Boca Raton, stopping at traffic light after traffic light. He had considered taking the Florida Turnpike, but figured staying on the well-lit road peppered with strip malls on both sides would make Renée feel better—or less bad.

In the distance, to the west over the Everglades, he heard the grumble of thunder and out of the corner of his eye saw a flash of lightning. That produced a smile. The heat was almost stifling in its intensity—South Florida at its hottest. A shower would cool things off—at least temporarily. It could also signal the beginning of the rainy season. The *experts*, and there seemed to be one on every corner in South Florida, said the hurricane season, and with it monsoon-like weather, started on June first. However, Mother Nature chose her own calendar, and it had little to do with the National Oceanic and Atmospheric Administration. Today was June fifteenth. There had been a few light showers, but not enough to signal the end of the dry months of the year.

Stopping at the signal at Clint Moore Road, Tom said, "Only a short distance to go. Abby lives in a gated community a few miles north. Want me to put the top down?"

No response. Renée leaned hard against the passenger door, her head against the window. She sat so she didn't have to look at Tom. She couldn't get any farther away and stay in the front seat.

"Yeah, probably not a good idea. It could rain. I heard thunder." He looked at her. "No more than ten minutes now. You'll like Abby. And I'm sure she'll like you."

Except for the quiet hum of the engine, sounds of their breathing, and the blast of radios in the cars around them, the car stayed quiet.

The light changed and Tom moved with the traffic.

He turned into the housing area, stopped and activated the gate, then headed for Abby's house. She'd bought the house after joining the 17th Judicial Circuit of the Office of the State Attorney in Broward County. After giving it careful consideration, she and Tom agreed that living outside her jurisdiction in a gated community would make it more difficult for someone she prosecuted to harass her. Thus, they looked in Palm Beach County and found the three-bedroom that Abby now occupied. Once they married, it would be their home.

Tom pulled into Abby's driveway and parked. "Here we are. I can almost taste that pizza. What toppings do you like?"

Renée hadn't moved, still squeezed against the door as far from Tom as she could get. She said nothing.

"Me, I'm an *empty the fridge* guy. Anything that will stick goes on before I pop the pizza in the oven."

No response.

"You really should tell me. The first thing Abby is going to say is, 'Get the crust out of the freezer and load it with whatever Renée likes. I hope you know, because I'm sure she doesn't want all that stuff you pile on. In fact, no one eats pizza like you do. I'll have a salad.'"

Silence.

"Okay. Wait and see. And since you're not helping me, Abby will accuse me of not asking."

Silence.

"Let's go in. I have to face her sooner or later." He opened his door, got out, and walked around the car. The passenger door inched open as he approached. He took it by the edge and swung it wide, then stepped back. *How can I reach her? How can I convince her I mean no harm? If our positions were reversed, would I trust me?*

In a soft voice, he said, "You're safe, Renée. I promise. No one is going to hurt you anymore. We're in a safe area, far from that dirty alley."

She gave him a hesitant look, then twisted in the seat, and got out. As soon as her feet hit the ground, she moved several feet away from Tom.

They walked toward the house. He glanced over his shoulder to insure Renée was behind him. She was, but keeping her distance.

"Abby," Tom called, opening the front door, "we're here. Load up the feed bags."

Abby appeared in the kitchen doorway. "Come in here and get the crust out of the freezer and load it with whatever Renée likes. I hope you asked her, because no one eats pizza like you do. I'll have a salad." She turned back into the kitchen.

Tom looked at Renée and winked. "Told 'ya."

A small smile played at the corners of Renée's mouth before she went serious again.

For the first time, Tom realized how cute she was—and the secret smile also revealed her youth. *She's certainly not eighteen.*

Tom and Renée joined Abby.

Abby's eyes widened when she looked at Renée, and she puckered her nose.

"Meet my fiancée, Abby. Abby, may I introduce our guest for tonight? Renée, this is Abby Archer. Abby, this is Renée, uh, uh. I'm so embarrassed. I forgot your last name."

Renée's head snapped up, and she looked around the kitchen. "Uh . . . Sto . . . Stover, that's it, Renée Stover."

"I'm so glad to meet you," Abby said, cutting her eyes at Tom. "It's nice to have you with us tonight."

"Would you like a shower before you eat?" Tom asked. "I think you'll have a better appetite if you remove a few layers of dirt." He softened his words with a smile, while hoping she'd agree on the cleansing.

14

"I don't have anything else to wear. I . . ."

"Now, that's a problem that can be solved." Tom placed his hand on Abby's shoulder. "Here's your opportunity to solve a dilemma. Renée would like to take a shower before dinner, but has nothing clean to put on. Think you can come up with something?"

Abby winked at Renée. "Like always, I'm way ahead of him. In fact, Lonnie will be here any minute with a change for Renée. So why don't you get her a couple of clean towels from the linen closet? I'll get the shampoo and conditioner and a bathrobe."

Renée flinched and retreated a couple of steps. "Who's Lonnie?"

"Sorry," Abby said. "Lonnie is our dearest friend. She had a teenage daughter named Mary Lou. I invited Lonnie over, and she's bringing some clothes that might fit you. I hope you don't mind." Abby broke eye contact with Renée and looked away.

"Mind? Uh, no, I don't mind. Can I shower now?"

Tom put on his stern face. "Not until you tell me what pizza toppings you like, young lady. If you don't tell me, I'll play *empty the fridge.*"

Renée smiled, her first real smile since Tom rescued her. "Sausage and pepperoni. No veggies. I don't like green stuff."

"Aha, I knew there was something about you I like," Tom said. "See, Abby. Not everyone is a health freak."

"Get the towels, then start the pizza. I'll show her where the bathroom is. I'll take care of you later." Abby kissed his cheek.

Tom followed Abby and Renée down the hall, stopping at the linen closet. After handing Renée three towels, he backed away and left Abby with her. He looked over his shoulder as they disappeared into the bathroom. *How'd I get so damn lucky? An old Special Forces grunt like me ending up with someone like Abby.*

He continued into the kitchen and, as instructed, pulled the frozen crust from the freezer and began to create a pizza. He spread the sauce thin, added a thick layer of cheese, then sprinkled on chunks of sausage and slices of pepperoni. When finished, he examined it with a critical eye, then added more sausage and pepperoni. "Perfect. Hmm, looks kinda small though. Lonnie should be here by the time it gets ready. Perhaps I should make another."

He repeated his performance and smiled at the two thick pies staring at him. "Close to pizza-heaven. Maybe I should go into business."

"You'd have to eat your product, you'd never sell any."

Tom turned as Abby came into the kitchen. "No fair to slip up on a master chef. How's our guest doing?"

"I may never get the shower clean, but I expect she'll come out looking a lot different."

"And about five pounds lighter. How old do you think she is?"

"I can't be sure, but not eighteen. I'm guessing early teens, thirteen, fourteen. No older than fifteen. Lonnie might have a better guess. She's spent a lot more time with teens that I have. She should be here by now."

"Is it just me, or does our *Renée* look kind of scrawny?"

"Hard to say under all that dirt, but I'd guess yes, almost undernourished. When Lonnie gets here, we'll ask her. She—"

The doorbell rang, cutting her off.

Tom said, "Wonder who that can be?"

"Oh, shut up and let Lonnie in. Did you pre-heat the oven yet? I see you made enough pizzas for your breakfast."

"Ouch, forgot in the excitement of creation. Crank it up to four-hundred." He headed toward the front of the house.

When Tom opened the door, Lonnie stood there holding a small suitcase. "Welcome to my humble abode," he said. "Well, Abby's humble abode. Mine is much more humbler."

"Humbler? Is that a word?" Lonnie asked, grinning. "Why am I asking you? Your vocabulary is straight out of Special Forces. Not many words over four letters."

"Give me a hug, you evil woman, then get in here. Abby will get jealous if I dally too long."

They hugged, as only close friends do.

"What's in the case?" Tom asked.

"Clothes for your guest. I had no idea about her size so I tried to grab a little of everything. Hopefully, some of it will fit."

"That's for you and Abby to figure out. Not a thing this man knows anything about. The female figure and the sizes that fit it remain a mystery to me."

"Sure. The only part about the female figure you notice is the chest."

"Not true," Tom said. "Especially if she's walking away from me."

Lonnie shook her head. "Where's Abby? I need adult conversation."

They walked into the kitchen where Abby stood at the counter, tossing a salad.

Abby and Lonnie touched cheeks, then Lonnie asked. "Where's your guest? I have some clothes for her to look at."

"In the shower. She might be there for a while. Lots of South Florida to wash off."

Lonnie chuckled. "What's her story, Tom? Abby gave me a quickie on why she's with you, but what was she doing in the alley?"

"She's not talking. Acts scared of me. I'm hoping she'll open up to you and Abby. After we eat, I'll make myself scarce. My guess is she's on the run."

"Duh," Abby said. "What was your first clue?"

"Be careful, or I won't give you any pizza. Never insult the hand that cooks for you."

"Oh, yeah," Abby said with mock sternness. "Like I'd eat that conglomeration. Lonnie, are you going to risk his creation, or would you like some wholesome salad?"

"I was married to a retired Special Forces type. Bring on the pizza. You'll change after you marry this character."

"You tell 'er," Tom said.

"No. Please. Anything but that," Abby said, chuckling.

Lonnie said, "For sure, one of you will change. While we're waiting, what can I do to help?"

"You can share a beer with me," Tom said. "Two Killian's on the way. Abby?"

"Oh, why not? How can I diet when you're pushing beer at me?"

"You could always say no. Uh-oh, forget those words were ever uttered," Tom said as Abby shook a knife at him. He stuck his head in the refrigerator and came up with three bottles, the distinctive Killian's horse head on the label.

"Uh, hello."

They turned and Tom saw Renée in the doorway, Abby's robe wrapped around her, and her hair clinging wet. Her eyes reminded him of the young girl in so many paintings—large and sad. Like they'd seen too much of life, and it was all bad. His heart leapt out to her.

CHAPTER FOUR

Abby stepped forward. "Renée, how was your shower? Feeling better?"

She pulled the robe tighter, her eyes darting around the kitchen. "Uh, are my clothes ready?"

"Oh, my," Abby said. "I got so busy supervising Tom, I completely forgot. I took them to the laundry room, then didn't put them in the washer. Sorry. I'll do it now." She looked toward Lonnie. "But before I do, there's someone I want you to meet. Remember, we told you a good friend was coming over. Well, this is Lonnie. Lonnie, this is Renée."

Lonnie extended her hand. "Nice to meet you. I have some clothes that might fit you—at least until yours are ready."

"Uh." Renée looked at the three of them, her eyes large and filled with question marks. "I, I guess."

"Good," Abby said. "Why don't the two of you use the guest room? Renée can go through the clothes and see if anything fits. I'll head for the laundry room to do what I should have already done. Tom, come help me."

Abby walked out of the kitchen with Tom in tow.

Pushing the laundry room door closed behind them, Tom said, "What was that all about? You sure don't need me to run a load of wash."

"We need to talk."

"Uh-oh, those dreaded words that bring fear to the heart of any man."

"Hush. This is serious. I've been thinking. I still think she's in her early teens. What are we going to do with her? She can stay here tonight, but I have to work tomorrow. I can't leave her here, and I'm sure not going to push her onto the street again. Can you keep her with you?"

"Not very likely. First, she's a young female, and I'm a crusty old bachelor. Second, she's afraid of me and would probably run as soon as I turned my back. If she takes off, who can say I'll find her again."

"Yeah, dammit. I hate it when you're right." Her smile said she was teasing. "So we need a solution." A frown creased her forehead. "I suppose I could call in sick, but I hate to do that. Or I could ask for a day of vacation. With the workload we have, that wouldn't make me very popular." She rubbed her temples, deep in thought, then her head snapped up. "No, I can't do that. Where is my mind? I'm in court tomorrow. I have to go in."

"Then it's up to me," Tom said. "Maybe I . . ." He paused. "Maybe I nothing. I can't think of a thing."

Both were quiet as the clock ticked deeper into the evening. After several minutes, Abby said, "How about Lonnie? She doesn't have a job or anything. Do you think she'd agree to come over and babysit Renée?"

Tom smacked his forehead. "Damn. The obvious can be so well hidden. Why babysit here? Maybe Lonnie would let Renée stay at her place for a few days. At least until we sort things out. That would solve everything."

Abby thought for a moment. "It's worth a try. Tell you what. I'll relieve Lonnie with Renée and send her in here. She was your friend before she became mine. You float it past her."

"Done," Tom said, leaning against the washer. "It's our best possible solution. I'll turn on the ol' Jeffries' charm, and we can watch her melt."

"Oh, yeah, I've seen that charm. You'd best play it straight." Abby blew him a kiss and walked out of the laundry room.

A few minutes later, Lonnie came in. "Abby said you need to see me. Sounds mysterious."

Tom chuckled. "Everything about me is mysterious. You should know that."

"Yeah, but it was Abby who sent me in?"

Tom filled her in on his and Abby's conversation. "So, we're in a bind. The best we can come up with is hope you'll take Renée with you."

"With me? No, I can't . . ." She frowned. "I don't know, Tom. You found her on the street. Suppose she's . . . she's . . . I don't know. I don't feel right about taking her into my home. She's obviously a runaway. How do we know what she's running from?"

"We don't," Tom said. "All we know is she's a young girl afraid of the world. The street is no place for her." He paused, then in a softer voice, added, "Lonnie, Mary Lou was a runaway, too. If someone had taken her in, things might have turned out differently."

Lonnie's eyes flared. "That's not fair, Tom. Renée isn't like Mary Lou. Mary Lou wasn't a . . . a bad girl. She just . . . just— Dammit, Tom." Tears sprang to her eyes. "I wish you hadn't said that."

Tom wrapped his arms around her and pulled her head onto his shoulder, feeling rotten. "I'm sorry. I didn't want to hurt you. But I don't want Renée to go back to where I found her tonight. Don't ask me why, but I feel responsible for her."

Lonnie's body shuddered, and then she sniffled and wiped her fingers under her eyes. "It still hurts so much. Losing Mary Lou, then Charlie . . ." She sighed. "You're right though. We can't let her out on the street. If she agrees, she can stay with me—until you find her family."

Tom whispered into her hair. "Thank you. Charlie would be proud of you, as am I. I knew you couldn't turn your back on Renée." He gently pushed her away. "Okay, you and Abby switch places again. It's up to you now to convince Renée. But I know she won't be able to refuse you."

Lonnie hugged him, then left the room.

Ten minutes passed while Tom twiddled his thumbs and thought of various scenarios for Renée. Any and all of them could be true. A teenager, defenseless in an alley with two punks. Too many ways to get into such a position.

Abby came in. "Lonnie's with her now. Her eyes were red. Did you make her cry?"

21

"I'm afraid so, but she agreed to offer Renée the choice. We'll see how it works out."

"I wish you could have done it without hurting her. But I know how close you feel to Lonnie. You'd never hurt her on purpose. We need to give them some time to bond a bit. Who knows, if she has no family, and Lonnie has no family . . ."

"Oh no, you don't. Don't start that female conniving. This is a short term thing."

"No conniving. Just thinking Renée, or whatever her real name is, will need a place to stay if we don't find her family. Now, your job is to search her jeans. Maybe she has some ID. Don't know about Renée, but I'm sure her last name isn't Stover."

"Okay, Sherlock. What makes you so sure?"

"Because she was stuck for a name until she looked straight at the stove. That's how. You were so interested in your pizza you missed it."

Tom considered what she'd said. "Very astute, my dear. Brilliant deduction on your part. You must be a lawyer." He pulled her into his arms. "That's why we make such a wonderful couple—brains and brawn. I've always admired your muscles." He kissed her neck.

She pulled away, stuck her tongue out at him, then relented and kissed him. "Go through her pockets. I'm not sure this T-shirt will ever come clean. And her bra and panties—ugh. She must have worn them for days."

Tom ran his hand into the right rear pocket of the jeans. "Well, what do we have here?" He pulled out a small card. "Looks like a school ID—one for a Samantha Renée Williams."

"Where's she from?"

"The card's for West Coral Lakes Middle School. Guess that puts her not far from here."

"Does it have a grade and birthday?"

Tom examined it, front and back. "Her birthday's July third. Age says thirteen. Guess she'll be fourteen in a couple of weeks. The card is for seventh grade."

"Uh-huh," Abby said. "This is even more serious than I thought, Tom. We can't allow a child like this back out on the street. She'll never make it. What you stopped last night would become commonplace. She doesn't stand a chance."

Tom rubbed his chin. "I agree. Should we confront her?"

"No," Abby said without hesitation. "We don't want her to run. What say we play along until we get more information? I'll check with the police tomorrow to see if anyone's looking for her. I'm sure there's no AMBER Alert. I'd have heard about it in the office. Can you take a run to her school? I know it's out for the summer, but maybe there'll be someone who knows her—summer school or something. Do you have time?"

"I'll make time." Tom paused, looking toward the kitchen. "She obviously needs help. Your idea about Lonnie is sounding better."

Abby put Renée's clothes in the washing machine and turned it on—using an extra ration of soap. "Okay, master chef, back to the kitchen. Your creations need you."

Tom couldn't have explained, even if asked, but Renée's situation dug deep into him. No way could he let her return to the world where he'd found her. Abby was right. Within twenty-four hours, some punk would have her down, raping her. After that, there was every chance she'd become the property of a pimp, who'd finish her education. Within a couple of weeks, maybe less, she'd be soliciting johns on some corner. Drugs would follow, then . . . He shuddered. Not going to happen.

As he and Abby stepped into the empty kitchen, he said, "I'll find her family. They can't be as bad as living on the street. Then we can take her home."

"Sure. But suppose she doesn't want to go home. Suppose she prefers to walk away, refuses our help. Kidnapping is unlawful, you know, no matter how much good we think we're doing. Child services will be our only recourse—as bad as they are. Before you say it, I will not turn my head on this. As an officer of the court, I simply cannot."

"Yeah. I might understand, but sometimes I wonder why I got mixed up with an Assistant State Attorney. You sure cramp my style."

"Because I'm irresistible. Watch your pizzas. I'm going to see how Lonnie and Renée are doing."

He peeked through the oven window. Not much to see. If you've seen one pizza cooking, you've seen them all. The timer said five more minutes.

He set the table, putting water glasses all around. His first impulse was to pour milk for Renée, but realized that would not be his best move. She said she was eighteen. Until he had things under better control, he'd support the lie. Instead, he put a diet cola beside her place, figuring every thirteen-year-old female in the world loved them.

Water for Abby and Lonnie. He looked longingly at another beer, but filled his glass with water, too. His paunch was showing. He'd have to kick up his workout routine and add more running.

As he finished preparing the table, the stove dinged. He took the pizzas out of the oven and sat them on top to cool prior to slicing. They smelled great.

Picking a slice of pepperoni off, he wondered what was keeping the women. How long could it take to go through a few clothes? He chuckled. Stupid question. It could take all night.

He walked into the hallway and called, "Chow's up. Do I have to eat alone?"

Renée's head popped out. "I'm hungry. The pizza smells good."

"Well, let's do it," Abby said. "We can look at the other stuff while Tom cleans up the kitchen."

"Yeah, right," Tom said. "Man cook. Woman clean. Man watch TV."

Lonnie took Renée by the arm. "This should be interesting. Why don't we eat while those two argue? We know Abby's going to win, however the word games will be interesting." She led Renée into the kitchen and examined the table. "Uh, only one problem, Tom. Are we supposed to eat with our fingers? I'm betting Renée is accustomed to a knife and fork."

Renée laughed, then put her hand over her mouth. It was a young girl's laugh, unrestricted, full of life.

Tom smiled. Then it clicked—why he was so drawn to Renée. She reminded him of his sister—many years ago when she was a budding teen. Sadness began to move in, but he stopped it by saying, "Abby doesn't let me play with knives. I was waiting—"

He wanted to bite his tongue as he saw the merriment disappear from Renée's face and fear return to her eyes. *Damn, why'd I have to remind her of the alley scene?*

Abby stepped into the breach. "Renée, will you help me finish the table? There's the silverware drawer." She pointed. "Get place settings for each of us. I'll put the salad out, and Tom can serve the pizza on a trivet."

"What can I do?" Lonnie asked.

"Sit and be ready for an experience extraordinaire," Tom said, slicing the pizza. Moving it to the table, he said, "There's more where this one came from. Hurry up, Abby. Our guests are hungry."

"Right here," Abby said, settling into her chair while placing a bowl of salad on the table.

For the next few minutes, silverware made more noise than voices as each concentrated on eating. Tom ate heartily, as he always did. Abby picked at her salad while limiting herself to one piece of pizza. Lonnie fell between the two of them, showing a good appetite, but not overindulging. Renée was clearly the winner of the eating contest. She ate as if it were her first meal in days, which it might have been.

Tom took away the empty pizza pan and replaced it with the second. That one too took a serious beating.

After dinner, Tom went into the laundry room and switched Renée's clothes from the washer to the dryer. He noted with satisfaction that they looked clean. Then, true to his word, he retired to the den, picked up a book and flipped on the television with the sound muted. From the kitchen, he could hear the soothing voices of the women.

He perked up when Renée asked, "Do you work, Ms. Archer?"

"It's Abby, and yes, I'm employed. I love it so much, it's hard to think of it as work. It's more like a new life, one that gives me great pleasure."

"What do you do?"

Tom sensed Abby hesitating. She was probably worried that the truth might spook Renée. So was he. How would she react to discover she was in the home of an Assistant State Attorney?

"I'm, ah, a lawyer."

"Really? A lawyer? That's what I want to be when I gr— Ah," Renée hesitated, and Tom could picture her trying to come up with a way out of what she'd almost said. "I've been thinking about law school. I mean, after I finish college." Her voice carried no strength, more like a little girl caught filching a cookie.

"Let's see if any of the other clothes fit," Lonnie said, rescuing her. "Abby, do you mind if we leave you with the rest of the clean up?"

"Of course not. Go. I'll join you as soon as I put these pizza tins into soak. Tom can clean them tomorrow. It's his cheese burned on."

Tom read, hearing an occasional giggle from the back of the house. He smiled. It was wonderful being in an environment where women laughed, and life was good. An unwelcome shudder ran through him as a picture from his past invaded. An operation while in uniform that went bad. The images raced through his memory.

CHAPTER FIVE

Lt. Sanchez and his patrol hunkered behind an earthen mound a hundred feet from the first mud hut in the village. It was noon, broiling hot, and quiet—as quiet as if the community were deserted.

Sanchez looked at the man on his right. "Sgt. Jeffries, what do you think?"

Tom, the senior NCO, studied the area, taking his time before answering. "Not what I expected. I thought there would be people doing what people do around here. Maybe we—"

"Not necessarily. Hey, Terp, what do we have here?"

The interpreter scratched his beard. "Not sure. Should be activity. Cooking fires. Strange, very strange."

"I don't like it," Sgt. Allen said. "Can we trust our intel?"

"Unless you've got something better," Lt. Sanchez said. "They say this village is friendly, but there could be a terrorist cell in the surrounding area. We have to question the villagers."

"So, we're going in?" Sgt. Allen asked.

Tom took another survey of the area, then studied the twelve men of the patrol. Eleven of them were well-trained Special Forces operatives, including Lt. Sanchez. He had no doubts about their loyalty or their abilities with the assortment of weapons they carried. Sanchez was a newbie in country, but showed promise, although a bit too by-the-book thus far. The last man was the weak link, a local national who had hired on because he spoke passable English. So far, he'd done a satisfactory job, but they hadn't had a situation as serious as this one. If the village were occupied by terrorists, the patrol would be heading into a trap—a possible

27

massacre. Tom accepted the responsibility of insuring that didn't happen.

Sanchez rolled onto his back. "We're moving in. Maintain interval and keep your eyes wide open. Two to each building. Watch out for booby traps and be alert for an ambush. But . . . don't shoot unless you're sure it's an enemy target. I don't want to have to explain any civilian deaths."

Tom's eyes tried to peer through the walls as he listened to the lieutenant's words. He hated those words. Damn PC world. He was reinforcing their rules of combat as handed down from above. In effect, he was telling the men they could only return fire. It didn't matter to the politicians in Washington that a first bullet could kill just as dead as a second, or tenth, or hundredth. However, all the men were pros, and he knew they'd follow the *don't shoot unless shot at* orders—all except the interpreter. Tom would stick with him in case he decided to change sides.

Sanchez nudged the interpreter. "Lead us in. Let them know we come in peace. Ask them to show themselves." Turning to Tom, he said, "We'll go in with our weapons over our heads. If anyone comes out, we'll talk to them. If there's no one there, we'll search, then call in transportation for home."

Sanchez stood and motioned the interpreter up with him. Tom rose beside him. The others dispersed to proper intervals and moved forward at a set pace. Each carried his weapon over his head, but with fingers inside the trigger guards.

A woman came out of the closest hut and said something in her native tongue.

The interpreter said, "She say we welcome."

As he spoke, another woman appeared from a second building, her head bowed in respect.

Tom had an uneasy feeling that something was awry. His instincts were usually correct. "I don't like it. Be ready."

As the last word left his mouth, gunfire erupted from the first hut, followed quickly by a burst from a second and a third. Tom dropped and returned fire. He looked to Sanchez and the interpreter, both of whom had fallen with the first volley. After checking Sanchez, Tom rolled to the interpreter, who lay like a bag of rags. Dead—both of them.

He looked left, then right, seeing three or four of the men in prone positions, returning fire. Most were not. They couldn't.

Several bullets slammed into the interpreter's body, which protected Tom. He heard a grunt from his left and turned to see blood spurt from Sgt. Allen's shoulder. Allen switched the weapon to the other side and continued to fire.

Tom had to do something. They were trapped in a killing zone. The enemy could chew them apart at leisure. Only one possibility. Tom yelled, "Cover me." He jumped up, then ran a zigzag route toward the first hut. Bullets whizzed all around him, but he continued to dodge left, then right, knowing those remaining in his patrol would give him covering fire.

He dived alongside the first hut, tossed a grenade through the window, then covered his ears. After the explosion, there were no sounds from inside.

He saw Sgt. Allen almost to the second house when he went down face first, apparently taking another hit. Tom scrambled toward Allen's target and heaved his second grenade. It flew true through the window and everything went quiet following the blast.

Fire continued from a third hut, but seemed to be slowing. Three men burst out of the front door and scrambled around the far side. Tom stood, then heard a sound from behind him. A robed figure had stumbled out of the second hut, bloody and carrying a rifle. Tom spun and let off a three-round burst and watched the figure fall against the doorframe, then crumple to the ground.

Tom saw no movement so he raced between the buildings, coming out the back as the terrorists cleared their house. He opened up, and they fell from the fusillade of bullets that tore into them.

Tom dropped and rolled alongside the remains of the hut, peeking into the courtyard. The two women who had greeted them were down, blood pooling around their bodies. The person who had exited the second hooch still lay in the doorway. No threat there. He looked toward his men and waved for them to stay put.

There were few acknowledgements.

After a few moments of quiet, Tom knew he couldn't wait any longer. He had to call in medevac for his wounded men and get the dead evacuated. *Leave no man behind* echoed in his head. Cpl. Nevers had the radio.

Tom dashed to Nevers' side and confirmed his suspicions. Dead. The radio had come through untouched, though, and Tom made the appropriate notifications.

An hour later, the area was secure, the wounded and dead evacuated. Tom and his captain made the rounds of the huts. Hut number one held three dead terrorists. Hut number two had three also, plus the one lying in the doorway. Tom turned the body over and gasped. It was a girl, probably a teenager. Her eyes stared wide in death, a haze covering them.

"Let's go, sergeant," the captain said. "She's dead. Looks like someone planted a tight shot pattern in her chest."

Tom stared at him, but said nothing. There was nothing to say.

They continued their search and discovered forty-eight bodies. Nine of them looked like terrorists, all killed by Tom. The other thirty-eight appeared to be the true villagers, ten men, nine women, and twenty children. Most appeared to have been killed from close range, exonerating Tom and his men. The forty-eighth was the girl Tom shot. Terrorist or villager? He would never know and would carry it to his grave.

The losses weighed heavily on Tom. Five of his troops killed, including Lt. Sanchez, and five with wounds ranging from serious to crippling. The interpreter, whom he'd distrusted, dead. Tom's conscience screamed that he should have done something different, something that would have produced different results. He was the senior NCO. He had the experience. He should have found a way to talk Lt. Sanchez into another approach. He should have looked before killing the girl. He saw her laying in the doorway, her life's blood covering the ground, pictured her eyes accusing him of acting without thinking. She was right. He would never forgive himself.

Tom leaned forward in his chair and shook his head, forcing the memories away, dragging himself back to the present. Enough.

That was then. He had to kill the girl. This was now. He had to save Renée.

A half-hour later, Abby walked in, followed by Renée and Lonnie. Renée wore a different set of clothing that almost fit.

"Well, we've lost our house guest," Abby said. "Lonnie hijacked her."

"Oh?" Tom said, pushing his recliner upright. "And how did this come about?"

Standing behind Renée, Lonnie winked. "I need the company, and both of you have to work. Seems like the perfect solution."

"Do you mind?" Renée asked. "Lonnie said she'd take me shopping for some new clothes tomorrow. Mine are all worn out, and these don't fit so good."

"Yes, I noticed," Tom said. "But, since your stuff is still wet, you must promise to come for dinner tomorrow night. You can pick up your old clothes and show off the new ones."

"I promise," Renée said, smiling. "I mean if it's okay with Lonnie and Abby."

"Works for me," Abby said.

"Free food is always good," Lonnie said. "We'll be here. Now, we'd better be on our way. Getting late for an old widow-lady like me. Are you ready, Renée?"

Renée nodded, then approached Abby. The hug she gave Abby was real, unlike the ones she probably gave her middle school friends. "Thank you for dinner . . . and for the shower."

When she came to Tom, he handed her three of his business cards. "Keep at least one of these with you at all times. It's my promise I'll be there, anywhere, anytime you need me. All you have to do is call." He kissed her on the cheek. He hoped no one saw it, but the moisture in his eyes threatened to overflow.

Tom and Abby walked Renée and Lonnie to her car. They exchanged more hugs, and then were alone. Arm in arm, they returned to the house with Abby's head resting against Tom's shoulder.

Inside, they turned to one another and kissed, a deep passionate kiss that said more than words ever could.

CHAPTER SIX

At seven a.m., Tom sat on the edge of the bed in his house, images of the previous night fresh in his mind. As he did every morning, he wondered what he'd done to accrue such luck. In spite of what Abby told him when they were together, he feared his glider might crash at any time. He didn't deserve someone like Abby—he wasn't worthy of her love. He was what he was, damaged goods with a darkness inside that would not go away.

He thought of Charlie Rogers, Lonnie's husband and Mary Lou's stepfather, how he died rescuing Tom when flames raged through Raul Santiago's home, incinerating everything in their path.

Other images flashed through his mind—jungle ambushes, urban assassinations, and intelligence missions where discovery meant torture and death. He remembered friends from his Special Forces days, friends who did not return.

As with every day, the memories ended with his sister—beautiful, innocent Katherine who never hurt anyone. Sis, who had such a wonderful future awaiting her. His sister who died at the hands of street scum later released by the so-called justice system. Sis, to whom he swore a vow on her grave—*No woman will ever go unavenged, not while I live.*

He reflected on the night in Dallas when he stopped at a convenience store for a six-pack on the way home. He was only another off-duty cop until he looked through the window and saw a robbery-in-progress. His police academy training took over, and he did everything right—called for backup, raced in, announced himself, and yelled for the thieves to lay down their weapons. He smiled at the memory of the first who spun toward him, raising his pistol. Tom recognized him as one of the thugs who killed his sister and got away with it. The creep's shot missed, but Tom didn't. A shoot-out ensued. The robbers didn't stand a chance—Tom's Special Forces experience raced to the fore and six quick shots later, they were dead, center of mass with each round. He felt even better when he saw that the others were two more of Katherine's assailants. Three down, two left to die.

When his relationship to the would-be robbers surfaced, the media attacked and tried to crucify him, scorning him as an out-of-control vigilante. They campaigned for his dismissal from the Dallas police force and his subsequent arrest. But the store clerk's calm, unemotional account of the facts could not be overcome. Internal Affairs cleared Tom, and he received a commendation.

The media frenzy convinced Tom he shouldn't be a policeman any longer. He had too much respect for those who wore the badge to taint them with his presence. His every move was scrutinized by a *journalist,* waiting to take him and the department down. He resigned and became a private investigator.

That wasn't enough. The media still hounded him, and he felt Katherine's presence wherever he went in the Dallas metropolitan area. It was time to move on. His good fortune took him to South Florida—where Abby resided.

Returning to the present, Tom frowned. The other two who participated in his sister's degradation and death were out there somewhere. They did a brief stint in prison on another charge, got out for *good behavior,* then disappeared. But someday, he'd cross their paths and complete his promise to Katherine. For scum like them, it was a small world.

Mary Lou Smithson's murder was next. He hadn't been able to save her, but he sent those who killed her into the fires of Hell, even though he lost his best friend, Charlie, doing it.

Now, there was Renée. She needed rescue, and he assumed that responsibility. If he didn't, who would? First though, he had to learn about her and what caused her to run.

He rose and padded into the kitchen where his automatic pot had produced fresh coffee. After pouring a cup, he sat at the table, took out his cell phone, and dialed Abby.

"You're up early, aren't you?" Abby said as she answered.

"What? I slept in because you wore me out last night. Usually, I wake the rooster."

Chuckling, Abby said, "Oh, sure. Speaking of which, I'll be glad when we're married. Then I won't have to be up so late. I can crash and leave you alone in front of the TV."

"I don't think so. I'm writing in the contract that we must go to bed at the same time—whatever hour I pick."

"Uh-huh. So, are you going to Renée's school?"

"Yes. I figure to hit there about ten. Things should be in full swing by then. More chance of finding someone who can fill me in on Renée."

"Call if you find out anything."

"You do the same. Don't forget to check as soon as you get to the office whether there's any paper on her. I don't want any surprises."

"I'll inquire even before I put my purse down. Is that fast enough?"

"You're learning. Guess I'm a good influence on you."

"Uh-huh. Gotta run. At ten, I'll be in front of the judge. See you tonight?"

"You betchum, Red Ryder."

"Ugh. I'm out of here."

The phone clicked in Tom's ear, and he again wondered how he'd gotten so lucky.

* * *

Tom parked in the visitor's lot and headed into the school. He stopped as he came alongside the entrance. A Broward County School Resource Officer car sat in a reserved space. "Schools aren't like they used to be," he mumbled. "Security everywhere."

Stepping inside, he came face to face with a desk and an armed officer. "Good morning," he said.

"Morning, sir," the guard said. "What's your business here today?"

Tom looked at the guard's nametag. "Officer Gomez, my name is Tom Jeffries, and I'm a private investigator. I'm looking for information on one of the students, a Samantha Renée Williams. Do you happen to know her?"

"Complete this form." The guard slid a clipboard to Tom with a pen attached.

Tom looked at the paper. Name, address, phone number, purpose of visit, name of student, person visited.

Tom filled in the blanks, leaving purpose of visit blank. Handing it to the guard, he said, "Kind of like visiting someone in jail." He smiled to take any sting out of his comment.

"Sorry, sir, but it's procedure. We do what we can to protect the children."

"No problem. Now, will you answer my question? Do you know her?"

The guard examined the form. "Can I see some ID, please?"

Tom showed his Private Investigator's license, which Officer Gomez examined as if he'd never seen one before. He copied Tom's license number onto the form. After he'd had ample time to memorize it, he said, "You'll have to go through the metal detector. Will you have a problem with that?"

Uh-oh. Should have thought of that. "Ah, I need to visit my car. Be right back."

Gomez smiled. "I'm not surprised. Get rid of everything metal except your car keys. I'll be here."

At the car, Tom popped the trunk, took off his sheath knife and ankle holster, then returned to Gomez, and passed through the metal detector.

"The office is down the hall, fourth door on the right," Gomez said. "They're expecting you."

"Thanks," Tom said, but didn't move. "This will be the third time I asked. Do you know Samantha Renée Williams?"

Gomez studied him. "I know most of the students here, one way or another. Some of them talk to me. Others I overhear. After a while, I become like a piece of the furniture, not noticed." He stopped and appeared to think. "Does that answer your question?"

"The first one. Do I get another?"

"Depends on what it is. But asking's free."

"Tell me about her. Does she have problems at home?"

Gomez stroked his chin, staring at Tom. "Like I said, main office is down the hall, fourth door on the right."

Tom nodded. "Okay, thanks."

He walked away, wondering if he'd seen something in the guard's eyes, some bit of knowledge he didn't want to share.

A few steps later, his phone rang, and when he checked the caller ID, he saw Abby's work number. "This makes my day much brighter. Speak to me, Sunshine."

"You're so full of it. I have something on Renée. First, there are no current reports on her. If she's a runaway, no one called it in. But, she has run before—on two separate occasions. The last one was during the winter and once the summer before. Each time, she was picked up within forty-eight hours and taken home."

"Anything about why?"

"Not that I know yet. I've requested copies of the reports, and I have a call in to the officers who found her. I'll let you know if they shed any light on the situation."

Tom thought a moment. "You saw her last night. Did you pick up any vibes about what would make her run?"

"My dear, it's been quite a while since I was thirteen, and about an equal amount of time since I've had any real contact with immature teenagers—well, discounting you."

"Hey, I'm not immature, but it's true you're robbing the cradle. I'm much too young for you."

"Yeah, sure—you dirty *old* man. But, back to Renée. She appeared pretty normal to me, although there did seem to be an undercurrent of unhappiness. I suppose that's to be expected in a runaway, though."

"And what she went through in that alley didn't help either. First, the two thugs threaten to rape her, then I scare her worse when I dump them on their butts. She had every right to have an undercurrent."

"There's that, too. By the way, I checked. There's no report of muggings in that area. I guess you got away with it. But, you really have to be more careful."

"What? I should have let them rape her?"

"No, of course not. But . . . Dammit, you can't settle every grievance with your fists or that fancy knife of yours. That's why we have policemen. Let them do their jobs."

"I'll never get in the way of them doing their jobs—when they're there to do them."

"I have to go. Court convenes at ten. Be careful, please."

"I was about to go into the admin office when the phone rang. Maybe they'll be able to tell me something." He hesitated, then added, "It's nice to have someone worry about me. I'm sorry to be such a bother. Talk to you later, Sunshine."

"I always wanted to be prematurely gray. Why else would I hook up with someone like you?" She chuckled. "You kind of light up my day, too." The line went dead.

Tom closed his phone and looked toward Gomez, who was paying close attention to a paper in his hands. Tom turned and finished his trip to the main office.

CHAPTER SEVEN

Tom opened the door to the main office and tapped on the doorframe as he walked in. "Hi, do you have a minute?"

A woman, working at her computer, turned and said, "Come in. I'll be with you in a moment. Let me save this." She made a few more clicks, then said, "What can I do for you?" The nameplate on her desk read, Ms. Lawrenson.

"I'm Tom Jeffries, a private investigator. I'm looking for information on Samantha Renée Williams. I believe she's a student here."

"Ms. Lawrenson said, "I talk to no one without knowing who they are. ID?"

Tom smiled and laid his PI credentials on the desk in front of her.

She picked the case up and eyed it as if attempting to burn the letters off the paper. "Okay, these give you one question—not that I agree to answer it."

"Is Samantha Renée Williams a student here?"

"Samantha? Yes. Well, during the normal school year, she is. She's not in summer school, though."

"Has she had any disciplinary problems?"

"That's a second question and not something I'll answer. Why are you asking?"

Tom hesitated, juggling possible approaches. "I have an interest in her. I'm not asking you to violate any school rules, but anything you can tell me might help her."

Ms. Lawrenson stared at him, a severe look on her face. "Maybe you should talk to the principal. We work under tight privacy rules for the protection of our students. She will have a better feel for what she can tell you."

"That's fine. Can I see her?"

"She's not in today. She's at a countywide training course. It lasts all week." Her fingers drummed on the desk.

"Is there anyone else I can talk to? Who's in charge in her stead?"

"It's summer school, Mr. Jeffries," she said, exasperation in her voice. "With all the budget cuts, we're lucky to have enough teachers. I'm sorry, but there is no one I can recommend."

Tom rubbed his forehead. "I understand. How about giving me Samantha's home address then? I'll talk with her parents."

"Her mother," Ms. Lawrenson said. "She doesn't have a father at home." Her lips set in a thin line.

"Okay, how about her mother's address?"

Ms. Lawrenson smiled a sardonic smile. "Sorry. Privacy rules. There's nothing I can tell you. Now, if you don't mind, I have to get this report out. District will be screaming in a few minutes if they don't receive it." She turned to her computer and rested her fingers on the keyboard.

Tom accepted that he'd been stonewalled by a pro. "Thank you, Ms. Lawrenson. I appreciate your position." He laid a business card on her desk. "If you should happen to think of anything you *can* tell me, please call. It could be very important to Samantha."

She hesitated, then slid the card into her center desk drawer. Her hands moved back to the keyboard, and she began to type, leaving Tom little choice but to leave.

Tom retraced his steps toward the exit, not happy with what he'd accomplished. As he came alongside the guard's desk, Gomez said, "Did you get what you needed?"

"Well, I know Samantha's not enrolled in summer school. Other than that, not a thing."

"Not surprising. Ms. L is known around here as the *Secretary from L.* She doesn't make it easy for anyone."

"Have you changed your mind? Or do I leave here empty-handed?"

Gomez ruffled some papers on his desk. "I didn't mean to be eavesdropping, but when you were on the phone, did I hear you say something about an alley and rape?"

Tom gave it a quick thought and decided he had nothing to lose by telling Gomez the whole story. "Yeah. Samantha ran away from home. I found her in an alley last night with a couple of miscreants who were about to introduce her to womanhood—the hard way. She was terrified. I took care of the problem, but ended up scaring her even more. She's with a female friend of mine now. She's not talking, though. I need to find her parents and get her home."

Gomez looked sad. "What a shame. You know, in this job you get to know these kids. You see them every day, you hear them talking about their hopes and dreams. You watch them laugh, play jokes on one another, share their good times, and moan about the bad ones. They come in as little boys and girls, ten-eleven years old. Three years later, they leave as young ladies and budding young men. In that way, it's the best job I've ever had."

He shook his head and stared at his hands. "The other side is you hear things you don't need to hear, their boyfriend-girlfriend problems, their broken hearts, their family problems. Some of the things make me want to pay the parents a visit." He took a deep breath. "But, of course, I don't—I can't. My job is to keep them safe while they're here in school. Anything beyond that is beyond the scope of my job."

He opened a drawer in his desk and took out several papers clipped together. He placed them on his desk, then pushed his chair back. "I gotta hit the head. You can find your way out, can't you?"

"Yeah. Thanks for talking to me. I understand how these kids can get under your skin. I'm an Army veteran. I felt the same way about my fellow soldiers."

Gomez stuck his hand out. "Keep Samantha safe." After shaking Tom's hand, Gomez walked away.

When Gomez turned a corner, Tom looked at the papers the guard left on his desk. It was a roster, listing students with their emergency contacts. He slid into Gomez's chair, pulled the stack to him, and flipped pages until he saw Samantha Renée Williams. Glancing over his shoulder to make sure no one was watching, he copied the phone numbers and the address. Only the mother's name was listed, Barbara Williams, no father. Tom closed the bundle and returned the pages to the center of Gomez's desk. Then he left the building.

Tom slid into his car, got the air conditioner running, and took out his phone. He was about to call Abby when he remembered her schedule—court at ten. It was ten-thirty. He would have to wait until later to feed Renée's mother's name to her. He would prefer to know her record, if any, before knocking on her door. Circumstances dictated doing things in reverse. After programming his GPS with Barbara Williams' address, he pulled out of the parking lot.

Tom drove the street looking for the right address. It appeared to be an upper middleclass neighborhood. The houses, mostly two stories, were well cared for. Mowed lawns and trimmed hedges. There were a variety of cars parked in the driveways and along the curb—everything from huge and expensive SUVs to low-end sedans. The common factor was they were all of recent vintage.

He parked in front of Williams' house. Except for its pink color, it looked like its neighbors. Tom noticed the houses came in only a couple of models and the differences were small. They all bore pastel colors, no two in the same hue side-by-side. A Mercedes sedan sat in the Williams' driveway.

He walked to the front door and rang the doorbell. Soft chimes played inside, then he heard steps. The door opened a couple of inches, a chain keeping it secure.

"Yes," a woman said, peering through the opening, half of her face visible.

"My name is Tom Jeffries. Are you Ms. Williams?"

"If I am?"

"I'm a private investigator, and I'm looking for the mother of Samantha Renée Williams. Would that be you?"

"What's she done now? And why a private eye? Usually, it's a cop banging on my door."

"Ma'am, as far as I know, she's done nothing illegal. May I come in? I'd really like to talk to you about her."

The half-face seemed to reflect on his request, then the door closed, and he heard the chain slip out of its sleeve. The door re-opened, this time wide enough for passage.

"Come on in. I can give you a few minutes. Then I have to get dressed. I have a lunch date."

Tom stepped through the doorway and saw an attractive woman in her thirties. She wore a robe with her blond hair in rollers. Dark roots showed. No-frame glasses covered her eyes.

"I'll make it as fast as I can," he said, following her as she led him down a hallway into a nicely furnished living room. While he was no expert on furniture, he opined it had not come from Walmart. Lots of leather and chrome. Modern and lacking any visual indications of wear and tear.

"Have a seat. Can I get you anything? Coffee, a soda?"

"No, thank you." Tom dropped onto the couch while Ms. Williams sat across from him in a recliner, leaned back, and crossed her legs. Her robe fell open, revealing attractive thighs. She glanced down, then left the opening.

"Okay, why are you looking for Sammi?" she asked.

Tom smiled. "Sammi? Is that her nickname?"

"That's what I call her. She doesn't like it, but I do, so I use it. Now, why are you looking for her?"

"I didn't say that's what I'm doing. I'm wondering why you haven't filed a missing persons report on her. I believe she's been gone for several days."

She sat forward, pulling her robe together over her knees. "What business is it of yours? If you know she's out there, you must know where she is. So, where is she? Tell her to get her ass home. I'm tired of her games."

"Why didn't you report her missing?"

Attractiveness fled her face as her eyes went cold. "Not that it's any of your business, but she does whatever the hell she pleases, so why should I bother the police? This is her third runaway. The first two times I got all worried and called the cops. They brought her home and acted like I was some kind of unfit parent. This time she can find her own way home." She shrugged as she relaxed. "That kid's been a pain in the ass since the day she was born."

Tom reflected on her words, interpreting her attitude. Not very difficult. She didn't care. "Where's her father? Is he in the picture?"

Ms. Williams let loose a short, choppy snort. "That son of a bitch walked out when she was two years old. Before she was three, we had a divorce. The only contact we have with him is the alimony and child support his bank transfers to my checking account every month. My lawyer hired someone like you to catch him in the rack with his bimbo. We cleaned his clock." She leaned back in the chair, a sneer on her lips. "So, when is she going to come crawling home?"

"Don't you want to know where she is or if she's in good health—if anything has happened to her?"

"Look. Let's cut the bullshit. I'm fed up with her crap. If you want her, keep her. After a few weeks, you'll feel like I do."

Tom wiped his fingers across his lips, fighting to hold his temper. He would gain nothing by telling her what he was thinking. After taking a deep breath and letting it out in a long, slow blow, he said, "I've taken enough of your time. You said you have to get dressed, so I'll leave." He stood. "Thank you for talking with me. You've been very enlightening. I'll let myself out."

She stood and faced him. "Tell Sammi her *mother misses* her." Her eyes put the lie to her words.

Tom walked from the house, his fingers entwined in front of him. By concentrating on squeezing them together, he stayed silent.

Once in his car, he slammed his palms against his steering wheel, then squeezed his hands into fists until his knuckles hurt. "How do women like that become mothers?" he said through clenched teeth. "She gives forced sterilization legitimacy."

He pulled away from the curb, drove down the street, and turned right. He thought he remembered seeing a strip mall nearby. And he needed one—needed someplace he could get out of the car and walk off his frustration. Two blocks away, he saw what he sought, wheeled in, and parked in front of a Publix Super Market.

He got out and began to walk the parking lot perimeter. The fourth time he passed his car, he felt his adrenaline flow slacken. He was over the hump. He remembered times when that same flow had saved his life. This time, though, he needed to control it. Strangling Barbara Williams was an attractive idea, but not a viable option.

He looked around, then entered a Starbucks and ordered an iced coffee. A chilled drink was in order to complete his cooling off process. He sat outside and sipped, taking a more objective look at Ms. Williams' words. They still stunk, still showed a callous woman who had no right to call herself a mother. What was he to do? He had no legal right to keep Renée from her mother, but he didn't want to send Renée home to that woman either. He hoped Abby would have some ideas.

The evening couldn't come soon enough.

CHAPTER EIGHT

Tom finished his Starbucks coffee, crumpled the cup, and put it in the trash. Then, he returned to considering his next step. Nothing came to mind that would lead to answers to the questions swirling in his head. Maybe Abby, since she wasn't as close to the situation, would have a more objective view of where to go. He checked his watch. No chance she was in her office unless the judge had declared a postponement or a mistrial. But, even if she wasn't there, he could still leave a message.

He called and, as expected, heard the announcement on her answering machine. Her voice made him feel better, though. "Hi, Sunshine. Call me as soon as you can. Love you." He hung up, a warm feeling in his chest.

He thought for a minute, then dialed Lonnie's cell number. When she answered, he asked, "How are things going?"

"I'm having a ball, and it looks like Renée is, too. We're in the mall. It's been a long time since I've had the pure pleasure of watching a young teen shop." She chuckled. "Even one who claims to be eighteen. She's a delight, Tom. I'm so glad Abby called last night."

"Hey, don't I get any credit? I brought her home."

"Nah, your ego's big enough."

"Will we see y'all tonight?"

"Yep. Renée and I will be there. She's already talking about showing off her new clothes to you and Abby."

"Sounds good to me."

When Tom hung up, a smile decorated his face. *Sometimes, I do the right thing.*

He walked to his car, opened the door, and climbed in. The heat was probably pushing one-hundred-thirty degrees inside, common for South Florida when parked in the direct sunlight. He started the engine, set the air conditioning to high, got out, leaving the driver's door open, and walked to the passenger side. Once he opened that one, he leaned against the side of the car, waiting for the interior to cool to a temperature a human could tolerate.

* * *

Abby pulled into the driveway at six o'clock. Tom met her at the car, opened her door, and helped her out. Pulling her to him, he said, "I missed you today," and kissed the tip of her nose.

"Not here, you big lug. My neighbors think I'm a nice girl."

"Oh, but you are. And I'm learning more about that every night."

She brushed his cheek with her lips. "I need to change. This suit and heels are fine for the courtroom, but don't work at home. If you'll grab my briefcase, please, I'll meet you inside." She slipped away from him and headed toward the house. Over her shoulder, she added, "I'll be in the bedroom getting comfortable—if you're looking for me."

Tom watched her walk through the doorway, his smile stretching his lips, grabbed her case, and followed. Once inside, he mixed a weak Scotch and water and carried it into the bedroom.

She took the drink, sipped, and said, "You're such a keeper. I should have arranged for someone like you a lot sooner."

"There is no one else like me," he groused. "And you'd better be careful. I might decide to share my talents with some other lady."

She put her arms around him and kissed him. "Not a chance. You're my slave forever."

"Hmm, I could learn—"

The telephone rang.

Abby unwound her arms and picked up the phone, blowing Tom a kiss as she did so.

"If nirvana had phones, it wouldn't be nirvana," Tom said, walking out of the room.

Once in the kitchen, Tom opened the refrigerator, grabbed a Killian's, and popped the cap. Nothing to do except wait for Abby to finish her conversation, then they'd figure something for dinner.

"That was Lonnie," Abby said, entering the room. "She and Renée will be here in about a half-hour. What's for dinner?"

"Your night tonight," Tom said. "I did last night."

"Yeah," Abby said, frowning. "I know. Steak. I have more salad makings, and we have four nice steaks in the fridge. I can nuke some potatoes, and we'll have a meal fit for hero private investigators. What say you?"

"I say you're setting me up to cook again tonight. You know I can't resist a good steak. I'll get the charcoal going. When Lonnie and Renée get here, we can throw the steaks on."

"So, what did you learn about Renée today?"

"Not much. She's run away twice before. She has no father in the picture, and her mother doesn't want her." He set his bottle on the counter. "I don't know what to do. We can't keep her, but we can't send her home, either. I'm hoping your fertile imagination will come up with some ideas."

"Wow. You draw trouble like Yankees draw mosquitoes. Let's get dinner going now. We can talk later after our guests leave."

Tom went into the backyard, uncovered his Weber grill, and poured in a generous heaping of charcoal. He doused it with lighter fluid, then tossed in a match and stepped back when it whooshed. The grill was one of the first things he bought after Abby accepted his proposal. He enjoyed a well-seared steak, sealing in its natural juices, and was pleasantly surprised to discover Abby did, too.

When the flames died down, he dropped the cooking grate in to allow the intense heat to sterilize it. After another moment, he put the dome on and walked inside to prepare the steaks.

A few minutes later, Lonnie and Renée arrived. Renée bounded in with a smile that lit up the room. "We had the greatest time today," she said. "Lonnie took me to the mall, and we shopped and shopped. Wait 'til you see my new outfits. How do you like the one I have on?" She took a ballerina's pose and pirouetted

The difference between the Renée of the previous night and this one was drastic. She'd been withdrawn, shy, even scared. Now she didn't seem to have a care in the world. And with every move, she threw a loving look at Lonnie.

When Renée dashed to the bedroom to change into another outfit, Abby said, "Okay, what did you drug her with? That's not the same girl we saw last night."

"Isn't she something?" Lonnie said. "I had so much fun today. Having Renée around could become habit forming." She stared toward the hallway where Renée had disappeared, sadness capturing her face. "She reminds me so much of Mary Lou at that age. They could have been sisters."

Tom glanced at Abby, worry tainting his face. "Did she have anything to say about her family?" he asked Lonnie.

"No. I tried to get her to talk about them a couple of times, but each time she changed the subject. I don't know any more than I knew last night." She sighed. "How about you? Did you find out anything?"

"A bit," Tom said. "But nothing definitive. Can you keep her a few more days?"

"Sure—"

Renée skidded around the corner. "Look at this awesome shirt and these really incredible shorts. Don't I look great?"

"Slow down, all of you," Tom said. "There are more important things to be addressed here."

Three heads, as one, swung toward him.

"I have coals out there burning at five-hundred degrees or better. They're ripe and ready to use. Renée, you're my question mark. I know Abby and Lonnie like their steaks medium, and if mine can't moo, it's overcooked. So how about you? How do you want yours done?"

"Uh . . ." Renée appeared a bit lost, then swung her head toward Lonnie. "Like Lonnie's. That's what I want." Her expression danced with joy.

Tom turned toward the steaks plated on the counter. A smile played around his mouth, and a satisfied glint dominated his eyes.

* * *

Dinner was one of the most satisfying Tom could remember in a long time. Between bites, Renée bubbled and gurgled like the young teen she was. It was as if everything was new to her, and she loved everything she tried. Tom could only watch in awe, a warm feeling growing in his gut. But when he remembered Renée's mother, the warmth became a cold knot. What was Renée's life like at home? His best guess was it didn't contain much of the unbridled joy he witnessed tonight.

After dinner, Lonnie and Renée helped clear the table, then announced they had to leave. Lonnie had an early medical appointment, and Renée couldn't wait to hit the community pool to show off the bikini Lonnie bought her. There had been no opportunity for Tom to tell Lonnie about his visit to Renée's mother.

After walking Lonnie and Renée to the car and waving them out of the driveway, Tom turned to Abby and said, "We need to talk."

"Oh, this should be good," Abby said. "My man using a woman's favorite line. I can hardly wait."

"Not about us. About Renée—and about Lonnie, unless my eyes deceived me."

Abby looked in the direction they had disappeared. "Yeah. Good things which could produce bad results might well be happening. I'm worried about Lonnie, Tom. She may be setting herself up to get hurt again."

Hand in hand, they walked into the house and settled on the living room sofa. Tom briefed Abby on his day. He tried not to slant it too much, but couldn't keep disappointment out of his voice.

"So, you're saying," Abby said, "that Renée's mother isn't fit to wear the title."

"Something like that. I can't come up with any other interpretation. If she'd been slobbering good and crying about her *poor baby*, I'd have reason to think she might be faking it. But she was direct—cold and direct. In no uncertain terms, she was saying she didn't care about Renée—no faking involved."

"What do we do?"

"Whoa, that's my line. You're the legal-beagle. Is there some loophole we can use to take her away from her mother?"

"And do what? That would be the same as jumping from a piranha tank to the shark pool. We'd have to turn her over to the authorities, and they'd place her with the Department of Children and Families. You know their track record. Renée would never tolerate that. She'd run in a flash—back out on the street. And next time, you might not stumble across her."

Tom wiped his hand over his face. "That takes us back to the beginning. What can we do?"

Abby squeezed his hand, her face screwed up in concentration. "How about the father? Know anything?"

"Not a whit. I can't even be sure his name is Williams. That could be the mother's maiden name. Or she could have changed it with the divorce. You know, you women change names like you change shoes."

"I'll ignore that for now, buster. How long have they been divorced?"

"Let me see. Ms. Williams said that by the time Renée was three, she had divorced him. That would make it ten, eleven years ago."

They sat silent for several minutes before Tom said, "Maybe we can trace Renée's dad and let him know what's happening. If we're really lucky, he'll go to court to reclaim his daughter."

Abby gazed into his eyes. "I'm looking for that little flame that says you're still awake and not dreaming. I love an optimist, and I love you, but there is such a thing as being too optimistic."

"Got a better idea?" Tom kissed her on the cheek. "I'm betting not."

"No, darn it. Where do we start?"

"Maybe you can find the court records of the divorce. That'll give us basic ID on him, maybe even an address. From there, I can attempt to track him down. He's got to be on the Internet. Everyone else is."

"Suppose he's dead or the divorce didn't occur in Broward County."

Tom frowned at her. "You do have a mean streak. If he's dead, we'll be sitting here like we are now, looking for another approach."

The Runaway

CHAPTER NINE

At six-thirty a.m., Tom shut off the alarm and rolled out of bed. He had nothing specific on his calendar—his day depended on others. First was Ken Dotson, his boss at the law firm of Dotson and Nelson.

After the senior partner at Bernstein, Goldsmith, Espinosa, and Bernstein dismissed him because of their differing definitions of loyalty to the law firm, Tom landed with the smaller office of Dotson and Nelson. The retainer wasn't as large, but neither were the number of associate attorneys looking over his shoulder. The smaller office meant less pressure, an environment he enjoyed. Enough independent cases came along which, added to the retainer, kept his creditors satisfied. He hadn't spoken with Ken in the last few days and thought it smart to check in with him. But he'd wait to make the call. Ken began his workday early, but refused phone calls until after nine. He said he used that time to catch up on case law that, otherwise, he couldn't work into his schedule.

Tom pulled on a pair of gym shorts and padded into the kitchen where his coffee pot had once again accomplished its miracle— brewed while he slept. He poured a cup, then went out front and to pick up his newspaper. Dropping at the kitchen table, he pictured Abby at home, dressing for work, and smiled. He loved the way she looked in the morning—her red hair mussed and her face pure, no makeup. It wouldn't be long before he saw her every day as she awakened. They hadn't set a date for the wedding yet, but he was ready for it to happen.

While reading the sports section—not much to read in June—he decided to call Lonnie. He needed to let her know what he learned about Renée's mother. If Renée acted out in some strange manner, it might help Lonnie understand.

He showered, shaved, and dressed for the day in slacks and a polo shirt. Of course, he wore his western boots, ankle holster, and sheath knife.

At seven-thirty, he called Lonnie. When she answered, he said, "Not too early for you, is it?"

"No way. Charlie used to say nothing good comes from wasting daylight. So, what's up?"

"I want to catch you up on what I learned yesterday. Didn't have a chance last night. Can we talk without Renée overhearing you?"

"She's in bed. Did you find her family?"

"Sorta." Tom gave Lonnie a step-by-step of his trip to the school and the visit with Renée's mother. When he finished, Lonnie said nothing.

"Lonnie? You still there?" he said after listening to the static on the line.

"Yes. I'm here. I'm . . . I'm speechless. I don't know what to say. Are you sure you didn't misunderstand her?"

"I'm sure. And her use of the nickname, Sammi, kind of sealed the deal. She said Renée hates it, but she uses it because she's her mother and she likes it."

"Sammi. I sure can't blame Renée. I've spent all my years with a gender-neutral name. I still get mad when I get mail addressed to Mr. Lonnie Rogers. It goes straight into the trash. And Sammi is even more masculine than Lonnie. I can imagine some of the gibes she gets from others—probably the same ones I've gotten. People think they're so cute."

"Abby's in court today, but she'll attempt to ID Renée's father. Once she does that, I'll track him down. Maybe he'll want to fight for his daughter—and be a better parent."

"I hope. She can stay with me until you get things under control. It's great having her around. She reminds me of . . . Uh, I have to get moving. My early medical appointment, remember?"

"Tell the doc you're healthy and have a heart of gold." Tom hung up, feeling better. Lonnie was a hell of a woman. Of course, if she hadn't been, Charlie would have never chosen her.

That thought of Charlie was like a stab to his chest. *Leave no man behind*—his military creed. Yet, he'd had to leave Charlie. The pain would never go away. Charlie had saved Tom's butt and paid with his life. But, thanks to Lonnie, Charlie's last few years had been his happiest.

At nine-thirty, he called Ken Dotson. "Tom Jeffries here. Anything for me?"

"Thanks for checking in. In the old days, I'd have sent you digging through musty records, but now through the magic of the Internet, I can have Donna do that."

"What are you looking for?"

"We have a case where the heirs are disputing the will." He chuckled. "If kids and siblings weren't greedy, I couldn't make a living. Anyway, I need the death certificate to establish the exact date and time of death. One of the daughters claims the will is dated after the death."

Tom smiled, then reflected on what Ken had said. "Death certificate. They're online, aren't they?"

"For the most part, they—"

"And birth certificates, too, I bet."

"Yes. Why your sudden interest?"

"Because I need one. I mean I need one for a client. I hadn't thought of cyberspace."

"Not so fast, Tom. For a birth certificate, you have to prove a valid reason for getting it. It's a personal record not released to just anyone."

"Oh." Disappointment flooded Tom. "So, to get a copy you have to be a relative or something?"

"That's about it. Parent, guardian, some other legal connection."

"Rats. How about a copy of a divorce decree?"

"That's a public record," Ken said. "All you do is pay the fees. You're really digging at something, aren't you? Can I help?"

Tom gave it quick thought. "Can I trade you for future services—at a discounted billing rate?"

Ken laughed. "Keep it simple, and I'll have Donna do it when she runs the records I need."

"Perfect. I love that arrangement."

"I'll get Donna on the line, and you can fill her in. Good luck with whatever you're doing."

Ken disappeared and a moment later, a female voice said, "Tom, you there? Ken says you have a search for me."

"Not an easy one, I'm afraid. I just realized how little info I have. The mother's name is Barbara Louise Williams, and the daughter is Samantha Renée Williams. I need name and address of the ex-husband."

"By ex, I assume you mean they're divorced. When?"

"Ten, eleven years ago."

"And you don't know his name, other than Mr. Williams?"

"I can't even be sure it's Williams. She might have reverted to her maiden name and changed her daughter's name. That's what I meant when I said I know so little."

"Keep saying it. You're right. Let's see. Divorce records at the state level are stored by the husband's name, so we're out of luck there. If you know the county, you may be able to do a physical search. What county was it?"

Tom said nothing.

"Ooookay, you don't know that either."

"The mother lives in Broward County now."

"Yeah, like people don't move around all the time. Do you have a date of birth on the daughter?"

"Yes, July first." Tom added the year. "If you can get a birth certificate, we can get the father's name off that, then find the divorce decree, which should have his address at that time."

"Uh-huh, and if I'd been born rich, I wouldn't be sitting here listening to you. Look. Ken likes you and says this is important, so I'll talk to some people. I know they won't give me a birth certificate without proper certification. Possibly, though, I can get them to read me the pertinent details—mother, father, and place of birth. Then, like you said, I can obtain a copy of the divorce decree. Would that do it?"

"You bet it would. Find it and I owe you and your husband a dinner."

"Don't have a husband, but I do have a boyfriend with expensive tastes."

"You're on. We'll double date—you and yours and Abby and me."

Tom hung up, feeling better. He dialed Abby's cell phone to let her know she didn't need to call in any IOUs to find Renée's father. He wanted to talk to her, but leaving a message would have to do. Her cell phone would be off while she was in court.

His phone rang. Tom frowned. Ken Dotson. "Hey, Ken, didn't we talk a few minutes ago? What's up?"

"I have something I'd like for you to look into—if you're so inclined."

"Inclined? You know I'm inclined. I'm on the books with you."

"Well, this one is off the books. It's not for the firm, it's for me. Kind of a personal favor, if you will."

"Oh, you mean like having Donna track something for me—*off the books?*"

"No, no. Of course not. I simply thought if you're not too busy . . ."

Tom chuckled. "Want me to come to the office?"

"Maybe we should meet for lunch," Ken said. "Like I said, it has nothing to do with the firm. I'd like to keep it between the two of us."

"You're spooking me," Tom said, a smile in his voice. "Okay, Surrelle's at noon?"

"You're on."

"And you're buying."

After saying their goodbyes, Tom hung up, puzzled at the strange conversation. He shrugged. Noon was only a couple of hours away.

* * *

After placing their orders at Surrelle's, Tom said, "Okay, why are you treating me to lunch?"

"Bear with me for a moment," Ken said. "My story might seem to wander a bit."

"Let'er rip. I'm all yours."

"My mother has a mah-jongg friend with a problem. Ellen, that's her name, is elderly, late seventies. She lives alone in a condo. There's a guy coming by once a week, extorting money from her. She's afraid of this man so she gives him what he demands—two-hundred dollars. Mom asked if I can do anything to help her. So, now I ask you. Can we do anything to help her?"

Tom gave Ken a quizzical look. "The answer is so obvious there must be a reason you haven't done it. Tell her to call the police and report this jerk."

"You're right. Too obvious. She's afraid to call, and I can't do it for the same reason. Let's face it. In our system today, she calls. The cops pick him up. He's back at her door the next day. Sad, but true. And that next visit might be a lot worse than the ones when he only demanded money. Also, Ellen thinks he's doing the same thing to other women in the area. She doesn't want to be responsible for anything happening to them."

Tom sipped his coffee. "This hoodlum sounds like a mother's delight. He deserves to have someone kneecap him."

Ken said nothing, his coffee getting his full attention.

"Uh-huh, I'm catching on. You think I'm the person who can stop him from bothering the ladies."

Ken looked up from studying the swirls in his cup. "I'd never ask you to do anything that would get you in trouble. However, it looks like he won't quit until he bleeds them dry. None of them are paupers, but they're not rolling in money either. They need help. With your background, I thought you might know some way to dissuade him."

Tom smiled and shook his head. "A man's reputation, whether it be true or false, follows him everywhere. Give me her name, address, and phone number. I'll see if I can think of a way to help."

Ken reached into his pocket, came out with a folded sheet of paper, and handed it to Tom.

"You must have been pretty sure I'd help you," Tom said with a grin.

Ken shrugged. "I had hopes. If not, I'd have taken this back to the office and shredded it."

Tom read, "Ellen Lowenstein, Unit 920, 121 Golden Isles Avenue, Coral Springs." The address was followed by a telephone number. "Looks fine. What night does our *collector* come by?"

"Wednesday. Tonight. He usually gets to her place about eight o'clock."

Tom thought for a moment. "Excuse me while I change my order." He waved for the waiter.

When the waiter came to the table, Tom said, "Change my order to the twenty-four ounce porterhouse, and bring me a Killian's. He's paying." He pointed to Ken.

When they were alone again, Tom leaned forward and said, "Now for your issue. Get the word to Ms. Lowenstein someone will call her this afternoon. Leave names out of it. No need to place her in the middle if anyone gets curious. I'll wait until after four to give you time. Then, you make sure you have an alibi for tonight. Might be good to spend the evening with your mother."

CHAPTER TEN

After Tom and Ken went their separate ways, Tom dialed Abby's cell phone, hoping to catch her before she returned to court. Nope, the phone was still off. He left a message. "Honey, don't bother to try and dig up that information we talked about. I found another way to get it—I hope. Also, I've picked up another assignment, which might keep me out tonight. I'll call later and let you know. I love you."

He closed the phone, a smile playing around his lips. It seemed that smile haunted him most of the time now—ever since Abby said, "Yes."

He spent the next hour checking out Ms. Lowenstein's neighborhood. After learning everything he needed to know about her parking lot and the environs, he headed to the library and settled into a comfortable chair, reading and people watching. After his years in the Army, he found watching civilians entertaining. It was a whole different world to him. At four-thirty, he walked outside, flipped his cell phone open, and punched in Ms. Lowenstein's number.

"Hello."

"Hello, Ms. Lowenstein. I'm a friend of Ken Dotson. Did his mother tell you I would call?"

"Oh, yes. Thank you, thank you, Mr., uh, she didn't tell me your name."

Tom said, "That's not necessary. What you don't know cannot hurt you, and you cannot tell. Do you expect your visitor tonight, and, if so, what time?"

"I understand," Ms. Lowenstein said. "Well, I think I do. Yes, it's tonight, and he usually shows up about eight o'clock. He's pretty punctual."

"That's good. Is there anything special that will help me recognize him?"

"He's big and wide. He almost fills the doorway when he walks in. Let me see, most of the time he has on jeans, a black T-shirt, and sneakers. Oh, he wears his hair in a bunch of little braids that stick out all over. Does that help?"

"Yes, that's good," Tom said. "What race is he?"

"Am I allowed to say? I, I don't want to get in trouble."

"Rest assured," Tom said, "the only person in trouble is the man taking your money."

"I think he's African-American. He's very dark. But he has some accent, so he might be Latino."

"Do you pay him in cash or a check?"

"Cash. I tried to give him a check one time, and he got very upset. What should I do tonight?"

"Nothing different. When he shows up, do exactly what you usually do. Give him the money. I'll take it from there."

"Will you be with him?" she asked. "I'm not clear on what's happening."

Tom sighed. "You don't need to know any more, ma'am. You'll get your money back tomorrow or the next day, and he will never bother you again. That's all you need to know."

"Oh, my. Can you do that?"

"Yes, ma'am. I can do that, and I will do that. You rest easy now." Tom hung up, a frown on his face. *What a bastard. Makes me glad I had special training. Thugs who prey on little old ladies need to learn. He will.*

* * *

At seven-thirty, Tom parked in a dark area of the condominium parking lot where he could watch the front entrance. He scooted down in the seat and began his vigil.

A maroon Mercedes entered at eight o'clock and pulled into a handicapped space. A huge black man, dressed as Ms. Lowenstein had described, got out and entered the building. He had no limp and did not appear handicapped, a point Tom filed for later reference.

Tom climbed from his car and moved to a spot in the shadows near the front of the building where he could intercept the extortionist. Twenty minutes later, the thug was back, a roll of bills in his hand, and whistling a happy tune. He shoved the money into his right front pocket as he took out his car keys.

Tom watched, wondering if his time in the building meant he had more than one *client*. Could be. Ken said his mother's mah-jongg friend thought he took money from others. Tom got ready to move as soon as the car door opened.

The hoodlum crawled into his car, and Tom raced forward. He jammed himself into the doorway to keep it open and pressed his knife against the man's side. "I hope you won't do anything to make me shove this knife through your T-shirt and into that roll of fat around your middle. Unlock your back door. We're going for a ride."

"What the hell you talkin' 'bout? I ain't going nowhere with you. Git that knife outta my way."

"I hoped we could do this on a friendly basis." He swiped the blade, opening a large slit in the T-shirt and drawing a bead of blood.

"Ow, you sombitch." He mopped his side with his hand. "I'm bleedin'."

"Next time, the cut will be deeper. And I'll keep doing it until you unlock the back door or your guts hang out. Which will it be?"

The thug hesitated, then the lock clicked. Tom switched his knife into his left hand and filled his right with his Colt .45. "Don't try anything while I'm getting in. This baby will blow a hole through your door, through you, and keep right on going." He opened the back door and entered. Once inside, he pressed the pistol against the back of the thug's head. "Drive. When you get to the street, turn right."

"I ain't—"

Tom gave him a sharp rap with the barrel. I didn't say talk. I said *drive*."

He drove.

Three blocks away, Tom directed him into a strip mall and had him go to the back of the buildings. "Park behind that post office where the lamps are burned out. We have some negotiating to do."

After they parked, and Tom was satisfied the area was quiet, he said, "Now, your name. I like to know who I'm dealing with."

"People call me Big. That's all you need to know. What's yours?"

Tom slapped him with the pistol. "You don't still don't get it, do you? Let me put it in terms you can understand. I'm not a patient man, and I *do not* like you. When we part company, you can be alive and go on to live your life however you choose, or you can be dead, bleeding all over the nice leather seats in this car. *Don't piss me off or I will-blow-your-head-off. Do you understand?*" Tom laid his pistol in his lap and switched the knife to his right hand. He then pricked the back of Big's neck at the hairline, drawing a small bubble of blood. "You will do what I tell you. Hand me your wallet. And, if you have any inclination to get cute while doing it, be my guest. This knife will slice your head off so fast, it'll be rolling in the floor before you feel a thing."

Big hesitated, then in slow motion twisted so he could reach behind him. He came out with his billfold and passed it over the seat.

Tom took the wallet and flipped it open. "Your driver's license says your name is Future Star Miller. Your parents had a strange sense of humor."

"My daddy played football. He thought I would, too."

"You seem to have missed the cut somewhere along the way. I can see why you prefer to be called Big, though."

"Yeah—"

"I don't give a rat's ass," Tom said. "I don't like Big, so I'll call you Star. Fits you better. How's that?"

Tom saw Big's jawbone grinding.

"Let's see what else you have in your wallet." He did a quick thumbing through the bills. "Looks like about three-hundred. That's a good start."

"Take it, sombitch, and let me go."

"You're half right. I'm taking it, but not letting you go. I only see two credit cards, both in your name. That surprises me. Where are the others?"

"What others?"

Tom sliced off a braid and slid it down Big's chest. "Don't play stupid with me, Star. I'm talking about the cards you stole and will either sell on the street or use yourself. But, not to worry, we'll come back to those. Is this list of names the people you've been ripping off?"

"Don't know nothing 'bout no list and no rippin' off."

Tom scanned the list and saw Ms. Lowenstein's name, as well as several other addresses in the building. "I'll take that as a yes. Now, give me that roll of bills in your right front pocket."

"I ain't got no roll in—"

"Wrong." He whacked off another braid. "You're going to look awful funny with braids on one side and bald on the other. Want to keep lying to me?"

Big rolled to his left, slid his hand into his pocket, and brought out a roll secured with a rubber band.

"That's good," Tom said. "Now hand it to me."

After a brief hesitancy, Big did.

"Another thou or so. That's not even worth your coming out tonight. Try the left pocket."

"C'mon, man. Leave me somethin'."

"Oh, I am. I'm going to leave you alive—if you cooperate and do what I tell you. Left pocket."

Big repeated his rotation in the opposite direction and handed Tom another roll. "That's all of it, all I got."

"Maybe. Let's see. How much do we have here?"

"Another thousand. Count it if you don't believe me."

"I will. Now, let's go back to the question about the credit cards. Let me have them."

"Man, I ain't got none, 'cept what's in my wallet, and you done got that. Now git outta my car and leave me alone."

Tom cut off two braids from the same side he'd removed the others. "We can keep this up a while longer. You have lots of these greasy things that should be removed. Is that what you want?"

"Whatever. You the tough guy with the nasty knife. Wanna put it down and meet me outside the car?"

Tom chuckled. "Damn, Star. You must think I'm really stupid. Fight with you, unarmed? You'd snap me in half. But this knife and my forty-five make us about even, wouldn't you say?"

"I don't give a shit. Let's git out, and you can keep them things. I'll still whoop your ass."

"I believe you, Star. I believe you. So, we won't do that. We'll stay right here until you're bald, then I'll look for something else to carve. Your ears stick out. Bet all the girls laugh at you. I can help you with that problem—just slice them right off." Tom rested the blade in the notch between Big's right ear and his head and exerted enough pressure to draw blood. "Yep, that would work. You'd be flat on the side of your head. No ears for anyone to make fun of."

Tom waited a moment, letting Big think whatever he chose. "Time's up. Give me the cards and your phony IDs."

"I keep 'em in the console. That's my safe. I'll have to open it to get them out."

Tom chuckled. "I'll bet they are. Let me see now. You're wearing jeans and a T-shirt. That means you either have an ankle holster or the gun is in your car. I suspect the latter. Could it be in the console?"

"Why you so suspicious? Want me to show you?"

Tom thought a moment. Not good. The console lid swung upward toward the rear of the car. That meant Big would have clear access without Tom being able to see inside. Not a situation guaranteeing a long life. "We'll skip the cards. You need to win one."

Big humphed. "Some hero you are. No guts. Sure you don't wanna try me?"

"Nope. We're almost finished here. Two more small points. I have the utmost respect for those who carry on their lives in spite of their handicaps. You parked in one of their spaces. That will not happen again. If I see your car in a handicapped space again, it will have four flat tires and many scratches when you return. Plus, there'll be a big, burly cop leaning on the hood. Got it?"

"You borin' me. Move on."

"Here's the last part of the deal. You're going to forget this part of town. All the people who live in this area are going to disappear from your address book. And, I hope you won't move your little shakedown operation to another neighborhood. Because if you do and I find out about it, we will meet again. The next time you won't like me at all."

"I don't like you now."

"Oh, that hurts my feelings." Tom snipped a braid. "Next time, it'll be body parts I'm cutting off, not these disgusting dreds. You need to change your hairstyle. Do we have an agreement?"

"You got the gun. You got the knife. I ain't got much choice, do I?"

"Very astute reasoning. I didn't expect that from you." Tom slipped fifty dollars into Big's wallet and put his driver's license and credit cards into their slots. "I don't want you to think I'm the type who would leave you penniless, so I'm giving you enough cash for a six-pack on the way home. Also, your credit cards in case you need a tank of gas. But remember, I know where you live. I have no qualms about staking out your place and blowing your head off if you mess with these little old ladies again. You're understanding me, aren't you?"

"Yeah, asshole. But it swings both ways, you know."

"Time will tell," Tom said. "Last thing. You wear your watch on your left wrist so I assume you're right-handed. Is that correct?"

"Yeah, so what?"

"Put your left hand over your right shoulder, fingers apart."

"Huh?"

"Just do it."

"This is stupid," Big said as he did as told.

Tom grabbed Big's pinkie and snapped the bone.

"Oww, you sombitch. You—" Big sat for a moment, holding his broken finger, sucking air through his teeth. After a moment, in a cold voice, he said, "You needs to know you 'bout to make your secon' mistake."

"Really? What's the first?"

"Messin' with me. Nobody messes with Big what don't pay for it."

Tom chuckled. "Can you hear the sweat dropping off me back here? I'm really scared." He paused, then said, "Okay, I'll bite. What's the second?"

"Not killing me while you gots the chance."

"Consider yourself lucky. I'm in a compassionate mood tonight. You should get yourself to the hospital. That could be a bad break." Tom put his knife away and picked up the pistol as he opened the door and stepped into the night. "Remember, you don't want to see me again."

Big started the engine, backed out, and threw gravel as he raced away.

Tom moved across the alley and fitted himself into a shadowed doorway. If Big returned, he planned to be ready for him.

Tom waited about thirty minutes then walked to Ms. Lowenstein's parking lot where he'd left his car.

CHAPTER ELEVEN

The ringing of the telephone woke Tom. He rolled over, picked it up, and mumbled, "Hello."

"She's gone. She left during the night."

"What . . . who?" Tom stuttered. "Who is this? What time is it?"

"Lonnie. It's six o'clock. Tom, I'm so sorry to wake you, but Renée is gone. I looked in her room, and she's not there. Where can she be?"

"Settle down, Lonnie. Let my head clear. I had a late night."

After retrieving his car from Ms. Lowenstein's parking lot the previous evening, Tom called Abby to see how her day went. She was exhausted after a tough day in court and said she was going to bed early, facing the promise of another nasty day.

Since he couldn't see Abby, Tom had decided to check in with some of his snitches. He liked to keep up to date on street-happenings. Buying a few beers now could pay off later. He pub-crawled until well after midnight, drinking with several different people. His head had hit the pillow about three. Now there was a panicky woman in his ear when all he wanted was sleep or, next best, coffee.

Tom said, "Check around the house. I'll call you back in ten." He clicked the off button, then swung himself out of bed, and looked at the clock. She was right. Six in the morning. He'd had three hours of fuzzy sleep—too many Killian's with too many different people.

He headed toward the kitchen where his coffeepot waited. The hour was too early for it to have performed the miracle of fresh coffee, but he could flip the switch. He thought he remembered preparing it when he got home.

Ten minutes later, he sat at the kitchen table, a hot cup of joe in front of him, the phone against his head. "Sorry, Lonnie. Now, what about Renée?"

"She's gone, Tom. I looked in every room in the house, and she's not here."

"Was she there when you went to bed last night?"

"Yes. I peeked in on her after watching the *Tonight Show*. She was sound asleep . . . or I thought she was."

"And she was gone when you got up?"

"Yes. But that's not the worst of it."

"Oh," Tom said. "What is?"

"I'm in her room now. She left her new clothes piled on the vanity. Oh, Tom, she's run away. Why?"

"I don't know. You relax, though. I'll find her. I can't promise she'll come back, but I won't leave her out there. There's too much evil looking for young girls like her."

Lonnie sobbed into Tom's ear. "What can we do? She's so naive, so innocent. Find her, Tom. *Please* find her."

"I'll do what I can. Settle down. Make a cup of tea or something. I'll hit the street. Maybe she returned to the area where I found her. In the meantime, dig through her room. Maybe she left a clue." He paused, considering the situation. "I suppose it's possible she went home. I'll call her mother."

"Yes. Maybe that's it. It could be. I bet she went home. Oh, Tom, I hope so."

"Don't get your hopes up too high. Like I said, I'll call. Have some coffee. Eat some cereal. I'll get back to you."

Tom hung up, feeling as low as he had in a long time. What was it about Renée that had gotten so close to him? Then he realized she reminded him of his sister as a young teen—the way she was when he left for the Army.

A deeper sadness settled over him. As he often did when alone, he spoke to his dead sister, Katherine. It had been his salvation on many a mission in hostile areas while a Special Forces operative. He knew some might call him nuts, but he dismissed their notions.

So far, she hadn't answered him. If she did, he might have to re-evaluate.

"Sis, I know I failed you, but whatever part of heaven you're in, put in a good word for me. I'll need all the help I can get. I don't think Renée went home. I think she's on the run, and nothing good can come from that."

Tom refilled his cup and headed for the shower. Thirty minutes later, he was back at the kitchen table, clean, shaved, dressed, and sipping fresh coffee. He watched the clock tick around to seven, wondering what time would be safe to call Barbara Williams, Renée's mother. If his impression of her were right, she'd be a late sleeper. He decided to give her until eight.

He called Abby and told her about Renée's absence.

She sounded as distraught as he was. "I wish I could help, but I'll be in court all day today. We're bringing in our *expert* witnesses, and I'm responsible for them. I'm so sorry."

"I understand. To be truthful, I'm not sure where I'll start. If she's not with her mom, and I'd give long odds on that one, about all I can do is drive around and hope I see her."

"Do you have a picture?"

"No. Never thought about taking one. I'm hoping Lonnie has one."

"Well, good luck. I'm sure you'll find her. Now, I have to dress and get out of here."

At eight o'clock, Tom called Renée's mom, who was not happy at being awakened. The call went as he anticipated. She had not seen Renée and wasn't holding her breath for Renée to come home. Furthermore, in spite of Tom's urgings, she refused to contact the police.

Her last words were, "*If you find her, keep her.*"

He called Lonnie and asked about pictures. His first piece of good luck. She had taken a couple of snapshots of Renée, so he swung by Lonnie's house and printed out several copies. He intended to spend the rest of the day showing the pictures around, hoping someone would know something. But first, he had to wrap up his confrontation with the thug the night before.

He headed for the law offices of Dotson and Nelson. En route, he called Ken. "I have a list for you and money to be distributed. I'm sure you and your mother can take care of it. I'm on another mission today. A young girl's life might be at stake."

"No problem," Ken said. "You do what you need to do. I'll make sure the money gets divided equally. Before you go, though, will there be any more, uh, interface with the extortionist?"

"I think not. But, if he shows up, let me know. I'll pay him another visit."

At the office, Tom delivered the bills and the list of people to Ken, who was effusive in his gratitude. "You need anything, let me know. It's yours."

"Same as yesterday," Tom said. "The info off the birth certificate and divorce decree I told Donna about. In fact, I need it worse today."

"Want to tell me why?"

"I'd rather not," Tom said. "One of those situations where the less you know, the better off you'll be in the long run. But rest assured, if I need legal help, I'll come running."

"You're on. And, somehow, we'll get the ID information for you."

* * *

"Get him in here." Lester Goodrich-Green said to his special bodyguard, Antoine, who leaned back in an expensive leather-covered, plush chair along the wall of the large office. Lester Goodrich-Green, who considered himself a special boss in his own world, pointed toward the waiting room beyond the closed, heavy oak door.

He prided himself on his *appearance* as a legitimate businessman. He owned the four-story building and the land around it, including a ten-acre lake that his office overlooked. Anyone taking a cursory look at his business ventures would find a slumlord with holdings in several major cities—everything legitimate. In reality, his wealth came from a variety of criminal activities, including extortion of those too weak to resist.

Mr. GG, as he insisted people refer to him, wore an expensive dark western suit, white satin shirt, and a fancy bolo tie. His boots were custom made, and his black 20X Stetson sat on a special stand he had made for it. A fancy alligator hatband stood out against the white beaver. Although Mr. GG was born in Brooklyn and had only visited Texas for business purposes, he enjoyed presenting himself as a westerner. His freshly shaved head reflected the concealed overhead lighting.

He watched as Antoine walked into the anteroom and motioned to a large man sitting on the edge of his chair. "Boss wants you."

Future Star Miller, aka *Big,* stood, glanced at the others in the room, then moved toward the doorway. His steps were heavy as if he carried a huge weight on his shoulders.

Mr. GG smiled, thinking, he knows he screwed up. He knows the price. Then he turned toward the window overlooking the lake and watched the fountains. The sun played on the water, creating rainbows through the spray.

"You want me, Mr. GG?"

Mr. GG ignored the voice, instead concentrating on a covey of ducks racing across the lake. First, one would gain an advantage, then another. "I enjoy watching nature at work. No fancy rules to live by. No asshole cops putting people in jail because of laws passed by another bunch of assholes. They do what comes naturally." He glanced at Big. "I stocked my lake with fish. Ducks showed up and they eat the fish. Ducks attract alligators who eat them." He spun his chair. "But who eats the alligators, Mr. Future Star Miller—or should I call you Big?"

Big stared, his mouth working, but no words coming out.

"I eat the alligators," Lester said in an authoritative voice. "I love alligator tail. Ever had any? Chewy, but tasty. I make fish food out of the rest of the meat and bones, and boots and other things out of the hide. So you see, it's a complete circle—from fish to ducks to alligators to fish." He propped his boots on the corner of his desk and relaxed. "Nice, aren't they?"

Big found his voice. "Yes, sir. Those are some mighty-nice boots."

"You bet your ass they are. Best money can make." He dropped his feet to the floor. "And that brings us to your problem, doesn't it? Money, the money you didn't turn in." He stopped and bored into Big with his eyes. "I understand you told my man some bullshit story about being robbed. You even have a broken pinkie to prove it. Oh, I'm so sad for you." He paused, then came back with a raised voice. "You know I'm not going to believe that crap. My people don't get robbed." He leaned forward. "They do the robbing. Right?"

Big swallowed hard, his face contorting into desperation. "It's the truth, Mr. GG. Some sombitch ambushed me and took it. That's the truth, I swear it is. And, and he even broke my finger. See. I had to go to the hospital and ever'thing."

"Uh-huh. My man says you should have collected about three thousand last night. Where is it?"

"It's . . . uh . . . like I said. Some bastard—"

Mr. GG slammed his open palm on the desk, the slap sounding like the crack of a pistol. "Don't give me that crap. Don't make me think I hired a collector so weak he can be taken down by one man, that I hired a collector who thinks he can steal from me, then blow smoke up my ass. I hired you because you're supposed to be able to take care of yourself. Are you telling me you're nothing more than a *big* baby? Do I need to assign a babysitter? Should I send somebody with you to collect from little old ladies? Or, should I cut my losses now and get rid of you? Answer me, *boy*."

"No sir. Let me be. I'll make it good. I promise."

"I know you will. In fact, I'm absolutely sure of it." He swiveled his chair toward the window overlooking the lake. "Come over here."

Big walked around the desk.

"Look out the window, this edge of the lake. See those two dark humps in the water, about three feet apart?"

"Yes, sir."

"That's one of my alligators, one of the small ones. He's just lying there, being as patient as a bird of prey floating on the wind. But if something bothers him, those jaws snap open and take care of the problem."

He looked at Big whose eyes bulged. "My outlook on life is like that gator's. I like to take things easy and let the world take care of itself. But like him, I have my limits—and I have Antoine. He is very loyal to me. Aren't you, Antoine?"

While Big looked toward him, the bodyguard nodded, no expression on his face.

"So, here's the deal," Lester said. "You *will* pay me six thousand by the end of the week or my alligators will have dark meat on the menu. Understand?"

"Yes, sir, Mr. GG. I understand. I sure do. I'll get the money."

"Good. I'm sure you will," Lester said, again staring out the window. Such a peaceful scene, so serene. He took a deep breath and felt himself relaxing. Yes, nature had a wonderful way of doing things.

After a moment, he turned back to his desk. "Antoine, take Mr. *Big* Miller out and give him some vigorous exercise. You know the routine. Mr. *Big*, this is to serve as a reminder that people who work for me turn in every dime they collect."

Antoine took Big by the arm and walked him toward the door.

"Oh, Antoine," Lester said. "While you're, uh, *discussing* this with him, convince him this kind of thing is only allowed to happen once. The second time he feeds my alligators."

CHAPTER TWELVE

Tom stopped at a bookstore and bought street maps of Miami-Dade, Broward, and Palm Beach Counties. Putting them together, he discovered the area stretched about a hundred-twenty miles north to south, and from ten to twenty-five miles wide. Almost every inch was built-out. He gave up counting towns. They clung together like grapes in a cluster with no clear boundaries between them. Finding one teenager who wanted to stay hidden would be as daunting as guessing the number of peas in a jar—or, in this case, finding one pea among many jars.

He decided to concentrate on the area in Broward County where he'd first seen her. Maybe she was there for a reason, and that reason was strong enough to draw her back.

His second thought was to contact Deputy Gomez at Renée's school. He remembered an impression of sympathy when Tom told him about Renée. At a minimum, Gomez should know the areas where runaways hung out.

And third were his snitches—if he could find them. Some of them had no desire to show their faces during the day. They didn't trust the system any more than Tom did, but for different reasons. Theirs usually had to do with some petty crime they'd committed. They were creatures of the night.

He checked the time—nine o'clock. He decided to head toward West Coral Lakes Middle School. Perhaps Gomez was on duty again.

Once he arrived, he put his weapons in the trunk of his car and walked into the school. Deputy Gomez sat at his desk.

"Hey, you're back," Gomez said. "Did you find Samantha's mother?"

"Yeah, I did." Tom frowned. "She'll never make mother of the year."

"I've heard that," Gomez said. "Is Samantha alright?"

"She was, but that's why I'm here. She took off again last night. I need to find her before something horrible happens to her. She's not near as tough as she thinks she is."

Gomez gave him a hard look. "Why'd she run? Did you—"

"Don't even ask. She was staying with a *female* friend of mine who was treating her like a queen. Something got to her and caused her to disappear. I can't leave her out there alone. Can you help me?"

Gomez rubbed his chin. "Sure wish I could, but I don't know her well enough to say."

"C'mon. You must hear the scuttlebutt among the kids as to the safe places to run so parents can't find them."

"There's some neighborhoods near the ocean I've heard them talk about. The kids say there are people who will take care of them."

"That doesn't sound good. What's the word at the station?"

Gomez shifted his gaze toward the empty hallway, then looked in the other direction, as if checking to see if anyone was close enough to overhear him. "Look, you're putting me on the spot here. You know I'm not allowed to talk to you."

"Yeah? So what? It's better to let a young girl fall between the cracks?"

Gomez appeared to think for a moment. "We do as much as we can. We run lots of patrols through the area, but a cop car is a signal to disappear. We've had a few successful stings in the past, but new lowlifes flood in faster than we can chase them out. You might want to walk the streets, but even if she's in that area, don't expect to see her. Kids have a way of staying out of sight—with a lot of help."

Tom sighed. "No different from too many parts of Florida. Actually, I shouldn't blame Florida on this one. There are jerks everywhere preying on kids. I plan to make sure Samantha Renée is not one of them. I appreciate your help. If you pick up anything, please let me know." Tom laid a business card on the desk. "Too bad these kids don't see more adults like you who care about them."

Both stayed silent for a moment, lost in their own worlds. Then Tom said, "What happens if I hit the local police station and report what has happened? Will they accept a report and look for her?"

Gomez tugged at an ear. "Hard to say. It's certainly not the normal missing person report. That should come from the mother. How can they know you're on the up and up? You have no relationship with the family."

Tom frowned. "Okay, another scenario. Do you believe me?"

Gomez stared at Tom a moment. "Let's say I have no reason not to, so yeah, I guess I do."

"Suppose you report her as missing? Can you get things moving?"

"Still not the normal missing person report. Look—"

"C'mon, Gomez. A young girl's life is at stake here. Can't we for once throw out the bureaucratic bullshit and do what's best for her?"

Silence filled the hallway as the two glared at one another. Gomez broke first. "I'll do what I can. At least, I can ask the local patrols to keep an eye out for her."

"It's a beginning," Tom said. "Here's a snapshot taken yesterday. While you're pushing from your end, I'll do what I can to find her." He stuck out his hand. "Allies?"

Gomez grinned as he took Tom's hand. "Allies."

"Call me if you get anything."

* * *

Tom drove to the strip mall where he first found Renée. Leaving his car in the front parking lot, he went in the convenience store, and approached the clerk. Tom surmised he might be from the Middle East.

The clerk's eyes grew large when Tom reached into his pocket.

"Hey, be cool," Tom said. "All I need is information." He removed the picture of Renée and held it out.

The confusion in the clerk's eyes told Tom there was a language problem. Not surprising. It was South Florida. In simple terms,

Tom asked if the man had seen Renée. After several tries, he got an emphatic shake of the head.

"No. No see her. She no here."

Figuring he'd gotten as much information as possible—perhaps not as much as the clerk knew, but all he could put into English—Tom thanked him and left.

Out front, he stopped and looked around. The alley where he'd first seen Renée attracted him. He turned alongside the convenience store and entered. Memories of Renée and the two thugs, Rocky and Jumbo, who were about to rape her, flooded his mind. His hands opened and clenched, opened and clenched. Anger filled him—anger at those who preyed on the helpless, anger at his inability to find Renée, anger at Renée's mother who should lose the title, and anger at a society that allowed such injustices to occur.

He walked down the alley. Everything was the same—rotting garbage, discarded boxes, trashcans, and debris of all types, everything with its unique foul odor. And the rats. They scurried into their holes as Tom encroached on their space. He imagined their wondering why a human would want to come here.

He exited the far end, having seen nothing interesting. The lot for overflow parking behind the strip mall stretched in front and to his right and left. He turned right and walked its perimeter.

He hadn't expected to find evidence of Renée, and he didn't. Not that the lot was clean, just that there was nothing of her. Back at the entrance to the alley, he went in. This time he stopped where he'd accosted the thugs. The blades from their knives still stuck from between the concrete blocks in the wall of the convenience store where he'd snapped them off. That brought a smile to his face. By now, they probably had replaced their weapons, but they'd remember Tom and maybe, spend time watching over their shoulders. The experience might make them less likely to attack a helpless female. Tom hoped so.

Other than the blades, he saw no indication of the confrontation he'd fought with Rocky and Jumbo. The blood they spilled was gone, sucked up by rats, or covered with a new layer of grime. The alley had recovered from the human incursion. How long had it been—two days, three days?

He returned to the front parking lot—through the stinking alley. Leaning against his car, he called Lonnie. "Any word from Renée?"

"No. But I did find something that worries me."

"What?"

"It's . . . it's like she was doodling on the desk pad. She wrote several times, *I won't go home. I can't go home. I won't go. I can't go. They can't make me go.* Why would she write that?"

Tom thought about it. "Did you say anything to her about going home?"

"No. When I first met her at your house, I asked if she wanted me to call her mother or someone for her. The look in her eyes was wild, as if she was afraid and would run at any second. I changed the subject fast and didn't bring it up again."

"Okay, that's not it. But somehow, she must have gotten the idea we'd send her home." He thought back through the last couple of days. "Remember when I called you yesterday morning? I told you about visiting her mother. You thought Renée was asleep. Maybe she wasn't. Maybe she heard us talking and imagined the worst."

Silence filled the line, then Lonnie said, "I bet that's it. After we hung up, I went to her room, and she was getting out of bed—or I thought she was. She put on a show of stretching and rubbing her eyes. It seemed . . . a bit phony—especially as I consider it now. I think you're right."

Tom sighed. "Knowing doesn't help us find her, though. I'll keep looking. You keep recalling every word she said. Maybe she dropped a hint somewhere."

"I'll do it. Find her, Tom. We have to find her."

Tom said good-bye and closed the phone. "Easier said than done. I have no idea where to look next."

He spent the rest of the afternoon cruising streets in Coral Lakes. He worked both commercial and residential areas. He saw a lot of young people, but Renée was not one of them.

At four-thirty, his phone rang. The caller ID read *Abby*. In spite of the disappointment he felt about Renée, his spirits lifted.

"Hi, Sunshine. You out of court for the day?"

"Yes," she answered. "Any word on Renée?"

"Nothing. Not a sniff. I hope your case went better."

"Not much. I'll tell you when I get home—if you're there. Will you be?" She hesitated. "I'd really like it if you were."

"I'll have a chilled martini waiting for you."

"That's wonderful. This has definitely been a two-olive day. I have to drop some files at the office, then I'm on the way."

* * *

Tom drove straight to Abby's house and let himself in with his key. Each time he used it, he blessed the day he met her. Then true to his word, he timed her arrival and met her at the car door, took her briefcase, and handed her a chilled glass filled with a clear liquid and three olives. "I figure three are better than two. Change while I pull something out of the freezer for dinner."

Abby took the glass, then put her other arm around his neck, pulling him to her. She kissed him, then said. "Why don't you move in with me? You could do this every day. Why do we keep living apart?"

Tom returned the kiss, then sipped from her martini. "Because I'm an old-fashioned guy. And because it wouldn't be good for the career of an up-and-coming Assistant State Attorney to be shacked up with a nobody. But I'm willing to elope any weekend you're free."

Abby nuzzled his neck. "Sounds good to me." She pulled back. "But I made my dear mother a promise, and I'm stuck with it. Now, let me in the house before the neighbors call the cops and accuse me of lewd and lascivious behavior."

Tom laughed and stepped aside. He followed her into the living room, placed her briefcase on a side table, and headed for the kitchen. He smiled when he heard Abby humming as she walked into the bedroom. For the umpteenth time, he thought, I'm such a lucky guy.

* * *

During dinner, Tom updated Abby on his unfruitful search for Renée, concluding by saying, "I feel like it's hopeless. There are a million places she could be. No way I can expect to *stumble* over her."

"It does seem like a long shot. Still, what's the alternative?"

They were quiet for a bit until Tom broke it by asking, "How about your day? How's the trial coming?"

"Not as bad as trying to find Renée, but I'm worried."

"Oh?"

Abby sipped her water, then smiled at Tom. "You know I shouldn't discuss a case with you—especially one in the courtroom."

"True, but you want to."

"Yes, I do. This is such a frustrating situation. It's spousal abuse. We have enough to put this guy away—pictures of her black and blue marks shaped like his hands and fists, the wife's statement right after the assault, medical experts testifying as to what probably caused the bruises, a urine sample with blood in it . . . the works."

"So?" Tom leaned forward. "Sounds like a slam dunk."

"It should be. But it's the oldest story in the book. The wife has changed her mind and was a weak, and I do mean weak, witness. You'd have thought she was married to the Pope—he never touched her, never hurt her, never even yelled at her. To make matters worse, the defense counsel packed the jury with women. And my first chair didn't try too hard to stop her. She has trotted out—"

"Whoa, I'm getting confused. She who?"

"Sorry. The defense attorney is Sheila Kennedy. She's good and produced witnesses who testified the wife is accident-prone—walks into furniture, trips easily, and other things that produce bruises. Each also said she's a slob, keeps a terrible house, her cooking is barely edible, and she's always browbeating and humiliating her husband in public. She even trotted out a *doctor* who said her type was prone to bruising."

"Is the jury buying it?"

"I'm terrified that they are. They appeared to be leaning forward in their chairs as the witnesses related what a terrible wife she is. If I'm any judge of people, they're picturing her as a rotten person, who hurts herself, or worse, deserves to get knocked around."

Tom frowned, a look of disbelief on his face. "Would a woman think that way? I mean, wouldn't they sympathize with the victim?"

"As nutty as it might sound, no. Many women are tougher on other women than they are on men. Of all the bosses I've worked for and all the co-workers I've had, the women have been the toughest. They can be your best friend, but the first to put a knife in your back on the job. I'm afraid the same thing is happening in this case."

"I defer to your knowledge of women." Tom ducked his head. "As you know, I have little experience in that area."

"You don't want to open that to discussion, do you?"

"Nope," Tom said, standing. "How about a cup of coffee? I brewed a short pot of decaf."

"Sounds good. And it won't keep me awake. Of course, it won't get this trial out off my mind either. We should wrap it and have it to the jury tomorrow. Then, I'm going to crash all weekend."

Tom set a cup of coffee in front of her. "Does that *crash* include me?"

"You bet it does. I expect to have my head in your lap while you watch your stupid games." She sipped. "Excellent. Just the way I like it—the right amount of milk and sweetener. Thank you."

"My goal is to please, my Sunshine."

Abby set her coffee swirling as she concentrated on stirring it. "Tom?"

"Uh-oh. I know that tone. What'd I do?"

"It's not what you did. It's what you haven't done." Abby laid her spoon beside her cup. "You haven't reported Renée's disappearance to the police. Don't you think you should?"

"You sure know how to hone in on a guy's insecurities. I've been arguing with myself all day about that. My head says I should. My heart says no."

"Why? Isn't it the logical thing to do?"

"I guess it's a combination of the look in her eyes when I mentioned the police after rescuing her—and her mother's attitude. Renée does not want to go home, and I can understand why. If we bring the police in and they find her, they'll either take her home or turn her over to the Department of Children and Families. Both are lousy solutions."

Abby frowned. "Staying on the street is better? No way, Tom."

"I know. I know. I'm hoping she'll show up at Lonnie's. Then, once she's there, we can come up with a better solution—like finding her father. Maybe I'll get his ID tomorrow and can start the search."

Abby rose and stood behind Tom, massaging his shoulders. "How long can we afford to wait? If we screw this up, the next time we see her might be in the morgue."

Tom took her hand. "I understand." He stood, turned, and kissed her. "I'm going to run now. I want to swing through the neighborhood again where I first saw her. Maybe I'll get lucky."

"If you're coming back, don't be surprised if you find me asleep. I'm exhausted."

"You get your rest. I have some people I hope I can find tonight. Once I'm finished, I'll head to my place."

CHAPTER THIRTEEN

Tom slept in on Friday morning, having spent most of the night searching the streets of Coral Lakes. He saw many young people in situations that did not bode well for them, but no sign of Renée.

His visit with snitches had been as unproductive. They explained, in no uncertain terms, they paid no attention to the runaway kids who inhabited the sidewalks, sleeping in doorways, panhandling, and far worse things. Getting mixed up with an underage female was a quick way to the slammer. Tom handed out pictures and told them he didn't want them involved, but to give him a call if they saw her.

As he sat at his breakfast table, nursing a cup of coffee, considering what to do for the day, the phone rang. "Tom Jeffries Investigations."

"Good morning. It's Donna, Mr. Dotson's legal assistant. I—"

"Donna. Good to hear from you. Hope you have the news I need."

"I do. Get a pencil and pad."

Tom sat his mug down and pulled a piece of paper toward him. Picking up a pen, he said, "Let fly. I'm ready to copy."

"Per the birth certificate, the father's name is James Robert Williams. When the divorce decree went through ten years ago, his address was 1999 Plano Road, Dallas, Texas. Is that what you needed?"

"Current address?"

"Not from me. Try the Internet. Couldn't be more than a few hundred Williams in Dallas."

"Right. Thanks, Donna. I'll let Ken know he owes you a bonus."

"That'll be the day. Good luck and remember, Mr. Dotson says you didn't hear anything from me or the law firm."

"Gotcha." Tom hung up, staring at the name. Williams. One of the most popular last names in the country, and Texas was no exception. And the others, James Robert. He frowned, wishing Williams' parents had shown a bit of imagination. Iggy, Digby, or something in that range of popularity would have been nice.

He took his coffee into his office and dropped into the chair in front of the computer. Connecting to the Internet, he searched on James Robert Williams, Dallas, Texas. A moment later, he had over four and a half million hits.

"Oh, no. This is impossible. Hey, Sis, think he goes by his initials?" He put in J R Williams, Dallas, Texas. That took him up to four-point-seven million hits.

He stared at the monitor. *Maybe he's at the same address.* He searched on 1999 Plano Road, Dallas, Texas. No such address. He leaned back in his chair, struggling to dredge up memories of his police days in Dallas. He remembered major reconstruction in the eastern part of the city where Plano Road was. Maybe they renumbered the streets as they renovated, widening streets, and wiping out whole neighborhoods.

After a few more searches without luck, he stood and headed for the kitchen. *Obviously, the Internet is not the solution. Guess I'll have to go to Dallas and find him—if he's still there.*

He refilled his cup and sat at the table with his pad and pen. Try as hard as he could, he found no answers. He caught himself drawing circles, no new ideas coming to mind. *I can't leave the area. Suppose Renée needs me. And I can't find Williams from here.* He stared at the ceiling, thinking back through the years, to his active days in Dallas. First, the police force. Then, his time after getting a PI license.

A shadow of a memory nagged at him. He squeezed his temples, trying to dig deeper. *Edwards.* The name leapt forward. *First name? Funny first name. Not standard. A game. A sport. A card—Jack, King, Ace. Yes, Ace Edwards.* Once he had the name, the memory flooded forward. Ace was an ex-Dallas cop, same as Tom. He hadn't known Ace well while in uniform, but he had been a friend of a friend. He had a good rep. Like Tom, Ace left the force and became a PI, only he did it first. Could he still be there, still be a PI?

Tom returned to the computer and searched on Ace Edwards, Dallas PI. There he was. His biography, resume, snail mail address, email address, and, most important, his telephone numbers—landline and cell. A feeling of exultation flooded through Tom as he copied the pertinent information to his hard drive.

Then the questions began. Could he hire Ace to find Williams, and how much would it cost? Would Ace take on such a daunting task? Tom pictured Renée as he'd first seen her—filthy, accosted by two thugs, and so frightened her skin was snow white under the dirt. Yes, he'd either hire Edwards or ask him about another PI who would do the legwork. James Robert Williams, father of Samantha Renée Williams, had to be found.

Tom checked the time on his computer—nine-thirty. Eight-thirty in Dallas. He picked up the phone and punched in Ace's landline number.

After the fourth ring, he heard, "You've got Ace Edwards, top PI in Dallas. If it's legal, I can do it. I specialize in finding those that others can't. Leave your name and number, and I'll get back to you."

"Ace, Tom Jeffries here, a voice from your past. Give me a call, please. I'm at . . ." He left his number and hung up, a smile on his face at Ace's recording and the confidence that came through in his voice. *Well, my man. I have a challenge for you.*

He checked the phone numbers he'd copied and punched in the second number—Ace's cell. It rang three times, and Tom resigned himself to leaving another message, then a voice said, "Ace Edwards, Private Investigator."

"Ace, this is Tom Jeffries. We were on the Dallas police force at the same time."

"Who? Jeffries? I don't remember— Wait, yes I do. Aren't you the cop who had the shootout in the convenience store and took out three would-be robbers? Then . . . then there was some kind of scandal. Wait, don't tell me. I'll . . . Yes. The media thought you should have had a kumbaya moment with them instead of dropping them in their tracks. You were all over the Dallas newspapers and TV. Same guy?"

Tom chuckled. "Good memory. In fact, too good. I was hoping folks had forgotten that."

"Not a chance. You came out of it a hero. Yeah, that's what happened. There was a big ceremony with the Chief and the Mayor. Even the Governor sent his congratulations. I remember standing at attention in full dress uniform while everyone treated you like royalty. So, where are you now? What can I do for you?"

"I'm in Florida with a PI shield like yours. I need a favor, a big one."

"If I can. Anything for one of my personal heroes. What is it?"

"Find someone."

Ace chuckled. "Now you've hit one of my specialties—Ace Edwards, finder of missing persons. What's the name?"

"James Robert Williams."

"Age?"

Tom thought a moment. *Renée is almost fourteen. He should have been at least nineteen, twenty when she was born . . .* "Thirty-three to forty-five."

"That's quite a spread," Ace said. "Can you narrow it any?"

"Sorry, but that's as good as I can do."

"Last known address."

Tom hesitated, knowing he had no good answer. "1999 Plano Road."

"In Dallas?"

"Yeah. In Dallas—several years ago."

"I'm sorry, Tom, but I know Plano Road pretty good." He hesitated. "I'm not sure there is a 1999. I did a stakeout in that area not long ago. If I'm remembering the right area, it's commercial—warehouses and light manufacturing. Are you sure about the address?"

"I wish I were. However, it's the best I have."

"Okay, let's move on. What's his profession?"

"I don't know."

"Physical description?"

"I don't have one."

Tom heard a deep sigh. "I'm getting the idea you have a name and nothing else. Is that right?"

"Not exactly," Tom said. "I have an address to go with the name—and the name of his daughter who needs him."

"Not sure about the address part. Daughter who needs him? I'm a sucker for a sob story. Give it to me."

Tom told Ace everything he knew about the Williams family. He finished by saying, "That's pretty much it. Renée refuses to go home to her mother, and her mother is perfectly happy with that. I'm hoping Renée and her father can bond, and he will give Renée a real home."

"Tom, you're a romantic. Do you really believe this Williams character will open his arms to a daughter after being out of her life for . . . for how long?"

"Ten years-plus."

"Stuff like this only happens in the movies. You're wasting your time."

"I know, but it's all I've got. I'm open to suggestions. Do you have one?"

Silence filled the line.

After about ten seconds, Tom asked, "Will you try to find James Robert Williams, father of Samantha Renée Williams?"

Silence refilled the line until Ace said, "I don't suppose you're collecting a fee for this. With the pain I hear in your voice, I'm assuming you're doing it *pro bono*, right?"

"No, not right. If I can save Renée from the street, it'll pay more than any case I've ever solved. It's that important to me, Ace."

"Crap. Of all the PI's, in all the towns around Dallas, you had to call me."

Tom chuckled. "If that was your imitation of Bogey, you'd better stay a PI."

"You're right. But I love *Casablanca*. Without putting you on the spot, I'm guessing you can't afford my usual rate, as low as it is."

"Only in gratitude, and room, board, and a tour guide if you visit Florida."

Ace let out a deep sigh that rippled into Tom's ear.

Tom could almost picture the gears in Ace's brain turning, trying to find a way to say no while wanting to say yes—or vice-versa. He said not a word, didn't even let his breath hit the microphone, waiting and hoping.

The clock ticked away about fifteen seconds. "Tell you what," Ace said. "I have a semi-partner. We often share cases, especially ones that are manpower intensive—like this one will be. I'll talk to her, and if she thinks we can help you, we will. How's that?"

"She?"

"Yes, Kit Levitt. Well, actually, her name is Carsen Levitt, but with that name in Texas, she has to be Kit. Get it?"

"Oh, yeah. I was in Texas for only a few years, but I know heroes of the Old West influence almost any situation. When will you talk to her?" Tom let out a long breath, relieved that Ace had made a partial agreement.

"As soon as you get off the phone. I don't think she has anything going today. But don't let your hopes get too high. The first thing she'll do is tell me there are probably thousands of Williams in the greater Dallas area, and at least half of them are James Robert. Then she'll ask me how much the case is paying. When I tell her you'll pay with your gratitude—well, she's very expressive when she's wound up. Get the picture?"

"For sure. I have one like that here in Florida. Her name is Abby. She's sugar and spice unless something riles her, then be ready to duck. She was a successful convoy commander in Iraq, successful because she can be as mean as a mama gator protecting her hatchlings. And she knows all the words that go with that. Yeah, I feel like I've already met your Kit."

"Glad to know you understand. Is there anything else about this Williams you can tell me?"

"Only that his ex-wife is named Barbara Louise Williams, and the daughter is Samantha Renée Williams."

"If I find him, what then?"

"Tell him I'll be in touch. Then get his contact info and feed it to me. I'll take it from there."

"We'll talk later."

The phone clicked in Tom's ear, but it felt like he and Ace had shaken hands. Tom frowned. *Now all I have to do is find Renée.*

CHAPTER FOURTEEN

Tom leaned back in his chair and let out a deep breath. Nothing was resolved, but he felt better. With Ace looking for Williams—well, if Kit agreed to help him—the situation might be ready for a reunion when he found Renée.

He wondered about the father. Tom didn't have any children, but he remembered his best friend, Charlie. Mary Lou was only his stepdaughter, yet Charlie would have fought a mountain lion to safeguard her. There was a bond between them that Tom someday hoped to feel. Perhaps, after he and Abby married, there would be a little Abigail. He smiled, thinking of a tiny bundle in a pink blanket, hair as red as her mother's. He vowed, "I'll never leave you, Little Abby. I'll be by your side forever."

A picture of Renée re-inserted itself into his head. "I don't know why you left, Mr. Williams," he whispered. "Maybe that witch you married, Renée's mother, chased you away. But I hope you don't disappoint me—and don't disappoint your daughter—when we track you down. I'm giving you another chance at the most precious thing in life—fatherhood."

Filled with fresh energy, he sent Abby a text message, hoping she'd read it when the court took a break. *Some progress. Things might be looking up. Good luck with case.*

He refilled his coffee in the kitchen and stared at the clock. Ten o'clock. What was Renée doing? Was she safe? Had she had breakfast? Did she have someone to protect her? How could a thirteen-year-old girl survive on the street?

His head dropped into his hands, and he spoke to his dead sister, as he often did. "Sis, if you can help her, please do. And help me find her. I have to save her before it's too late."

The seconds turned into minutes and then passed in clumps of fives. Thirty minutes later, his phone rang. Caller ID showed the Dallas area code.

"Tom Jeffries, Investigations."

"Glad to know I dialed the right number. It's Ace. I talked to Kit, and she did exactly what I said she would. Told me I was nuts, an old softy, that we can't possibly find the right James Robert Williams among the hundreds, maybe thousands, in the area. Then she chomped on me some more because there are no fees involved."

"So?" Tom said, disappointed. "It's a no-go."

"Of course not. I told you she's one sweet lady. Once she enumerated all the reasons we couldn't do it, she said she'd get right on it. She's putting together a list of Williamses as we speak. She'll handle the computer side of things, and I'll wear out the telephone."

"Ace, if you were here, I'd kiss you—although I'd rather kiss Kit."

"No kisses, but you do owe us a trip to Disneyland. Neither of us has been."

Tom chuckled. "You're on. Let me know when. Abby and I will join you."

"Okay. I'm hanging up. I need to get to work. Lots of phone calls to make."

"Thanks, Ace. Talk to you later."

Tom disconnected, relief flooding through him. When this was over, he'd find some way to pay Ace and Kit. It might not work out, but at least he was doing something. Now it was time to get on the street. Maybe, just maybe . . .

* * *

Lester Goodrich-Green—Mr. GG—sat at the head of his teak conference table. He let his eyes roam the faces of those he had called to the meeting. There was his target of the day, Future Star Miller, who preferred to be called Big. Beside him sat Antoine,

Lester's number one bodyguard who acknowledged no last name. Then Snowcone Wilson, so called because of his snow-white hair, and last, Howard. No one knew whether Howard's first name was Howard, Anthony, or something different. Howard only answered to Howard.

Big's face was swollen, and he looked uncomfortable trying to sit upright. He rubbed his gut and took short breaths as if each one hurt.

"So. What do we have?" Lester said. "Did you find the man who—how did he say it—*robbed* Mr. Miller?"

"We think so," Antoine said. "Last night, Big spotted a man he thinks did it. He was driving a red Chrysler convertible, and Big thinks he remembers one in the parking lot where he was jumped."

"Is that right, Mr. Miller?" Lester asked, a note of skepticism in his voice.

"Yes sir. I'm pretty sure it was him."

"Since I don't see him here with you this morning, I assume you recovered my money, plus interest, then let him go. Is that right?"

"Ah, no sir," Big stammered. "Ah . . ."

"It was my decision not to take him at that time," Antoine said. "He was talking to a boy I've used in the past. He's good for giving bad tips to the cops or anyone else that asks. Anyway, Red Chrysler showed my boy something. I was curious. If he was selling out, I needed to know. Like you, Mr. GG, I take care of those who would double cross me—and I like to do it fast. Besides, we only have Big's word for the so-called hijacking."

Big squirmed in his chair. "But—"

"I hope your decision was the right one, Antoine." Mr. GG rubbed his thick lips. "I do not take it lightly when money that belongs to me is not properly delivered." He glowered at Big, then turned back to Antoine. "What did you find out?"

"His name is Tom Jeffries. He's a private investigator in Coral Lakes. I have his phone number and email address from the business card he gave my man. I can track him any time I want to. But most interesting is he's looking for a girl, a teenager. He gave him a picture and asked that he keep a watch for her. He promised a reward if he found her."

"Antoine," Mr. GG said, frowning. "I have a lot of faith in you, but there are limits. Where are you going with this? Don't disappoint me."

"Jeffries wants her and doesn't know where she is. Why shouldn't we collect his reward? We can always pick him up later."

Mr. GG considered Antoine's words, then chuckled. "I said I have faith in you. Your idea has merit. I'll consider it. Who is she?"

"Her name is Samantha Renée Williams. He believes she's on our streets. We should have no problem finding her. Here's the flyer he passed out."

After looking at the picture, Mr. GG returned it to Antoine. "Keep an eye out for her, but don't move until I tell you. Use Snowcone and Howard." He turned toward Big. "You still owe me six thousand. If you don't pay by the end of the week, the amount doubles. Meeting adjourned."

Big cringed, then rose with the other three. Everyone stood at attention until Mr. GG left the room.

* * *

Tom's slow-crawl through Coral Lakes' streets did little except irritate the drivers behind him. Honking horns demanded he speed up. Again, he saw young girls, but not Renée. His eyes felt strained and gritty, and he was tired of looking. Maybe another hour, then he'd call it quits until the sun went down.

About three o'clock, he saw a couple of familiar faces. He searched his mind. Who were they? His memory clicked in. Rocky and Jumbo from the alley. Tom didn't know how they'd greet him, but they did know Renée. He hadn't seen them since their brief knife fight when he interrupted their attempted rape of Renée. Apparently, the knocks he gave them hadn't been too serious. On the one hand, he was glad they were healthy enough to walk the streets. On the other, he hoped they'd been hurt bad enough to think twice before accosting another female.

He debated stopping and talking to them. They might run, they might want to fight, or, if Sis had done her job in heaven and lined up the angels, they might have news of Renée and talk to him.

He pulled to the curb and got out of his car. "Yo, Jumbo, Rocky." He held both hands up to show he was unarmed.

They stopped and turned toward him. "How you know us?" Jumbo said. "Do I know you?" He squinted. "Yeah, you looks familiar. You ever seen him before, Rocky?"

Rocky glared. "Yeah, yeah, I seen him. Ain't he . . . yeah, he is. That's the honky what broke our knives and left us in that stinking alley."

"Good memory," Tom said. "Glad to see you up and around. No hard feelings on my part. How about you?"

"I got hard feelings," Rocky said. "I gotta knot on my head and my arm still hurts where you cracked it with that bad-ass knife of yourn. You bet yo' ass I got hard feelings."

"I was hoping you wouldn't hold a grudge. I'd like to be your friend. What about you, Jumbo? Can we be friends?"

Jumbo stared at him. "You the craziest white man I ever seen. You broke a gallon of milk on my head, and I ain't gonna think about that pile of shit you left me layin' in. Now you want to be my friend?"

"Sure," Tom said, smiling. "I see no reason we shouldn't be. It's such a small world. I'll even buy you new switchblades, better than the ones you had."

"Alright, what's yo' jive?" Rocky said. "You up to somethin'. What is it?"

"Don't get excited," Tom said, reaching behind him. "I need my wallet." He pulled it from his left rear pocket, and took out four twenties, holding two in each hand. "Here. This should replace your knives."

Both stared at the money, their eyes alternating between Tom's hands and his face. After a moment, they inched close enough to grab the money, then stepped back.

"We'll talk," Jumbo said, stuffing the money in his baggy jeans. "But you need to make it fast. We busy men."

"I'm sure," Tom said. "I need to get something from the car." He opened the passenger door and took out an eight by ten envelope. "I'm looking for this girl. She's only thirteen. Have you seen her in the last few days?" He handed a picture of Renée to each of them. He watched as they examined it, wondering if they would recognize her. If they did, they were good actors—no sign of recognition. Maybe because in the photograph, she was clean, dressed in nice clothes, and had her hair combed. She looked little like the girl they assaulted.

After a moment, Jumbo said, "Why you want to find her? She your squeeze? Kinda young for an old fart like you, ain't she?"

"Nah," Rocky said. "I heard people like him likes 'em young."

"She's a friend," Tom said. "That's all. She's on the street. I'm afraid she'll get in trouble or get hurt. She could even bump into some thuggish people who'd try to take advantage of her. I don't want her turning tricks or selling drugs. You get my drift?" His words poured out hard and clipped, chasing the smiles off their faces.

"I can go there," Rocky said. "There's some bad dudes that would hurt a little girl like this."

Tom raised an eyebrow at Rocky before asking, "Have you seen her?"

Jumbo stared at the picture, twisting it around in the light. "I mighta. Coulda seen her last night. But I can't be sure. You got any more of them twenties? The knife I want cost at least sixty dollars."

"Yeah, me, too," Rocky said. "Me and Jumbo was together when we mighta come across her. We know a man what's got knives with pretty pearl handles and a silver release button."

Tom fished out two more twenties. "I might want to see those blades after you get them. I'm sure they'll be as good as you say." He tore the twenties in half and gave one piece to each of them. "Where'd you see her? And when?"

Jumbo's face flashed disappointment as he stared at the half-bill. "You hard, man. Hard."

"I've been told that before. I'm waiting."

"She mighta been on the corner of First Street and Third Avenue. The one we seen was with another girl."

"What were they doing?" Tom asked.

"Crossin' the street as far as I seen. You see anythin' different, Rocky?"

"Naw. Same thing. Two teenage white girls walking along. If I'd knowed you was lookin' for 'em, I coulda told 'em."

Tom wiped his hand across his mouth. "Which way were they going?"

"Down Third Avenue, headin' south." Jumbo appeared to think for a moment. "They looked alright. Didn't seem scared or nothing."

Tom took four business cards from his wallet. "Here. Each of you take two of these. Her name is Renée. Give Renée a card and tell her to contact me. Tell her it's important."

"How 'bout the other girl?" Jumbo said. "You want her to call?"

Tom hesitated, thinking. It was a good question. "Yes, tell her to contact me, too. And if you see either one of them, you call." He took out two more cards and handed them over.

Jumbo took off his baseball cap and scratched his head. "You asking right much. I mean, me and Rocky got a business to run. If we have to do stuff like this, we be missin' out on sales. What's in it for us?"

Tom stared him down. "Three things. First, I'll make it worth your while. Second, you'll feel good because you're doing the right thing. And third, I won't take you into that alley where we met and stomp the hell out of you."

Jumbo sneered at him. "Could go the other way, but I'm a man of peace, so I'll take your deal." He looked at Rocky. "How 'bout you?"

"Yeah. I can do that. We keep our eyes peeled. If we see her or that other girl, we call you, and you pay us."

"Good," Tom said. "Put out the word to your customers, too. Whoever finds her gets a good payday. But she has to be unhurt. If anyone has done her bad, I'll track them down and do worse to them—much worse—than I did to you. Spread the word."

Jumbo and Rocky nodded.

Tom turned and started toward his car.

"Hey," Jumbo called. "How 'bout the other half of these?" He held up his half-bill as Rocky did the same.

"Sorry. I must have forgotten," Tom said. "Here. You can tape them together." He handed over the two halves, then returned to his car, not sure he'd accomplished anything, but feeling better for the effort.

Tom sat in his car, watching Jumbo and Rocky walk away. They high-fived, probably gloating about how they'd put one over on the honky. There was no doubt their loyalty was for sale, but had he offered enough to buy it—even in a matter as small to them as a young, white runaway on the street? He wouldn't know unless one of them called.

He considered his next move. There was little point in continuing to burn gas driving the streets. He had several pictures in the hands of people who knew the hideaways better than he did. One of them would be far more likely to spot her, no matter how many miles he drove. No good ideas came to mind, so he decided to park near the corner of First Street and Third Avenue. If she walked past once, maybe she'd do it again.

He drove to a strip mall off the intersection and parked where he could watch the sidewalk. He lowered the windows and prepared for a sweaty vigil. Late June in South Florida was no place to perform a stakeout during the day.

An hour later, all he had accomplished was sweating off about five pounds. He was hot, miserable, and frustrated. *Where are you, Renée? And, more important, are you safe?*

He started the engine and kicked the air conditioner to high. After a moment, he raised the windows. Once the car cooled, he'd decide what to do next. He mopped his brow with the back of his hand, feeling better as the cool wind from the vents struck his face.

CHAPTER FIFTEEN

Mr. GG told his secretary to send Antoine into his office. He absentmindedly tapped a pencil on his notepad while he waited. The top page of the pad contained swirls, circles, half-written words, and other examples of his doodling—evidence he'd been thinking. It was a habit that relaxed him whenever he needed to make a decision with long-range implications.

When Antoine had settled in a chair in front of his desk, Mr. GG said, "I've considered your idea about snatching that girl, and decided it's a go. It galls me when someone puts something over on me, and, if I believe Mr. Miller, Jeffries did just that. I considered pulling him in and teaching him never to mess with our people again, then make his body disappear. That would satisfy my need for him to suffer physical pain. But that wouldn't be as good as watching him twist in an emotional noose. That's the worst kind of suffering, the kind you're hopeless to understand or do anything about."

He leaned back, placing his hands over his paunch. "So here's what I want you to do. Take Snowcone, Howard, and Big and get the girl. Bring her here and put her in the basement. You know which room. We'll find out why this Jeffries is looking for her. If it's because they're relatives or something closer, we'll let him know we have her and lead him in circles looking for her. It should be quite amusing."

Antoine chuckled. "I like it, Mr. GG. I like it a lot. But do I have to take Big? I don't have much faith in him."

"Yes. There's a lesson he must learn. Plus, he's the one I want exposed if anything goes wrong. Let him make the actual snatch.

You and the others stay in the car out of sight. That way, he's the only one the police will be able to ID."

"Suppose the cops grab him and he talks?"

"Simple," Lester said. "He dies while we laugh at them with our airtight alibi. There will be several young ladies and some other men who will testify that you, Snowcone, and Howard were with them distributing DNA."

* * *

Abby left the courtroom, her stomach feeling like it had been slammed with a thick lawbook. How could the jury find him not guilty? The pictures, the scars, the experts' testimonies. Everything said he beat her with regularity. Yet, a majority of the jurors bought the story that her injuries came about because she was accident-prone. Worse yet, most of them were women. Ridiculous. American jurisprudence at its worst. It was one of those times when she agreed with Tom.

"So, what's your next case?" Wilbur Taylor, her first chair, said. "I have a home burglary. The police caught him dead to rights, but the defense refuses to plead out."

"What? How can you simply walk away from what we just saw? Don't you realize what will happen to her? The next time he has a couple of drinks, he'll remember she hauled him into court, and he'll beat the hell out of her. We'll see him again. I hope it's not on a murder charge."

Taylor stopped and placed his hand on Abby's arm, halting her. "You need to learn to turn it loose after the jury votes. Yes, I feel sorry for her. Yes, I think he's guilty as hell, and I'm upset that he beat the rap. But none of that changes a word. Our court system says he's not guilty. End of case. Time to look forward, not backward. We have too many pending cases to live in the past."

Abby took several deep breaths, considering what he'd said. He was right, but she couldn't be that callous. He'd been in the office ten years. How many such injustices had he lived through? She could only hope she never developed so much scar tissue she didn't feel it anymore.

"Wilbur, if I ever become as blasé about justice as you are, I hope I have the good sense to recognize it and quit. I'd prefer to chase ambulances than have no remorse when criminals walk free. I will never, ever be like you. Now, I have to visit the ladies' room."

As she spun away, she saw the shocked look on his face. Fine. He deserved it.

She stopped at the mirror, fluffed her hair, and retouched her make-up. What little she wore really didn't need freshening, but she wanted to kill enough time for Wilbur to leave the area. She shouldn't have been so curt with him, but damn it, a woman's health was at stake, maybe her life. How could he be so unconcerned? Or was he right? Should she become a hard case like him? Should she simply adopt the attitude of whatever happened in the courtroom stayed in the courtroom? She thought of Tom, knowing what he'd say. Then she thought of Katherine, Tom's sister, and how the justice system failed her. No way could Abby grow a shell like Wilbur Taylor's. No way would she allow that to happen.

Tom. She remembered the text message he sent her. *Some progress. Things might be looking up. Good luck with case.* That's what she needed. Good news. As she walked out of the bathroom, she hit autodial for his number.

"Hi, Sunshine. What's up?"

Hearing his voice and his out-of-nowhere nickname for her lifted her mood. "Not much. What did you mean things are looking up?"

"Let me see. First, I got an ID on Renée's father, a James Robert Williams, who lived in Dallas at the time of the divorce. Then I contacted an old acquaintance, who agreed to try to track him down. If they can—"

"They?"

"Oh. Forgot to say. My friend is Ace Edwards and he works with another PI named Kit. He wanted to bring her in because she—"

"Kit? She? Tom, after the day I've had, please keep it simple. My puzzle solving abilities aren't in the best condition."

"Bad news?" Tom said, his voice losing its upbeat tone.

"The worst. The guy walked on all charges. Not even a slap on the wrist."

"I'm so sorry. I know how deeply you felt about this case. I don't suppose there's any way to go after him again."

Abby sighed. "Not unless—no, make that not until he does it again. It's a shame his wife will have to suffer more."

"Why doesn't she leave him? Surely, she knows it'll be the same thing all over again."

"Social services is working with her, but leaving is not in the DNA of abused wives. The same things that allow them to take the abuse keep them in the relationship. There are volumes written about it, but no one has found the solution."

The line stayed silent for a moment, then Tom said, "Want I should talk to him?"

"Who? Talk to whom?"

"The husband. Maybe I can impress on him the disadvantages of hurting his wife."

Abby hesitated. Could Tom scare him enough to keep him from abusing his wife? Yes, she believed he could. She shook her head. No way. She had sworn an oath. "Tom, you know that's not possible. My heart might say yes, but my brain says you have to stay away from him. The justice system might not be perfect, but it's the best one ever developed. It has spoken. Life moves on."

"And an innocent person pays," Tom said. "It's an old story to me—not one I have much respect for."

"Please, Tom. Leave it alone. Don't make me think I can't share myself with you. Let's change the subject. You were telling me about your friend in Texas, Kit somebody. You said he's a she. How's she going to help?"

Tom exhaled, then switched with her. "Ace figures she'll use the Internet to track Williams while he works the phone. No way of knowing if any of it will produce anything. Williams could be living in Alaska or Timbuktu by now."

"We can keep our fingers crossed, though. There's always the chance he's still in Dallas."

Tom chuckled. "That's one of the things I love about you. Ever the optimist."

"Beats the alternative. I hope to be home by six. Will you be there?"

"Martini or Killian's?"

"How about opening a bottle of Riesling? In fact, chill another bottle. I feel like a wet night." She hesitated. "And Tom, will you stay tonight? I don't want to sleep alone."

"Of course. Whenever you need me, I promise to be there."

During their conversation, Abby had exited the courthouse and now stood beside her car. "I have to go into the office and check a few things. I'll get out of there as fast as I can, though."

"Before six?"

"If I can make it."

"I'll be waiting."

Abby disconnected, feeling better—not much, but better. At least Tom had a successful day.

She walked through the big doors of the courthouse into the South Florida humidity. She'd be sweating long before she reached her car.

"Hello, Ms. Archer."

She started, not expecting to be addressed. When she turned to the speaker, she was even more startled—the abusive husband, Angel Rodriguez.

"Hope you have a nice weekend. Mine will be much better since I'll be spending it with my wife. No more jail time, right?"

* * *

Tom heard the click as the line went dead, then closed his phone. He stared at it, considering what she'd told him. Another jury duped by a slick defense counsel. Tom didn't blame the lawyer though. It was the justice system—a system that gave all the advantages to the guilty. When would it change? When would the victim get top billing? Most likely, never. If history was a measuring stick, it would get worse. Soon, criminals would own the streets while honest citizens had no choice but to cower within their homes.

If guns are outlawed, only outlaws will have guns. The pro-gun adage came to mind. Tom wasn't a part of the *everyone needs a gun* crowd, but he believed the flow of illegal guns could never be stopped. Street sales would continue, same as drugs remained available in spite of the many laws and actions against them. As long as there were illegal guns, there would be people using them, and as long as there were people to use them, there would be illegal guns. A strong justice system could control crime, yet its dilution was almost beyond repair after so many years of bleeding hearts whining about the poor accused.

Tom remembered the judge's ruling when the men who raped and killed his sister appeared in court. *The fruit of the poisonous tree doctrine* freed them—not because there was doubt about their guilt, but because the police had crossed some imaginary line. That ruling had almost cost another young woman her life. Although she lived to talk about it, she would live with the memories of gang rape forever. Tom wondered if the judge had felt any remorse when the five were arrested the second time. He hoped he had. He hoped he had lain awake at night, cursing himself for turning them loose. Tom hoped he burned in the flames of hell for letting them go the first time.

He looked along First Street and Third Avenue again. A few pedestrians, but none that could be Renée. He figured he might as well move on, might as well head for Abby's. Hopefully, one of his snitches would see Renée—or maybe Jumbo and Rocky would spot her—and call him.

* * *

After dinner and cleaning the kitchen, Tom and Abby moved to the couch where she curled up in the protective shelter of his arm, a cable news channel on mute portraying the worst in the news. Neither appeared to care what the talking heads thought was important.

The atmosphere was almost somber. Abby seemed trapped in the courtroom, apparently replaying every word of the trial. Every so often, she let out a sad sigh and shook her head.

Tom couldn't get the sight of Renée walking dark streets out of his mind. Where was she? How was she? Could she survive in such a dangerous environment? And even more important, how could he find her?

When they went to bed, their lovemaking was subdued, gentle, passionate, but carrying a hint of the sadness they both felt about the circumstances surrounding them.

Abby rested her head on Tom's chest, her warm body entwined with his. "We have to help her. We must find a way to save her."

"Yes," Tom said. "We can't let her become another victim of a callous society."

It never occurred to them they were each talking about a different female.

CHAPTER SIXTEEN

At seven p.m., with Howard driving, the black sedan rolled down the block, the passengers surveying the sidewalks. Big rode shotgun while Snowcone and Antoine occupied the back.

"Remember, Big," Antoine said, "when we spot her, your job is to get her in the car fast. I don't want her screaming her head off either. If you lose control, we leave you. Understand?"

"You got no reason to worry," Big said. "I'll throw her over my shoulder if I have to. Make sure you're ready to grab her when I stuff her in the backseat."

They continued to drive the streets, examining each young girl they saw. Although light was lost from the sun's setting, streetlights and storefronts filled in, making pedestrians almost as visible as high noon. Antoine kept peeking at the picture, trying to burn her image into his brain.

"Two girls walking away from us," Howard said, pointing to his left.

"Can't tell from the back. Go another block and make a U-turn."

As they came back toward the girls, Antoine compared the picture to them. "They look alike. It could be either of them. Stop alongside. Big, get the right one."

The car stopped, and Big stepped out, leaving his door open. Snowcone opened the back door.

"Which one of you is Samantha Renée Williams?" Big said, walking toward the two females.

"Who wants to know and why?" the girl closest to him said.

"Don't give me none of your damn lip. Answer my question. Which one of you is Samantha Renée Williams?"

The girl who had spoken stared at him, then turned to her friend. "Give me my purse. I need to talk to this man." When her friend didn't move, she snatched the red purse with a gold chain off her shoulder. Turning toward the car, she said, "I'm Samantha. What do you want?"

Big grabbed her arm and quickstepped her to the car. "My friend in the back seat wants to meet you. You're coming with us."

She opened her mouth to scream, and Big clamped a big hand over it. As Snowcone stepped out, Big threw her into the backseat. He jumped into the front and pointed a gun at the second girl, who watched as if in a daze. "You ain't seen a thing. Keep your mouth shut, or we'll find you."

Howard threw the car in gear and sped away.

* * *

Lester sat in a dark corner of the basement room studying the situation. He preferred to be a passive participant, seated where he could watch, but not be seen. Antoine would extract the information he wanted. He had never failed in the past.

The room had special features not found in any other place in the U.S.—or none that Lester knew about. It bore more of a resemblance to the torture chambers of medieval Europe or perhaps, Spain during the Inquisition.

Lester had chosen one of the less punishing devices for the girl, one he had personally designed. While he had no qualms about disemboweling a man, he had a soft spot for young people—unless they tested his patience too much. Antoine reported that the girl refused to utter a word during their trip to the facility. However, Lester believed he could still use a softer approach on her.

Antoine, Snowcone, and Howard finished strapping her into a special chair. It was made of polished stainless steel with pneumatic legs, each with a separate control, allowing the seat to be tilted in any direction. As soon as her arms were secured, Antoine raised the chair so her feet could not touch the floor, then extended the rear legs an extra two inches. She slipped to the front, only to have a retractor trigger the flexible band around her waist, causing it to jerk her back. The slide and jerk would continue until Antoine got the answers he wanted. Only one person had defied them long enough to frustrate Lester. To test his belief in the chair, he instructed Antoine to leave the prisoner overnight. When they re-joined him in the morning, he was broken. He begged to talk.

Lester smiled at that memory. The high-fat content of the feed he made had especially pleased the fish in his lake. To commemorate the occasion, he harvested an alligator for a new pair of boots.

Antoine walked around the chair, a smile playing as Samantha slipped and was jerked, slipped and was jerked. "Okay, I'm ready if you are."

"Ready for what?" Slip-jerk. "What do you want from me?" Slip-jerk.

"We're interested in the man who is looking for you. He took something that belongs to us, so we took something that belongs to him. That seems fair, doesn't it?"

"I don't belong to nobody. I'm my own person." Slip-jerk.

"Maybe. But he is looking for you. I'm sure you're aware of that. What is your relationship with him?"

"I don't know him." Slip-jerk. "Never seen him in my life. I know he's got a poster out, but I don't know why." Slip-jerk. "Now let me out of this damn chair."

"Oh, Samantha. I had hoped you would cooperate. Obviously, you're not in the mood—yet. I'll have some food brought in for you, then my friends and I will have dinner. We should be back in a half-hour or so. You might be friendlier by then."

He nodded toward Snowcone who walked into the hallway.

He was back ten minutes later with a bowl of tomato soup and a diet cola, both with covers with a small hole and a long straw. The food sat in recessed compartments on a modified lap tray.

Antoine adjusted the legs on her chair so she quit sliding, then placed the tray in her lap. He took another strap, looped it around her neck, then connected it to each side of the tray. "This will make sure your food doesn't end up on the floor. Sorry, but you'll have to sip through the straws. I can't undo your arms."

Once he was sure the tray was in the position he wanted, he elevated the rear legs. The slip-jerk routine began again. "Enjoy your meal. I'll be back."

As he and Snowcone walked through the doorway, Antoine nodded at Howard who sat in the shadows behind her.

Lester watched them leave, then rose and exited a door in his corner.

Antoine waited in the hall. "I think a half-hour should be enough to get her talking. She's cocky, but that chair will break her down."

"I agree," Lester said. "Dinner should be ready. We'll talk to her again after we eat."

* * *

An hour later, Antoine waited until Lester had hidden himself in his viewing corner, then opened the door and walked in.

Lester smiled as he settled into a comfortable lounger. The chair had apparently worked. The girl's sobs could be heard through the room. She was beaten.

Antoine faced her. "Are you ready to answer my questions?"

"Yes," she said through her tears. Slip-jerk.

"Good. I'm going to level the chair, but if you don't cooperate, I'll have to raise the legs again. Okay?"

"Yes. Please stop it."

Antoine evened the height of the four legs. "Now, Samantha, who is the man searching for you?"

She sniffled, leaning forward as far as she could, as if relieving pain in her middle. "I don't know him. I really don't. I'm not Samantha. My name is Jeannie."

"Samantha, Samantha, Samantha. You disappoint me. I guess it's the chair again." Antoine stepped around her.

"No. Please. I'm telling you the truth. I covered for her. Her name is Samantha Renée Williams, but she goes by Renée. She's the girl I was with. Honest, I'm not her. Please don't torture me anymore."

Antoine stopped and studied her, then walked into the darkened corner where Lester sat. "I think we have the wrong girl. Big screwed up."

Lester scratched his chin. "If you're right, Big has become a liability we can't afford. Go back and ask her why she pretended to be Samantha."

Antoine crossed to her and asked.

"Renée is young and scared. She doesn't know how to live on the street. I've been helping her. When that big man approached us, I could see how terrified she was. I don't know why, but I decided to protect her."

"Weren't you scared? Why would you do that?"

"There's guys like him everywhere. They usually run when I show them my knife. He didn't look like much."

Antoine reached behind him and picked up a knife. "You mean this one?"

"Yes. Can I have it back when I leave? You're not going to hold me are you? I need that knife."

"We'll see. Now, what do you think of the guy who grabbed you now?

"Same thing. He's . . . uh, soft, will scare easy. Not like you. You scare me. And this chair is the worst thing I've ever seen. Please let me go."

"If I let you go, what will you do?"

"Nothing. I won't tell anyone. I'll just go back on the street like you found me."

"Will you help us find the real Samantha?"

"Yes. I know where she hangs out. Please don't leave me in this chair again. I'll take you right there."

Again, Antoine consulted with Lester.

Lester said, "We'll take her back to the neighborhood where Big grabbed her. Tell Big I want her eliminated, and he is to do it. After he's finished, return him here. I have plans for him."

Antoine waved Snowcone over.

"Make sure Big leaves her where she can be found and make sure the Samantha Renée Williams ID is in her bag. That'll send a message to the bum who took our money. He'll know he's next."

"Gotcha," Antoine said. He turned to Snowcone. "Take Big and Howard. Pack her in the car and have Big kill her. Hide the body and purse in plain sight, then bring Big back here. The boss needs him."

CHAPTER SEVENTEEN

Tom's cell phone jolted him awake. He jumped out of bed and looked around, hoping to grab it before it woke Abby. Another ring led Tom to the dresser where he'd left the phone along with his billfold, pocket change, and keys. The caller ID read *Blocked*.

He answered, "Tom Jeffries, Private Investigations," as he walked out of the bedroom.

"Lt. Richards, Coral Lakes Police Department here. Do you know a young girl named Samantha Williams?"

Tom shook his head. "Hold it, Lieutenant. You woke me from a sound sleep. How about slowing down and giving it to me again."

"We've met before. I'm Lt. Jim Richards of CLPD. I asked if you know a Samantha Williams. Seems pretty simple to me. Late night?"

"No, not a late night. I'm just not accustomed to being awakened by a surly policeman. Do you always block your number? Afraid I wouldn't answer?"

"Close. So do you know the girl?"

"Why do you ask?" Tom's stomach rolled. *What has Renée gotten herself into that has drawn the attention of the police?*

"If you know her, tell me. If you don't, go back to sleep. And this time, the truth would be nice to hear. As I recall, you chose to lie the last time I asked for your help."

Richards referred to Tom's failure to identify the body of Mary Lou Rogers, the seventeen-year-old stepdaughter of Tom's best friend, Charlie. The gang who killed her left her naked with no identification other than Tom's business card stuck between her fingers. When Richards showed Tom the body in the county morgue, Tom chose not to identify her. He felt he owed Charlie that opportunity. Apparently, Richards held a grudge about it.

"We've been there, Lieutenant. I did *not* lie. For good reasons, I chose not to tell you everything I knew. I believe that falls under Freedom of Speech, which is protected by the First Amendment. And, before you accuse me of hindering your investigation, I didn't do that either. I promptly notified her stepfather within the hour, and he told you who she was. If you need time to refresh yourself on our Constitutional rights, I'll hang up and you can call me later."

There was a brief pause. "Okay, let me try again," Richards said, his voice tight. "If I hurt your silken feelings, I apologize, but I need to know if you know this young woman. Do you?"

"Same question. Why?" *He's playing games. He must have something on Renée. I hope it's not drugs. Maybe she got swept up in some kind of sting. I'll call Ken Dotson as soon as I get this cop off the phone. Ken owes me one.*

Richards sighed. "I'm standing in the morgue, doing what I least like to do. I'm staring at the body of a teenage girl. She carried ID of Samantha Renée Williams. She also had your business card. If you know her, I'd appreciate it if you would take time out of your busy schedule and come down here and formally identify her. Then, I can get on with trying to find the bastard that killed her. Have I explained enough for your satisfaction?"

Tom was in the process of pouring a cup of coffee. The coffee splattered on the counter, splashing him. He set the pot down, afraid he'd drop it, grabbed a dishtowel, and dabbed at his arm. *No, not possible. He has to be wrong. Slow it down, Tom. Slow it down.* After mopping the counter, he walked to the breakfast nook and settled into a chair. "She's dead? Is that what you said? What makes you think it's Renée?"

"From your voice, I gather you knew her. Look, Jeffries, I'm not sure of anything right now—anything except there is a dead teenage girl on the slab. I need formal identification before I can move on. Will you come down here?"

Tom's head spun, guilt ripping at him as badly as when he learned of his sister's death. It couldn't be Renée. It just couldn't be.

But there was only one way to find out. "It'll take at least an hour to get there. I'm up in Palm Beach County."

"Fine. If I'm not here, ask for Dr. Gonzalez. And, Jeffries, I'm sorry. I don't like you much, but I shouldn't have let my feelings intrude. I'll wait to hear what you say."

Tom disconnected, disoriented, not wanting to believe what he'd heard. Why? How? What could have happened to Renée? He stumbled into the bedroom and headed for the shower.

"Who was on the phone so early?" Abby asked. "Tom, what's wrong? You look— Oh my God, who's hurt? Lonnie? Is it Lonnie?"

"No, no. Not Lonnie." Tom sat on the edge of the bed. "Renée. That was Lt. Richards. He thinks Renée is in the morgue. I have to go in and identify her."

"Please, no," Abby said. "It can't be true. Not Renée. She was so . . ." Tears ran from her eyes as she covered them with her hands.

Tom held her a moment, then took a deep breath. "I need to shower. Then I'll head down to Coral Lakes. Why don't you go back to sleep?"

"As if I could." She sniffled. "No, I'll go with you."

"Abby, I love you. But this is something I'd rather do alone. Don't ask me why. It's just the way I feel."

She gave him a long look. "I understand. It's part of that hideaway you have inside you which is not open to anyone, even me. I've seen you retreat into it before. I couldn't touch you then, and I can't touch you now. But for reasons I don't understand, Renée got closer than anyone in a long time. Do what you have to do. Phone me as soon as you know something."

He started out of the room.

"Oh, no," Abby said. "I have to go into the office for a while. I'll try to wrap it up by noon. Call my cell."

* * *

The sign stood in front alongside the entrance to the building.
City Morgue
Entry by Permission Only
Again, he wondered why such a sign was necessary. *Entry by Permission Only.* Surely, no one would want to visit the county

112

morgue when they didn't have to. Then he remembered the media. Yes, they would consider it *news* if they could gain entry, even better if they could get videos of autopsies and bodies.

He looked around and saw an unmarked police car parked in an *official* slot. He wondered if it belonged to Richards.

Without enthusiasm, he opened his car door and got out, thinking there is a teenage girl in there ready for autopsy. He remembered the last time he was here, called to identify another young woman who would never enjoy the pleasures life could bring. He remembered how cold Mary Lou had looked, how the bruises around her throat stood out against the whiteness of her skin—and how dead she was. He couldn't bring himself to identify her, feeling like it would be a betrayal of his friend, Charlie. He didn't, and he made an enemy. Now there was another body and the same police officer standing over it. Tom hoped he would be unable to identify this one—for real.

He walked into the reception area. "I'm Tom Jeffries. I'm here to meet Lt. Richards."

"Yes," the young blond receptionist said, "he said I should expect you. Please sign in." She turned a clipboard toward him.

As Tom filled out the form, she called on the phone and announced his presence. A moment later, Richards appeared through a doorway leading to the rear of the building.

"Thank you for coming in, Mr. Jeffries. Anytime you're ready, we can go back. Everything is prepared for you."

"How about you give me some details first? What happened to her?"

"I'll tell you what I know." He waved Tom to a couple of chairs in the corner. "We don't have much yet. We received a nine-one-one call about a body in a dumpster. When my partner, Detective Summers and I arrived, we found the young woman. She'd been shot in the back."

"Executed?"

"I don't play semantics with death. All I know is she was dead."

"Was she . . . did she have on clothes?"

"Yes. And the M.E.'s preliminary findings say she had not been raped, if that's what you're thinking. Right now, we have no motive for the murder."

Tom released the deep breath he'd been holding. "Thank God for small favors. How was she dressed?"

"I'll show you what she wore. Mr. Jeffries, I really would like to get on with this. All I can tell you now is that a purse was in the dumpster with her. There was an ID card in the name of Samantha Renée Williams and one of your business cards in the purse."

"Is that all?"

"A couple of dollars, some change, and lipstick. I have a complete inventory list in the back."

Tom didn't move.

"Sir, can we get this over with?"

"Yes. Sorry if I seem to be dragging my feet. It's not something I'm anxious to do."

"I understand, but the sooner we have an ID, the sooner we can begin to backtrack her. Hopefully, that will lead us to her killer."

"You're right. Let's do it."

They walked through the doors leading to the back of the building and down a corridor. At an unmarked door, Richards stopped and pulled a paper mask from a box and slipped it over his nose and mouth. He handed one to Jeffries. "We also have Vick's if you want it."

Tom took the mask. "This will do. That stuff makes my eyes water too much." He slipped it on.

They entered a large room with cold storage vaults arranged in a horseshoe around three of the walls. In the center were several stainless steel tables, each with a drain. Tom's stomach lurched at the sight.

"She's over here," Richards said, walking toward a table with a figure covered in a white sheet.

Tom followed him.

"It's not pretty, but her face is not too marked." He hesitated and pulled back the sheet.

Tom stared, at first shocked. It was horrible. A beautiful young girl lay on the table, her face relaxed in the permanence of death.

He wanted to gag, but forced it down. Instead, he walked to the other side and peered at her. A feeling of disgust settled over him. Could it be? There were definite similarities. The hair, the nose—even the eyes. He leaned closer, and a feeling of peace and satisfaction replaced the disgust. There was a dead girl on the table, no doubt about that. But it was not Renée. First, he felt relief, then guilt flooded him. A young girl had lost her life. How could he feel relief that he didn't know her?

He let out a breath he hadn't realized he held. "Sorry, Lieutenant, I can't help you. I've never seen this girl before."

"Are you sure?" Richards stared at him. "Can I believe you this time, or are you playing games again?"

"Trust me. This is not the Samantha Renée Williams I know. There are similarities, but this girl looks older. Renée is a young-looking, almost fourteen-year-old. How old would you say this girl is?"

"Judging by my daughter, Chelsea, who is twelve, I'd guess mid-teens, maybe sixteen, seventeen."

"Me, too. It's not Renée."

"Why did she have Williams' ID?"

"Beats me. Maybe her name is the same."

"Not likely, is it?" Richards rubbed his chin. "Any idea why she'd have your business card?"

"Not really. I spread them around as thick as I can. You never know where the next call might originate. There are many places she could have picked one up."

"Yeah, but yours carried your special message. Come over here."

As they walked, Tom said, "We had this conversation once before. Have you forgotten that I write *If I can help, call me* on the back of my cards? And before you ask again, yes I sign them."

"I might remember something about that. Still seems strange though."

Tom shook his head. "I don't see anything strange about it. I need work. I do what I can to get it. Now, can I see her purse, what she was carrying?"

"Why? You said you don't know her."

"I don't," Tom said, "but you asked for my help. I'm trying to give it to you."

Again, Richards stared at Tom, doubt in his eyes. "Over here." He walked to the side of the room where several clear plastic baggies lay on a counter. "This is the purse we found. These other bags have the items that were in it. Here's the ID and this one holds your business card. Feel free to look, but don't open anything."

Tom picked up the bag with the purse and turned it around, examining it. Red plastic with a gold chain that could be worn over the shoulder. She hadn't had it when he found her in the alley, but it could be something Lonnie bought her. He'd have to ask.

He checked the ID card. The date of birth put her age at eighteen. Apparently, the forger figured she couldn't pass for twenty-one, but eighteen made her old enough for everything except buying booze. The picture was blurred. Could fit a thousand different girls.

"You know this card is a bad counterfeit, don't you?" Tom said.

He scowled. "No. I floated in on a garbage scow this morning and am learning how to be a policeman. Of course, I know it's phony. But I go with what I have, and what I have is an ID with the name Samantha Renée Williams on it. Now, from what you tell me, I'm back to Jane Doe. You ever see the purse before?"

Tom glanced at it laying on the counter. "No. I never saw Renée with one like it. I suppose she could have picked it up somewhere though. I simply *do not* know."

"Okay, one more time, and I'll leave it alone," Richards said. "Have you ever seen the victim before?"

"No. Never. Now, a question for you. Where did you find her? You said a dumpster. Where is it located?"

"Behind a Pizza Hut on Third Ave. In the two-hundred block."

"Yeah, I know the area. Kinda rough."

Richards took the plastic bag from Tom's hand as he locked eyes with him. "I don't like that look, Jeffries. Stay out of it. I'm pretty sure you're not leveling with me, that you have some scheme up your sleeve."

"Scheme? I have no idea what you're talking about. Now, one for you. What killed her?"

"Gunshot. Under the sheet, there is some heavy bruising. My guess is someone punched her in the midsection several times. My best guess is somehow she got loose and ran. The bastard shot her through the back."

"Sad, very sad," Tom said. "Like I said though, she's not the Samantha Renée Williams I know."

"I believe you. But there is more to it, isn't there?"

Tom moved toward the exit. "I don't know her. You asked me to come here for an identification. I can't give you one. Good luck, Lieutenant. I hope you find her killer."

CHAPTER EIGHTEEN

Tom sat in his car, air conditioner blasting. Even in the morning, a car left in the sun could heat to sauna-plus temperatures—and his had. He was tempted to lower the top to assist the AC in expelling the oven temperature air, however, he'd then be faced with the bright sun. Instead, he chose to drop the windows a couple of inches.

He opened his phone and hit autodial for Abby's number.

"Tom, was it Renée?" She answered as if she'd been staring at the phone, willing it to ring.

"No. Not Renée."

Abby's sigh of relief sounded loud. "Thank God. Do you know who it was?"

"No," Tom said in a resigned voice. "Another teenage girl, murdered in the prime of life. Another young unidentified corpse found in a dumpster. Why, Abby, why? When does it stop?"

"I don't know, Tom. The police catch all they can, and we put them away when juries allow it. There's nothing new here. It's been going on forever. We have little hope of stopping it. Our best is to make the cost as high as possible."

"I know," Tom said. "But it doesn't help that the system works against the victims. Look what happened with your wife-beater. Free to do it again. If the police are fortunate enough to catch the ones who murdered this girl, I'll lay you odds they have a previous arrest record. The cycle is non-ending."

"Why did Lt. Richards think it was Renée?"

"A purse was found in the dumpster. There was a phony ID in Renée's name. No other identification."

"You said found it in the dumpster? How do they know it belonged to the body?"

"They don't. And that's part of my fear. It could have been thrown into the dumpster before or after the body. Renée could be . . . I have to find her. She's either out there somewhere, or something dire has happened to her. I have to know which. And if I happen to stumble across the slime that murdered that teenager, they're history."

"No, Tom. You can't take the law into your own hands. Please, don't. Let the police handle it."

"Yeah, like they handled my sister's case. Like they handled the wife-beater. Like they brought the *Thorns on Roses* gang down."

"You know those were aberrations. It doesn't happen that way every time."

"Too often for me. It should never happen."

Abby sighed. "Have you talked with Lonnie? Maybe she's heard from Renée."

"I'll give her a yell. But I think she'd have called if she knew anything."

"How about Renée's mother? Maybe—"

"You're kidding, right? She's about the last one Renée would contact."

"It can't hurt to try," Abby said in a quieter tone. "The bond between mother and daughter is often stronger than either believes. If Renée's in trouble, she might dash for home."

"Okay. For you, I'll do it. But I'm not optimistic."

"I wish I had more time, but I have to run. Case meeting coming up. We'll talk tonight, all right?" She hesitated, then said, "Please don't do anything foolish."

"I never do," Tom said. "What you might consider foolish, I consider justice. And proper justice is never foolish. Until tonight, Sunshine. I love you."

"Love you, too."

The phone went dead in Tom's hand. He stared at it a moment, wishing he and Abby could somehow escape the ugliness in the world. Couldn't happen. He called Lonnie.

"Have you heard anything from Renée?" he asked when she answered.

"No, have you?"

"Same." He debated a microsecond about telling Lonnie what happened to the Jane Doe, then decided not to. No need worrying her more than necessary. "I was just hoping."

"I'll let you know if I hear from her," Lonnie said. "Well, I will after I give her the biggest hug in South Florida."

"One question," Tom said, a pause in his voice. "Did you buy her a red plastic purse with a long, gold-colored chain?"

"Yes. It was love at first sight. As soon as she saw it, she asked if she could have it. I realized last night it was the only thing from our shopping trip she took with her. Why do you ask?"

Tom hesitated—truth or duck the issue. "One of my snitches said he saw a young girl with a purse like that. It could have been Renée." Sometimes a small lie was justified—or so he hoped.

"Where? Was she alright?"

Crap. One lie always leads to another. "She was fine. I'm concentrating on the area where he saw her. If it was Renée, I'll find her."

"Oh, I hope so, Tom. I hope so."

"So do I, Lonnie. I'll talk to you later."

They rang off and Tom stared at his phone again. Abby's suggestion he call Renée's mother sounded like a waste of time to him, but it was a loose end he should explore.

He punched in the Williams number and listened to it ring, torn between wishing he'd get her answering machine and the desire to have the conversation behind him. Putting it off wouldn't make it more enjoyable later—probably the reverse.

"Hello."

Tom's disappointment soared. "Ms. Williams, this is Tom Jeffries. Remember I—"

"I well remember you, Mr. Jeffries. What do you want? Haven't you meddled in my life enough?"

"I'm sorry you feel that way. I only have Renée's best interest at heart."

I assume you mean Sammi's best interest. Renée was her father's choice. I don't acknowledge it."

Tom swallowed, grinding his teeth for a moment. "Yes, Ms. Williams, Sammi. Have you—"

"Mr. Jeffries, we have nothing to discuss. I recall that I was very specific when we last spoke. Renée is a juvenile delinquent who has brought me nothing but pain. I don't care where she is, I don't care what she's doing, and if she ever shows up at my door again, I'll turn her over the authorities as incorrigible. Is that simple enough for you?"

Tom counted to five while swallowing the words he wanted to say. "I have a serious question if you'll grant me a moment, then I'll leave you alone. Fair enough?"

"Ask. I have better things to do than waste my time on you and that kid."

"Have you seen Sammi since we last talked?"

Loud laughter answered him. "Hell no. She knows if she comes back here, I'll have her put in jail. I don't expect to ever hear from her again, and even that will be too soon. Now, you've asked your stupid question, and I have a luncheon date. Keep her if you like her so much. Do not call again."

The phone clicked in Tom's ear, leaving him with a guilty feeling for not telling her about the dead girl with Renée's ID. But why bother? She didn't care. He wondered why the Creator allowed some women to have children.

Tom's stomach growled, and he realized he was hungry. Not only was he hungry, but he suffered from caffeine withdrawal. His morning had been interrupted by Lt. Richards—not enough coffee and no breakfast. Time to rectify the situation. He backed out and headed for Denny's. Perhaps an orgy of calories and an overdose of coffee would awaken his brain and snap him out of his doldrums.

* * *

Lt. Richards sat on a steel folding chair, staring at the sheet-draped body on the table. "Who are you? Why did you have to die? What did you do to cause some asshole to put bullets into your back?" He rested his face in his hands, picturing his daughter,

Chelsea. *How can I ensure you a long life when kids are killed every day?*

"Lieutenant," a voice said, "Are you all right?"

Richards looked up and saw Dr. Gonzales standing beside him. He was dressed in a surgical gown and paper booties. He had slid his face shield up onto his head.

"Yeah. It gets so old. Too many kids dying. What can we do, doc? Obviously, tracking the killers and arresting them isn't the solution. We put one away and two more take his place. I feel like a hamster in his wheel—running as hard as I can, but getting nowhere."

"I wish I had a solution. I don't, and no one else does. I'll document how she died, and you'll find the murderer. Then tomorrow, we'll start over again with another one. Death is always a waste, even sadder when it's one with so much life to live." He sat in a chair near Richards and looked at the table.

A great sadness radiated through the room.

Richards' cell phone rang, and he looked at the caller ID. CLPD. "Hello."

"Hey, boss, you finished with Jeffries? Did he know the girl?"

"Yeah, Phil, we wrapped up a few minutes ago. He didn't know her—or said he didn't. I'm not sure, but he seemed sincere. Have you come up with anything?"

"Not really," Phil Summers, Lt. Richards' partner, said. "I put everything in the system. DNA, prints, description, and name as we had it. We might have results on the prints this afternoon—if she's in the database. You know the story on DNA, at least two weeks."

"Yeah," Richards said. "Maybe we should hire those television guys. Fifteen-minutes tops." He forced a chuckle.

"You're off script, boss. I'm the comic in our team. If you'll quit stealing my lines, I'll bring you up on what else I've done. I'm running her description and picture against missing persons reports in the state. Results should be in soon. That's it. Any other ideas?"

"Only the usual. Put some uniforms in the area where we found the body. Ask anyone and everyone if they saw anything. Maybe it'll turn up a witness." Richards thought for a moment. "Give them

Jeffries' description, too. My gut says he'll be all over that area. I want to know what he's doing. I still don't trust him. Tell our guys not to bother him, just record his activities. Then meet me at the scene. Maybe we missed something in the dark."

"Gotcha."

* * *

Tom finished his breakfast and pushed his plate away.

"More coffee, hon?" the waitress asked as she approached his table.

He looked at his cup. "One more—and the check, please."

She fumbled in her apron, then produced his bill, laying it on the table. "Thank you. Pay the cashier. Come back to see us now."

She walked away while Tom added sweetener to his cup. As he stirred the coffee, his mind raced ahead. What to do now? No-brainer. Renée was there, on the street. If he didn't find her, she could end up like the other girl. Why did the Jane Doe have Renée's ID—and probably her purse? Did she steal it? If so, why? Renée didn't have any money or any valuables worth stealing. And who made the fake ID for her? Nothing made sense. Nothing except he needed to find Renée.

Tom rose, left a tip on the table, and walked toward the cashier. All his efforts at finding Renée had proven fruitless. But now he had a clue, a small one, but a clue that might point toward her. The dumpster. If her purse was in it, she may have been in the area. Time to take a look. Of course, that meant circumventing the police who were probably crawling all over it.

CHAPTER NINETEEN

Tom parked in a strip mall a block from the Pizza Hut. From there, he saw several police cars and uniforms working the crime scene. He got out of the car and hesitated as his sunglasses fogged. Late June—hot and humid.

He walked toward the activity around the restaurant, feeling the sweat building. The temperature was already in the mid-eighties, heading into the nineties. The weather forecast was for possible showers in the afternoon. That would be the standard until November when the hurricane season ostensibly ended. During the intervening months, there would be many media-threats of hurricanes. The letters of the alphabet would bend to the frenzy of naming tropical storms and subtropical storms while each broadcast caused a run on milk and bread at the supermarket. But, there was always the chance an actual hurricane could hit, and that made the panic-calls almost worthwhile. For today, though, it was only hot and humid with a threat of showers.

The authorities had strung tape, isolating the rear of the Pizza Hut. "What happened?" Tom asked one of the policemen on crowd-control.

"Body in the dumpster. That's all I know," He lifted his cap and ran his hand over his baldhead, beads of sweat forming behind his wipe.

Tom showed his PI badge. "Okay if I go in? I might be able to help."

"You're kidding, right?" the policeman said, glancing over his shoulder. "I let you in there, and the lieut will take a bite of my ass a yard wide. Nah, you best stay on that side of the line."

"Would that be Lt. Richards you're talking about? If so, I understand. He *can* be a bit of a grouch." Tom thanked the cop and worked his way through the crowd until he had a better view. Officers in what appeared to be haz-mat suits were taking everything out of the dumpster and bagging it. One was inside the container passing the stuff out. Three others bagged and tagged. Even from where he stood, the stench wafted, causing several in the crowd to pinch their noses—but stand their ground. Tom's eyes watered while he hoped he'd see a reaction that meant they'd found something important. Didn't happen.

"Yo, man, what you doin' here?"

Tom felt a point dig into his back as he began to pivot. He stepped forward and continued his turn. "Same as you. Curious about all the activity. Do you know what they're doing?"

Jumbo stood in front of him, an open switchblade in his hand, belly high to Tom. Rocky bounced beside him.

Tom glanced around, wondering if anyone was watching. All eyes were on the dumpster.

"I heard they found a body," Jumbo said. "A young, white bitch. But that ain't your problem. Your problem is me and Rocky got business with you." He turned his head toward Rocky on his left. "Ain't we, Rocky?"

Tom saw that Rocky also held an open switchblade. His was along the seam of his baggy jeans, partially hidden in his right hand.

Rocky nodded. "You tol' us you wanted to see our new blades when we got 'em. We here to show 'em to you. Now, you gon' take a walk with us, and we show you better. Ain't that right, Jumbo?"

"You got it," Jumbo said, a sinister smile forming.

"Fair enough," Tom said, swallowing to hide his surprise at their sudden appearance. He hadn't thought they had the guts to make a play on him—in broad daylight, no less. "I assume you boys want to pick up where we left off, try your luck again. Where and when?"

"When is right now. Where is down the street and up the alley." Rocky grinned as he pointed.

"With these cops around?" Tom said. "That's stupid. They'll be all over me when they hear you two screaming. No, I definitely don't think this is the right time or place. Let me check my calendar. I'm sure we can come up with a mutually beneficial arrangement."

"Lord, he shore do talk pretty, don't he, Jumbo?"

"Yeah, he sho do. But he don't make much sense. I s'pect it'll be him doin' the screamin', don't you?"

Rocky wiped his switchblade on his pants leg. "He'll find out. Yep, he'll find out. You ready, *Jeffries*?"

"Almost," Tom said, pulling on his earlobe. "I was just thinking, though. We can make a better deal. I'm not inclined to spend the rest of my life in jail for killing you. And, I'm betting you wouldn't like it either—if you were lucky enough to get me. I have another idea." He paused, waiting to see if they would bite on his comment.

Jumbo cut his eyes at Rocky, then back to Tom. "What kinda idea?"

"There's two of you and one of me." Tom hesitated, seeing an expression he didn't trust on Jumbo's face. "What say we put the knives away and go bare knuckles? If you guys whip me, you can brag all over town you took down Tom Jeffries, ex-Army Special Forces and ex-cop. That should make you big men for a while." Tom stopped and looked from one to the other.

"We might could do that," Jumbo said. "But let's say I git a heart attack or somethin', and you beat up on Rocky? What you git out of it?"

"Hey, why you say he whup me?" Rocky said. "I can take him."

Jumbo laughed. "You know, I b'lieve you. But, s'pose you broke your ankle or somethin'. I still want to know what he gits."

"Good thinking," Tom said. "Proves I've been right about you all the time."

"What you mean?"

"You're smart. Both of you are too smart to be street bums. You could go back to school, make something of yourselves. I can see you now—"

"Now you gon' too far," Jumbo said. "Nobody'd believe that stuff. If you win, what's the deal?"

"Yeah, I suppose I did. So, here's what I'm thinking. You know I'm looking for a young girl. If I win, you put out the word that you're her street-protection. Let everybody know if they mess with her, they're messing with you. Then you find her. When you deliver her to me . . . no, you tell me where she is, and I'll go to her. When I have her back, each of you gets a Ben Franklin. What say?"

A puzzled expression on his face, Rocky looked at Jumbo. "What's a Ben Franklin?"

"I think it's a hundred-dollar bill. Is that right?"

"Yep," Tom said. "Do we have an understanding?"

"Sure," Jumbo said. "Now let's go to the alley." He folded his knife and dropped it into his pocket, motioning for Rocky to do the same.

The three of them walked away together.

They turned into the alley and moved to the end nearest the unloading area behind the stores. "This is far 'nough," Jumbo said. "Before we start, you need to meet my friend. Sticks, you can come in now."

A tall man wearing a muscle shirt and tight jeans stepped into the alley. His chest was so broad, the shirt looked like a thong separating his pecs. The jeans were in danger of splitting over his huge quads. He stood at least six-six with a shaved head. Every inch screamed muscle.

"Put your knife away," Jumbo said. "The man wants to fight bare knuckles." His smile said the rest of it—he had no doubts about Sticks' prowess.

Sticks stared at the blade he carried in his right hand, an eight-inch fillet knife, then slipped it into a sheath he wore on his belt. "Yeah, that's more fun."

Tom shifted his gaze from Sticks to Jumbo. "Good call, my man. We didn't set any numbers, did we? I admire a man who takes advantage of another's oversights" He stuck out his hand. "Sticks, I'm Tom Jeffries. I guess we're going to go a few rounds.

Before we get started though, that's some physique you have. Where do you work out?"

Sticks looked at Jumbo, a questioning look on his face. When Jumbo shrugged, Sticks took Tom's hand and mumbled, "Glad to meet—"

Tom dug his heels in, grabbed Sticks' wrist with his left hand, then spun, slamming Sticks into the concrete wall. Fortunately for Sticks, his chest hit first with a resounding thud. The crack that sounded when his forehead caught up brought a smile to Tom's face. Sticks crumpled and didn't move.

"Oh, that's too bad," Tom said. "I think your boy lost his urge to fight. Who's next? One at a time or both at once? Let's go."

When no one moved, Tom stepped forward and buried his fist in Jumbo's flabby stomach. Jumbo folded like a worn dollar bill, settling onto his knees before toppling forward.

Before Rocky could move, Tom spun and cracked his forearm alongside Rocky's head. Rocky joined Sticks and Jumbo.

"I win," Tom said. He checked each man's carotid and found it normal. "I would say sweet dreams and leave you here, but I wouldn't know if you'll live up to our agreement."

He toed Jumbo. "C'mon. A punch like that shouldn't put you out. You wouldn't be faking, would you?"

Jumbo rolled over, still holding his stomach. "You just don't give a man a chance, do you?"

"Can't. You're too good. If I hadn't struck first, you'd have kicked my butt. Now, let me help you up." He reached toward Jumbo with his left hand.

Jumbo took it, and Tom hauled him to his feet, ready to strike with his right if Jumbo tried anything. He didn't. He stood there rubbing his gut.

"Is Rocky gon' be alright?"

"Yeah, he'll come around most any time. Now, we made a deal, right?"

Jumbo looked at Rocky, then Sticks. "Yeah," he grumbled. "We said we hep you. We will."

"Fine—" Tom stopped as Rocky rolled over and groaned.

"Damn, Muster Jeffries. You a mean man. My head feel like somebody throwed a brick. Why you hit me so hard?"

Tom smiled. "Like I told Jumbo, I had to. Here, let me help you up." He pulled Rocky to his feet.

"What about Sticks?" Rocky said.

"He's okay," Tom said. "We should leave him there, though. Don't want him embarrassed when he wakes up."

"Embarrassed, hell," Jumbo said. "He's gone be breakin' somethin', and I don't want it to be me. Let's get out of here."

Rocky led the way out of the alley with Jumbo close behind, both walking at a brisk pace.

Tom smiled at their antics and followed. He steered Jumbo and Rocky out of the immediate area of the alley mouth, walked thirty or forty feet away where it was quiet, then stopped. "Before we separate and you search for my friend, who was in the dumpster?"

Jumbo stared toward the Pizza Hut where the police still clustered. "All we know is what we heard on the street. But we don't trust no gossip in this neighborhood."

"Yeah?"

Rocky shuffled his feet, his head hanging. "Uh, that girl ain't part of our deal. You got any more of them Pres'dent Jacksons? My mem'ry ain't as good as it used to be. There's some days—"

"Must be the envir'nment," Jumbo said. "I got the same problem. I heard that carbon oxide is doin' it. Comes from cars and everythin'. Ain't safe 'round here no more."

Tom stared at them a moment, suppressing a grin, then sighed and reached for his wallet. He took out two twenties, held them up and tore them in half. "One for you and one for you," he said, handing each a half-bill. "Note that I kept the ends with the serial numbers. I can turn mine in for a new twenty. Now, want to revisit my question?"

Jumbo stared at his half, a sour expression on his face. "Wha'd you ask?"

"Who was in the dumpster?"

"Cops ain't talkin'. One of 'em asked me if I knowed, so I asked him the same thing. He walked off."

Tom waved the two half-bills in the air. "Jumbo, you need to learn who you can bullshit and who you can't. Now, I'm going to find somebody on the street who'll talk to me. When they do, they'll be a few bucks richer. That could be you, but not if you want to play games all day. Maybe you and Rocky better step over there and get your stories straight before I kick your asses again and move on."

Jumbo bowed his neck. "You think you so tough. I say me and Rocky can take you. You sucker-punched me."

"Whoa," Rocky said, rubbing the side of his head. "Jumbo don't mean nothing by his mouth. We's lovers, not fighters. Ain't that right, Jumbo?" He elbowed his buddy.

"Yeah, I'm a lover, but I can take his ass if he fight fair." Jumbo glowered.

Tom stepped forward, invading Jumbo's space. "Someday, you're going to crowd me until you're a dead man. But not today. Today, you want my money, more than you want to die. And I want the information you have. So, why don't we knock off the crap, and you talk to me? Who was the girl?"

Jumbo looked at Rocky and nodded.

"All we know is she call herself Jeannie," Rocky said. "Showed up three, four weeks ago. Worked at a Burger King a coupla blocks over. Slept in the park. Coupla guys tried her, and she pull a knife on them. Said she'd cut their balls off. Way I heard it, she slashed one of 'em across the arm. They believed her then and left her alone. Word is she was one mean bitch."

Tom sighed. "She'd have to be to survive in this neighborhood." He thought a moment. "Yesterday, you said you saw my friend with another girl. Was that other girl Jeannie?"

"Coulda been," Jumbo said. "Can't be sure. We didn't get a good look at either one of 'em. Runaway girls come and go around here. Best not to pay too much attention. Ask the guys who run the greasy burger joints. New staff every week."

"I'll bet," Tom said and handed them the two halves of the bills. He took out several business cards. "Remember our deal. Spread these around. Tell your friends I need to find her. I'll pay when I have her back." He turned toward the dumpster and the police, then spun back to Jumbo and Rocky. "You might also spread the word that if anybody hurts her, they'll answer to me. They *will* bleed—a lot. Now, find Samantha Renée Williams."

CHAPTER TWENTY

Tom smiled as he watched Jumbo and Rocky shuffle away, each supporting his oversized baggy jeans. He wondered what would happen if they had to run. Their jeans would drop to their ankles while their faces bounced off the sidewalk. On the one hand, not a pretty sight. On the other, well worth seeing.

He walked along the street, thinking about what to do with what he'd learned. He should report it to Lt. Richards—if Richards weren't such a jerk. Had to do it though. He adjusted his direction so he'd front the crime scene. Once there, he spoke to the officer monitoring the perimeter and keeping the curious at bay. "Please ask Lt. Richards to come over. I have some information for him."

"You're that PI, aren't you? The one that wanted in earlier?"

"Yep. Same guy. I haven't changed a bit."

"Thought I recognized your hat. Not too many like that around here. Tell me what you got, and I'll get it to him."

"That's true," Tom said, taking off his Western hat and looking at it. "And that's a shame. A true beaver is well worth the investment." He placed it on his head, caressing the brim. "Back to my request. I'm trying to do this by the book. Ask him to come over. If you don't, I'm moving on. I'm sure he'll be interested in your badge number when I talk to him later."

The officer scowled. "Smart ass." He walked toward a group of plainclothes officers. A moment later, a man carrying his jacket over his shoulder detached himself and moved in Tom's direction. His wilted white shirt had the top button undone and showed sweat stains under the armpits. His tie had been loosened and hung like a limp rag down his chest.

"Mr. Jeffries, I'm Phil Summers, Lt. Richards' partner. He's tied up right now. Can I help you?"

Tom nodded. "I remember you. Might not have picked you out of a lineup, but I remember you had a better attitude than your boss."

Summers chuckled. "Yeah, he can get a bit testy when it comes to PIs. The officer said you have something for us."

Tom stared at the dumpster where the CSI types had finished their bagging and were now dusting everything in sight. "The lieutenant said he needs an ID on the victim. Her name might be Jeannie, and she might have worked at the Burger King a couple of blocks over. I can't vouch for its veracity, but that's what I heard."

"The lieutenant said you didn't know her. When did you learn this?"

Tom smiled and rubbed his chin. "You're more tactful than your boss. Is that your discreet way of asking if I lied to him earlier?"

Phil laughed. "You got me. Did you?"

"No. I learned the possible ID after I left him. It may not be true. If not, don't blame me."

Phil pulled out his notebook and flipped it to a fresh page. "Jeannie. Is that two n's or one?"

"Take your pick. I only heard it pronounced."

"Burger King. What was that address?"

"Phil, you're wasting our time." Tom shook his head. "You know I didn't give an address. I said a couple of blocks to the east. I'm sure you can find it. Ask one of the chubby uniforms who patrol this area. I bet they eat there often."

Phil glanced around and his eyes appeared to stop on an overweight officer. "I'll do that. Are you going to the Burger King?"

"Nope. I've done my citizen's duty. Now, I have other things to do."

Phil stuck out his hand. "Thanks. I appreciate your stepping up. Got a card? I'll give you a call if the info is correct."

Tom gave him a business card. Written on the back was, *If I can help, call me.* It was signed *Tom* in his handwriting.

"I see you're still doing that," Phil said. "How's business?"

"Good enough for an occasional six-pack. Not enough for a keg. Let me know what you learn about Jeannie." He turned and headed for his car. As he walked, he scanned side to side, hoping to spot Renée, thinking the excitement might have brought her out. He didn't see her.

Once at his car, he opened both doors, started the engine, then leaned against the front, while the air conditioner did its job. His mind wandered over possible actions he might take to find Renée. Nothing came to mind that he hadn't already tried. Well, there was one new thing. He hadn't checked the Burger King where Jeannie worked. If Renée traveled with Jeannie, she might be known there. Worth a try. He figured Detective Summers would forgive him for the small prevarication.

Tom's phone rang. The caller ID showed Lonnie's number.

Before Tom could say hello, Lonnie said, "Tom, she's here. She came home. You need to get here quick as you can. She—"

"Slow down, Lonnie. Are you saying Renée came home?"

"Yes. She showed up a few minutes ago. But you gotta get here. She ran into her room, then collapsed on the bed, hysterical. I can't get a thing out of her. Please hurry."

Tom ran around his car and closed the passenger door, then jumped in the driver's side, glad he'd started the engine and A/C before. Jerking the shift into Drive, he raced toward the parking lot exit. "I'm on the way, Lonnie. Make sure she doesn't run again. Hold her, lock her in her room, anything. Just keep her there."

"I'll try, but hurry."

"Ten minutes. Hanging up." He punched the Off button, then concentrated on the road. Any place else, he might have gotten a ticket for speeding and reckless driving, but it was South Florida. His driving didn't exceed the norm—well, not much.

He wheeled into Lonnie's driveway, slammed the transmission into Park, and dashed for her front door. It swung open when he was five feet away.

"I'm so glad you're here," Lonnie said. "She's in her room. She quit crying, but all she'll say is she has to talk to you."

"Gotcha." He never slowed as he went through the living room and down the hall. At the bedroom door, he forced himself to stop and take a deep breath. No need to scare her by bursting in like a rodeo bull.

When he had himself under control, he opened the door and looked around. No doubt it was a girl's room. The walls were a soft pink and several stuffed animals occupied shelves and a desk. The bedspread and pillow shams matched the walls. Renée lay on the bed, face down. Her rumpled clothing, same as he'd seen her in that first evening, was in sore need of a washing. Two Teddy bears were on the floor, looking like they'd tumbled off the bed.

"Renée. I'm glad you came back," Tom said from the doorway.

Her head popped up, and she rolled off the bed and ran to him. "Oh, Mr. Jeffries. Can you help her? Please, please, help my friend. I don't know anyone else to ask."

Tom's heart sank while he hoped he was wrong. Don't let it be Jeannie, he thought. "Help who, Renée? Who are you talking about?"

"My best friend, Jeannie. She's in trouble and needs someone like you. Someone with a knife like yours. Please, please, Mr. Jeffries."

Tom's heart took another nosedive, joining his stomach as they both plunged. He swallowed a huge lump that threatened to fill his throat. "What kind of trouble? What happened to her? What do you want me to do?" He had to keep her talking. Telling her Jeannie's fate would only terrify her, maybe send her into shock, or worse, send her back onto the street.

Renée pressed her head into Tom's shoulder, her tears saturating his shirt. "Some bad people took her. She saved me, and they took her. I'm so scared. Can you get her back?"

Tom took a deep breath. His heart cried as he struggled to keep a straight face. If he gave in to what he felt, it wouldn't help either of them—especially Renée. He glanced over his shoulder and saw Lonnie in the doorway.

"Renée, you're not making much sense. Let's go to the kitchen. Did you have breakfast? If not, I'm sure Lonnie has something she can put together. Maybe some food will help you feel better. I know I can use a cup of coffee."

Lonnie disappeared, leaving Tom to hope she had headed for the kitchen.

"So?" Tom continued. "What do you think? Breakfast, some juice, and you explain what you'd like me to do?"

Renée turned him loose, sniffled, and nodded. He took her hand and led her from the bedroom.

Walking into the kitchen, Tom saw Lonnie with her head in the refrigerator.

She stood, saying, "I'm betting someone is hungry. How about some juice while I scramble a few eggs and burn some bacon?" Her mouth curled into a smile that didn't reach her eyes.

"Sounds good to me," Tom said. "Except I'd prefer coffee if you have it." He looked at Renée. "What say you, my friend?"

Renée sniffled again. "I am hungry—if it's not too much trouble." She glanced at Tom. "I can wait until later."

Lonnie chuckled. "No trouble, my love. Breakfast is my favorite meal to cook. It's so easy. Scramble eggs, throw some bacon in the pan, and toast a few slices of bread. Nothing brainy required. I just let my fingers do the walking."

Tom smiled. "You're showing your age. Renée's generation has never heard that expression. She doesn't have a clue what you're talking about."

"Ouch. Old, very old," Lonnie said, grinning at Renée. "Is that true? Have you never heard, *Let your fingers do the walking*?"

Renée shook her head. "I don't understand it. Fingers? Fingers can't walk."

"Oh, my," Lonnie said. "Your education is sadly lacking. I shall have to take you under my wing—but not until you've had a good breakfast. You two wait in the living room. I need twenty minutes or so, and having you look over my shoulder will only slow me down. But first, a large glass of orange juice for Renée and a cup of coffee for Tom." She poured a generous portion from a juice carton and handed it to Renée. "Here."

Lonnie crossed the room, took down a cup, and filled it from the pot. "And for Tom, coffee. Sweetener is there." She pointed to the breakfast table. "Now, out of here, both of you."

"I give," Tom said. "Renée, shall we adjourn to the living room?"

Renée's face lit up as she sipped from the glass. "I think we should. Miss Lonnie sounds serious." Then she went sad again.

They walked out of the kitchen and settled on the couch. "Feeling better?" Tom asked. "If so, why don't you start at the beginning? Why did you run away from Lonnie?"

Renée bowed her head. "I heard her on the phone talking to you about my mother. I was afraid you'd take me home. I'm never going back there." She hesitated, then continued, "And, I needed to talk to Jeannie. She didn't know where I was."

"Fair enough," Tom said. "But you returned. Why?"

Renée wiped her cheeks with the backs of her thumbs, then mumbled, "I had to. You're the only person I know who can help Jeannie."

"We'll have to see about that," Tom said, rubbing his forehead. "I have several questions first. Who is Jeannie? How do you know her? What happened to her? Start with those."

Renée sighed, sipped, then set her glass on the side table. "Jeannie is a girl I met last week. She's so smart. She knows how to live on the street. She took care of me for a few days—taught me how to sleep in the park, how to get money from the old men who come into our area to look for girls. She was really nice to me. Some people said we look a lot alike. They even asked if we are sisters."

"Was she a prostitute? Did she do drugs?"

"Oh, no, Mr. Jeffries. She'd never do that. She said she's seen too many other girls die from drugs or some pimp beating them to death. She told me there was always a better way than that. She made me swear I wouldn't turn tricks or ever get hooked. She was my friend." Renée looked at her hands and rubbed them together. "My best friend."

"I understand. You said you met her last week. That would have been before you were in that alley. Is that right?"

"Yes sir."

"Where was she when I found you?"

"Working. She worked at Burger King. She said she could get me a job there as soon as I got my new ID card. We were going to get a room together." Her voice failed as tears flowed. "I was on my way to Burger King when those two grabbed me."

"All right. Now, pull yourself together and tell me exactly what happened." He took a handful of tissues from the nearby box and handed them to her while he thought about where to go next. Did she have any idea of Jeannie's fate? "Dry your eyes and blow your nose. I can't help unless I know the details. Where is Jeannie?"

Renée did what he said, then struggled with her voice. "I don't know where she is. Last night, we were walking on the sidewalk when a car slowed beside us. The man in the front seat put his window down and said, 'Hey, is one of you Samantha Williams?'"

Renée sniffled. "I was so scared I couldn't say a word. The only people who knew that name are Jeannie and the man who made my ID card. I told everybody else my name is Renée.

"Before I could move, Jeannie said, 'Who wants to know and why?' The car stopped and a man got out. He was big and ugly looking. He came at us. 'Don't give me none of your damn lip,' he said. 'Just answer the question. Which one of you is Samantha Renée Williams?'" Renée stopped talking, fear stalking her face as if she were reliving the scene.

Tom waited a moment, preferring she continue on her own. When she didn't, he touched her forearm. "What happened next? How'd you get away?"

"Jeannie. Jeannie saved me. She turned to me and said, 'Give me my purse. I have to talk to this man.' I had no idea what she meant. I just stood there like a statue. She snatched my purse off my shoulder, the little red one with the gold chain that Lonnie gave me. She forced hers into my hand, slung mine over her shoulder, and met the man before he got to me. 'I'm Samantha,' she said. 'What do you want?'

"He grabbed her arm. 'My friend in the back seat wants to meet you,' he said. 'You're coming with us.' Then he . . . he opened the car door and shoved her in. As he got in the front, he pointed a gun at me. 'You ain't seen a thing. Keep your mouth shut, or we'll find you.'" Tears rolled again, and her hands flew to her face as sobs racked her body.

Tom pulled Renée to him, feeling her pain and wishing he had a magic elixir to soothe it. Instead, he had truth, which would make it worse.

Lonnie came in from the kitchen. "Breakfast is ready." She hesitated, looking at Renée, then sat on the couch on the other side of her.

Tom took his arm away as Lonnie absorbed Renée against her body, stroking her hair, cooing at her, calming her as only a woman can do. "It's over, Renée. You're safe. You're here with Tom and me. No one can touch you now."

Tom looked into Lonnie's eyes and saw a depth of compassion he'd never seen before. He was seeing Lonnie as Charlie saw her. He was seeing the reason Charlie loved her so. He mouthed, "Thank you," as she continued to minister to Renée's psyche.

Tom's mind flooded with questions about what to do next. Should he tell Renée her friend was dead? Murdered. Most likely by the men who kidnapped her off the street? Should he tell her Jeannie saved her life by impersonating her, that if Jeannie hadn't stepped up, it would be Renée in the morgue? No. That approach couldn't be right. He decided to withhold that knowledge until he'd discussed it with Abby and Lonnie. They would know how to break the news to her. But first, he and Lonnie had to calm Renée. They had to wrap themselves around her so she knew she was safe. They had to convince her she should stay with Lonnie.

Then, he had to hope that Ace and Kit found Renée's father— and her father was a reputable person who wanted her to live with him. Of course, that didn't begin to address the question of whether Renée would accept her father in her life again. Tom had no way of knowing what poison her mother had spewed about him. The thought of Renée's dad being a jerk worse than her mother was just too much to swallow. The unknowns far outweighed the knowns.

And there were the most important questions. Who were the people looking for Samantha Renée Williams? Why were they looking for her? And most important of the three, were they still looking?

Randy Rawls

CHAPTER TWENTY-ONE

Under Lonnie's soothing influence, Renée became less agitated. At what appeared to be the perfect moment, Lonnie led her toward the kitchen, telling her it was time she ate. Tom marveled at Lonnie's magic. Only a few minutes before, Renée had been a distraught youngster whose heart appeared broken. Now, with Lonnie at her elbow, she was a more mature teen, looking forward to brunch.

Tom took a deep breath and pulled out his cell phone. While Lonnie had things under control, he needed to let Abby know Renée had showed up at Lonnie's. He hit speed dial.

Abby answered on the fourth ring. "Tom, glad you called. What's up?"

Tom gave her a quick rundown on Renée's unannounced appearance at Lonnie's. "I need to get more info from Renée, but I have to take it slow and easy. I don't want to spook her again. Why don't you come by here when you leave work? You three can do that female bonding thing. It'll help Renée relax."

"Oh? Are you setting Lonnie's social calendar now?"

"Do you think I should clear it with her first? How can she resist such a wonderful idea?"

"Just ask her."

"Hang on. I'll walk into the kitchen where she and Renée are closer than two dogs on a freezing night." He walked to the door. "Hey, Lonnie. Abby wants to know if it's okay if she comes by for a visit. What do you say?"

"Of course. Sounds great to me. How about you, Renée?"

"I like it," Renée said.

Tom spoke into the phone. "Did you hear that? Both of them think I'm a genius."

"Uh-huh. With the way you worded it, they didn't have much choice. You're really something, Tom Jeffries. Look, I'm almost finished here so I won't be long. There were a couple of cases I needed to review. I'm about as up to date as I'll get on a first pass. Monday promises to be a busy day. Now, if I can get you off the phone, I'll put things away and be ready to leave."

"It's great to feel loved. See you soon, Sunshine."

* * *

Abby disconnected, took off her reading glasses, and squeezed the bridge of her nose. Her eyes were tired, a feeling they had too often after several hours of study. The glasses were supermarket specials. Her optometrist said they were fine to use, and a lot cheaper, until her vision problem went beyond their capability. After that, the bad news, a full-time prescription.

Taking a mirror out of her desk, she squinted into it. Everything was fuzzy. She slipped her glasses on and her vision cleared so she could see how she looked in glasses. No way. When the optometrist gave her the bad news, she'd tell him to schedule an exam for contacts. Or maybe LASIK. Yeah, that's what she'd do—talk to him about laser surgery.

She put the files away, then straightened her desk. Walking into a mess on Monday set a bad tone for the week. She took her coffee cup to the kitchenette down the hall, washed it, and left it on the rack. Then she returned to her office and took off her *office-sweater*, smiling as she thought, sweat outside, freeze inside—the reality of South Florida.

Picking up her purse, she headed out of the building.

"Hope you're having a nice weekend," a man's voice said as she stepped into the sunlight.

She turned and saw Angel Rodriguez, the husband from the wife-beating case, leaning against the building. "What are you doing here?"

"Enjoying the weather. Beautiful day, isn't it?" He pushed off the wall and walked away, tipping his baseball cap.

"Wait a minute," Abby said. "I want to talk to you. Are you stalking me? If you are, I'll have you back in jail before—"

"Sorry, don't have any more time now. My wife is waiting for me. Have a nice day." He sauntered down the steps and turned onto the sidewalk, leaving Abby with her mouth agape.

That guy is so spooky, she thought. Maybe I should call a cop. "For what?" she mumbled, giving voice to her mental process. "He didn't do anything except wish me a nice day. Hard to make a case out of that—even for a wife-beater." She headed toward her car—opposite the direction Rodriguez went—resisting the impulse to look over her shoulder. A cold chill ran through her, making her wish for her sweater. What was his game—if it was a game?

* * *

Lonnie, Renée, and Tom sat in the living room. Whether it was the food or Lonnie's reassuring presence, Renée was in a more loquacious mood.

"I need to ask a few more questions," Tom said. "Are you willing?"

As Lonnie squeezed her arm, Renée smiled and said, "If it will help find Jeannie, I'll answer anything I can."

"Good. Think of the vehicle that stopped beside you. Was it a car, an SUV, pickup truck, what?"

Renée hesitated, then said, "Like yours, except it had four doors."

"A convertible?"

"No." Renée looked at Lonnie, as if seeking reassurance. "Not a top like yours. It had a real top. I meant it was a car-type car, not a SUV or pickup truck."

"I understand," Tom said. "What color was it?"

"It was a real dark color, black or maybe dark blue. It was hard to tell because it was night, but I think black."

"Do you know what kind of car it was?"

"No. All I know is it was a dark colored four-door car." She thought for a moment. "It was kinda boxy, you know, like square corners. The woman I lived with, Barbara Williams, has a Lexus. It wasn't rounded off like hers. Do you know what I mean?"

Tom glanced at Lonnie and saw she had heard the same thing he had—use of the name, Barbara Williams, rather than mother or mom. Lonnie's eyes were wide, and she wore a shocked expression. More proof Renée's had not been a loving household.

"That's fine. Maybe we can look at some pictures later." Tom shifted in his seat, "Let's talk about the man who got out of the car for a moment. Was he tall, short? What can you remember about him?"

"Tall," Renée said with no hesitation. "As tall as you. And big, wide, you know. He was so big. And black, an African-American." She stopped as if waiting for the next question.

"How was he dressed? Jeans, shorts, T-shirt?"

"Oh, no. He had on a dark suit with a tie." She frowned. "I think the shirt was white."

"So he was well-dressed?"

"He even wore a hat. Not a cowboy one like yours, but a nice-looking dressy one like they wear in old movies."

Tom nodded as he made notes. *Large, black, suit, hat, four-door square(?) sedan*

"When he spoke, was there anything special about him?"

"No. He talked like everybody else. He did have a deep voice, though."

Tom jotted *deep voice* in his pad.

"Where were you when Jeannie went with the men?"

"I think it was Fourth Avenue. I don't know the street names very good. But it was across from a Pizza Hut. I remember that. Jeannie and I ate there sometimes."

"What did you do after Jeannie got into the car, and it drove off?"

Renée hung her head. "I didn't know what to do. I wanted to get somebody to help, but didn't know anyone. I couldn't yell for the police. They'd have— I . . . I hid. I went into the park and hid in a big hedge. It's one of the places Jeannie showed me. There's a hole big enough to sleep in. I was afraid to come out, afraid they were looking for me. I stayed there until midnight. The only person I could think of who could help is you. But, I couldn't remember how to get to your house. So, I started walking to Lonnie's. It took me a long time because at first, every time I saw a car, I ran behind a bush." She ran her sleeve under her nose. "Did I do all right? I didn't know anything else to do."

"You did fine," Tom said as Lonnie gave her a squeeze. "The only other thing you could have done was find a policeman."

Renée looked scared. "No, I couldn't do that. No. Never. They'd make me go home, and she'd lock me in my room again."

Tom saw Lonnie's arm tighten around Renée, pulling her closer, comforting her. He averted his eyes, not wanting Renée to see the rage burning there. What kind of woman was Barbara Williams? Obviously, she was far worse than his first thoughts after meeting her. The dear Ms. Williams needed some of her own medicine.

He rose and walked into the kitchen with a heavy tread. As he reached for the coffee pot, he remembered her words about alimony and child support. Suppose she lost one—or both. He wondered if he could make that happen.

CHAPTER TWENTY-TWO

Detective Summers stuck his head into Lt. Richards' office. "Hey, chief, Got something here that'll interest you."

Richards looked up from his keyboard. "So, bring it in. It has to be better than this paperwork."

Summers dropped into a straight-backed chair. "Yeah, every time a new restriction comes down the line, it takes twelve pages of reports to prove you've not in violation. Wonder how it was in the old days before all this BS started?"

"You interrupted me to whine?" Richards drummed his fingers. "I thought you had something to say."

"Oh, I do, chief. One of the uniforms picked up a strange bit. It might, but probably doesn't, apply to the Jane Doe in the Pizza Hut dumpster. But I thought I should run it past you and let you make the call. I can come back later, though, if you're busy. It'll keep."

"Is there any chance you'll tell me today, or does the build-up continue forever?" Richards said, turning away from the computer. "Did you check out the supposed Jeannie who works at Burger King?"

"Yes, and she does. Maybe, did. They haven't seen her since early yesterday. She missed her shift this morning. The manager said that's no big deal, though. The kids he hires often treat the job like a trip to the dentist—something to miss whenever they can. Guy has a pretty good sense of humor. But then, I guess—"

"This is why you interrupted me?"

"Not exactly. But you did ask. And any time you ask a question, you know I—"

"Phil, I always enjoy our little tête-à-têtes, but this is neither the time nor the day for one. Why are you here?"

"Jeffries."

"What does that mean?"

"Jeffries is looking for Samantha Renée Williams. He's passing around her picture with his business card attached. Word is he's offering a reward." He laid one of Tom's flyers on Richards' desk.

"So?"

"So, I find it interesting. It could mean he knows more than he told us."

Richards leaned back in his chair, placed his hands behind his head, and stared at the ceiling. After a moment, his palms slapped down onto the desk. His eyes were hard as they locked onto Summers. "Phil, you may have hit the jackpot here. Try this scenario." He paused. "There is something going on between Jeffries and this Williams person."

"Take another look, chief. That's not a *person* in that picture. She's not much, if any, older than your daughter. She's a kid."

Richards picked up the picture and examined it. His eyes changed, softness taking over. "Okay, I reword what I said. For reasons unknown, Jeffries is hot on the trail of this young girl. Maybe she's a relative, maybe the daughter of a friend. Who knows? But this we do know. Jane Doe, or Jeannie, as he called her, was on the street with Williams' ID. Now the speculative part. Jeffries found out and grabbed her. He figured she could lead him to Williams. After all, if she stole the ID, she would know where Williams was at that time. Jeannie didn't cooperate even though he punched her around. She broke away and ran. He put a bullet through her back to stop her or keep her from identifying him—or any of many other possible reasons. He had to get rid of the body, so he placed her in the dumpster." He paused. "What do you say to that?"

Summers was quiet, appearing to consider what Richards said. "Not bad, chief, except why did he throw the purse into the same trash bin?"

"Why not? It's worthless to him without Jeannie. Plus, we don't know what he took out before ditching it."

Summers pulled on his earlobe. "One more. Why did he leave his business card in the purse?"

Richards rubbed his chin, then fumbled through a stack of papers on his desk. "Ah, here it is." He read, and then smiled. "The card was in an inner zippered compartment. Obviously, Jeffries overlooked it in his rush. Check and checkmate."

"Gotta hand it to you. That's a neat package with a glitzy bow on top. But my gut says no. I just don't see Jeffries that way."

Richards drummed his fingers a few seconds. "Correct me if I go wrong, Phil, but here's what we know about him. One, after the slime who murdered his sister appeared to get away with it, Jeffries resigned from the Army and became a street cop. Two, he staged a shoot-out with three of them. They died. He became a hero. Three, after the parades, tickertape, and awards, he gave up his badge and stuck out a shingle as a PI. Four, soon thereafter, the other two miscreants disappeared without a trace. Five, Jeffries moved to Florida." He paused and drilled Summers with his gaze. "Did I misstate anything?

"No, that's what—"

"Good. There's more. That *more* is the latest surrounding Jeffries. Our Jane Doe—his Jeannie—-Samantha Renée Williams, and him. Need I say more?"

"You left out that he's also ex-special forces. However, I think you're letting a series of coincidences lead you too far. I don't see Jeffries as a suspect."

Richards leaned back in his chair again, clasping his hands behind his head, one of his favorite positions. "So, you would rule him out?"

Summers sighed. "No. I wouldn't go off on him, though. What do you want to do—put a tail on him?"

"You know we don't have the manpower." Richards thought for a moment. "Okay, you think I'm overboard on him. I suppose it's possible. But we'll keep his name near the top of the list. And, right now, he's the only one on the list. Get it out in the briefings. Anytime his name comes up, I want to know about it." He paused, thinking. "Let's find out who this Williams kid is. See what you can come up with."

* * *

Abby arrived, and it became a three-girl thing—Lonnie, Renée, and Abby. Tom leaned against the doorframe to the kitchen, watching with pride as the three of them bonded. It was safe for him to leave for the street to look for Jeannie's killers. It was either find them or risk their finding Renée—the real Renée.

He stuck his head into the kitchen. "When you have a moment, check some car sites on the computer. Maybe Renée will recognize the kind the kidnapper drove. I'm going to hit the area where Jeannie disappeared. Maybe someone saw something."

The answers were there somewhere. His job was to find them. Should be a snap—*not*. He waved and headed out the front door to his car.

As he drove, his cell phone sounded. He hit the Chrysler Uconnect button on the steering wheel and said, "Tom Jeffries, private investigations."

"Ace here. We have a problem. No, we have a huge problem. Do you have any idea how many James Robert Williams there are in the Dallas-Ft Worth Metroplex? Not to mention those listed as James R., J. R., or J. Robert. We're in a quagmire here, Tom, and I'm not sure there's a bottom. Kit has come up with about a thousand-plus variations on the name. It will take forever to track all of them. To get what you want, we'll need more luck than a leprechaun."

"That bad, eh?"

"That bad, maybe worse."

"So, you're giving up? Is that why you called?"

"Hey, don't put words in my mouth. I still have Kit, and she's good at this kind of thing. I just want you to know it's going to be a long hard trail. No guess how long it'll take to find your man—if we find him at all. How much urgency are you up against?"

"A lot. There's a thirteen-year-old girl waiting for him. No, that's too optimistic. I hope she will take to him. I hope he will take to her. It's not quite an amateur space launch, but it's the best I have. They haven't been father-daughter for ten years."

"You *do* have a jellyfish by the tentacle. From what you said before, I assume she doesn't want her mother and vice-versa."

"Bingo. Give the little man with the cigar a mustache. Her father is my only hope. If I can't find him, or he doesn't want her, she goes to the Department of Children and Families. I don't know how they are in Texas, but I wouldn't put a baby alligator with them here." Tom hesitated, then in a softer voice added, "Ace, her only chance is her father. I know it's a stretch, but don't give up."

"Give up? Hey, that's not in my vocabulary. I never give up." Ace chuckled. "You've got the Ace and Kit duo on the trail. We've crossed rougher terrain than this. She has already uncovered the emails of several hundred and fired out a message to them. My finger is sore from punching in telephone numbers. Heck, my cats, Sweeper and Striker, are even helping. Every time I let up, one of them swipes me on the leg. We're doing all we can, Tom, and will keep at it. You take care of that young lady. We're doing our best. I'll ask Kit to send you a copy of the message she's saturating the Internet with."

Tom turned into the Burger King parking lot. "Thanks, Ace. You tell Kit I'll name my first daughter after her. I'd offer you the same for a son, but can't picture him having to live up to a name like Ace."

"Couldn't be an Ace. My name is Arthur Conan Edwards, acronym Ace. Your son would be Arthur Conan Jeffries, acronym . . . unpronounceable. I'm back to work." His laughter sounded as he disconnected.

Tom parked, got out, and entered the fast food restaurant.

* * *

Thirty minutes later, Tom left the Burger King, a long look on his face. He had spoken with the manager and each of the employees. They all knew Jeannie, described her as a nice person and a hard worker. They didn't know where she lived or any of her friends, other than Renée. They'd seen Jeannie and Renée together a few times, but couldn't add anything more. All in all, he'd learned nothing worthwhile.

A breeze had blown up bringing in storm clouds from the Everglades. Judging by their advance, he figured it would be raining within thirty minutes. That would kill any chance he had of finding one or more of his snitches. He climbed into his car and pondered what to do. He was fresh out of ideas. Maybe he should stop for the day. He opened his phone and dialed Abby's number.

After the customary hellos, he said, "I'm thinking about coming in. There's a storm brewing, and I don't really have any more leads. Anything happening there?"

"Renée found the car. Well, what she thinks is the car. She picked out a Chrysler 300, said it had the squarish look like the one the big guy was in. How does that sound?"

Tom thought for a moment. Yes, the 300 had a distinctive look that was memorable because of its boxiness. Could be. "That changes things. I think I'll prowl the streets, at least until the storm hits. Maybe I'll get lucky and spot it."

Abby cut in. "Tom, listen to yourself. The computer showed that basic shape covering several years and they're still making it. There are probably hundreds of them in the area."

"You're right. Well, I can cruise and copy license numbers. Perhaps we'll get lucky when you run the plates, and a name will pop up."

"Wait a minute. Who says I'm running the plates?"

"Why else would I hang out with an Assistant SA?"

Abby laughed. "You'd better have a better reason than that or you'll be sleeping alone."

"You got it, Sunshine."

Thirty minutes later, Tom had collected eight license numbers when the storm hit. The rain poured, lowering visibility to a point Tom couldn't read plates anymore. He parked and waited, a feeling of frustration flooding through him. The rain stayed constant, the frustration rose, and Tom packed it in and went home.

Randy Rawls

CHAPTER TWENTY-THREE

On Sunday afternoon, Lt. Jim Richards sat in his recliner, feet up and head back, drifting in and out of sleep. He wore shorts, an old T-shirt, and sandals, his lounge-around attire. The end table beside the chair held a half-finished beer and what was left of a serving of nachos.

A major league baseball game beamed from the TV set. The announcers kept up a constant chatter, proving their egos were more important than what the players were doing.

Occasionally, something other than pitch and catch would occur and the announcers would treat it like New Year's Eve, causing Richards to awaken. He would peek, take in the situation, and as the announcers went back to their self-aggrandizement, fall asleep again.

"Dad, can I talk to you?"

Richards opened his eyes to see his twelve-year-old daughter, Chelsea, standing in the doorway. He smiled, thinking what a glorious sight she was. Whereas he was dressed like a bum, she looked like she had a date with a Prince holding a glass slipper. In his opinion, it would be the Prince who would get the best of the deal. "Sure, hon. Come on in. I was just watching the game."

"I know. You were snoring." She giggled and squeezed into the recliner beside him. Her next words were too serious for one so young. "I heard you telling Mom about that young girl who was killed. Why, Dad? I don't understand why things like that happen. I mean, I know it's your job to find them and all, but why are people so mean?"

Richards sighed, his mind racing. Obviously, he couldn't give her his full truth. He cleared his throat. "The simple answer is because there are bad people in the world who will hurt anyone. The hard answer is I don't know. If she's like so many others, she was in the wrong place at the wrong time. People who prey on teenagers don't usually care who it is. They see someone who fits the profile and go after her. This time, it happened to be the young girl we're calling Jeannie."

"I'm sorry for her, Dad."

"So am I." He kissed Chelsea's forehead and in a softer voice repeated, "So am I."

Chelsea snuggled in beside him and opened a book. "Do you mind if I read while you sleep the game?"

"Sure, wise guy, if I can turn up the sound." He pulled her to him and mussed her hair.

"Dad, don't do that. Mom will say I never comb it."

Richards smiled. "Sorry. Read your book. I'll be good. I'll even turn down the game."

As Chelsea appeared to lose herself in the story, Jim's mind drifted to Jeannie's case. Studying his daughter, he knew he had to catch the murderer. Who could say Chelsea wouldn't be next? But first, they had to have a firm identification of the girl.

He rose. "Keep my spot warm. I'll be back."

He walked into the kitchen and picked up his cell phone. He had hoped for a peaceful afternoon, but it was not to be. Time to wreck it. He speed dialed Summers' number.

"Hey, chief. It's Sunday. Doesn't my contract say I have this one off?"

"Of course, and I would never violate your *contract*. I'll only keep you a moment. Tomorrow morning, I want you all over the *Jeannie* case. I want to know everything, and I want it yesterday."

"Okay."

"And while you're at it, find out what Jeffries is up to. Don't come into the office until you have some answers."

"Like, forever?"

"Sure. But don't expect a paycheck until you deliver those answers."

"I knew there had to be a fly in the beer."

* * *

Summers took Richards at his word and spent his Monday digging. The day moved into mid-afternoon, and he had little to show for his efforts. He'd discovered more of Tom's flyers, but nothing new of substance. Either people weren't talking or they didn't know anything—at least the ones he spoke to. The lack of chatter on the street made him wonder how big the hit on *Jeannie* had been. If it were a simple grudge thing, he'd expect to hear something, anything. But total silence . . . His gut told him that was abnormal.

Summers had worked with Richards for five years. Every time they had a case involving a teenage or younger girl, Richards took it personal. It ate at him far more than any situation involving an adult. Summers suspected his boss saw his daughter in every young victim.

He didn't want to face Richards with nothing to report so he decided to dodge for a while. He stopped by the Central Broward County District Office of the Broward Sheriff's Office. He knew an old case he could run past Chief Lauerhill, justifying his visit.

He parked and entered through the public entrance. Sgt. Carl Michaels manned the desk. He and Michaels broke in together longer ago than Summers wanted to remember.

"Phil, you slumming?" Michaels said.

"No, just thought I'd drop by and see if you guys had anything new on that string of burglaries that went down about six months ago. Is the chief in?"

"Just missed her. She had a medical appointment. Come on back, I want you to meet someone."

Summers entered the desk sergeant's inner sanctum through the bulletproof Plexiglas door. He saw a second officer sitting with Michaels. The nametag on his uniform read Gomez.

"Meet Santiago Gomez, my neighbor," Michaels said. "Of course, with that moniker, we call him Sandy. He's the School Resource Officer at Coral Lakes Middle. Front line of policing, I say. He's also part of our Citizen Observer Patrol and has applied to become a deputy. Can't imagine why. Sandy, this is Phil

Summers. Ignore his scowl. He's one of the good guys, even if he is a detective."

Gomez stood and stuck out his hand. "A pleasure to meet you, sir. Some day, I hope to be plain clothes, too. Of course, first I have to get out of the school and land a real police job."

"Be careful what you wish for," Summers said. "There are days I'd trade jobs with you. In fact, this is one of those days."

"Oh," Michaels said. "Is the mighty Richards-Summers team stymied?"

"Not exactly. Well, yeah, exactly. You might have read about the teenage girl found in a dumpster. That's ours, and we're not having a lot of luck with it. About all we've learned so far is she might be connected to another young girl named Samantha Renée Williams. She—"

"Excuse me. Who did you say?" Garcia asked.

"Samantha Renée— Wait a minute. You're a School Resource Officer?"

"Ah . . . yeah."

"Did you interrupt because the name Samantha Renée Williams means something to you?"

Gomez looked at Michaels, then back to Summers. "Is that an official question? I mean, there are rules I have to live by. Are you asking me as a law officer or as a friend of Carl's?"

Summers studied Gomez. "I don't want to get you into any trouble with the school board. If it would help, I can take you downtown."

"Whoa," Michaels said. "Sandy didn't mean anything like that." He turned to his friend. "I'm sure it's okay to talk to him, Sandy. I'll be your witness that it's an official inquiry."

Gomez rubbed his chin, his eyes bouncing between the two officers. "Yeah, she goes to my school. What do you want to know?"

Summers shook his head. "Sometimes, this is the most ridiculous business. I spent the last week chasing around Broward County trying to get a lead on her, then I walk in here, and bam, you're standing there." He turned to Michaels. "Is there some place Sandy and I can talk?"

"Sure. Through that door, first office on the right. I'll make sure no one bothers you. Grab some coffee on the way in, if you want."

Forty-five minutes later, Summers left the station, shaking his head. Crazy how answers to your most difficult questions rushed to intercept you sometimes. So Jeffries had been tracking Samantha Renée Williams and had gone to her school, looking for information. However, based on the flyers he'd been handing out, he must not have found her.

* * *

Summers sat in his car, his cell phone in his hand, replaying Gomez's story in his mind. He tugged on his earlobe thinking how often a case was like splitting a diamond. The cleavage-plane might be difficult to find, but it was there, and all it needed was the right tap and everything opened. Gomez just might be the cleavage-plane he'd been seeking. However, Jeffries' lack of forthrightness disappointed him.

He dialed Richards' number and waited.

"About time you called in. I didn't know today was a holiday."

"You told me not to call until I had answers. Are you ready?"

"Make it good."

Summers filled his boss in on Gomez's story, especially Tom's tracking of Samantha Renée Williams and her mother. He finished by saying, "I have the mother's name, phone number, and address. Do you want to go with me?"

"Yes. I'll meet you there. Call and let her know we're coming."

"Suppose she's not home?"

"Then you'd better stop me before I get too far from the office. That way, I can head for home and an early evening with my family."

* * *

"We're investigating the death of a young woman, one we think your daughter knew," Richards said. "We'd like to speak with her. Is she here?"

Barbara Williams sat at the kitchen table, her hands clenched, a worried look on her face. She wore fashionably ragged jeans, an expensive-looking T-shirt, and flip-flops. Her face bore minimal make-up, only a light touch of lipstick. Her shoulders hunched forward.

In a hesitant voice, she said, "No, she's not here right now. What makes you think she knows anything?"

Richards looked at her eyes, wondering if he saw fear. *Why should she be afraid? Something about her daughter?* "Do you know a man named Tom Jeffries?"

She started. "No. I mean, yes. He . . ." Her voice died away as her face contorted. "Why . . . do you ask?"

"We know he has an interest in your daughter. We just don't know why. When did you meet him?"

She took her time answering, her face passing through several looks—from distress to sadness to something that almost appeared to be satisfaction.

Richards said nothing, watching her, wondering why she appeared to be stalling.

After almost a minute passed, she said, "He came here." She sniffled. "It was after Sammi didn't come home. He . . . he told me not to call the police. He said if I did, something bad would happen to her. I . . . I—" Sobs interrupted as tears slithered down her cheeks. She pulled a tissue from her sleeve and held it under her nose as she cut her eyes from Richards to Summers.

Richards leaned forward in his chair. "Take it easy, Ms. Williams. Compose yourself. Tell us the whole story." He turned to Summers. "Maybe you could get her some water."

Summers stood and looked in cabinets until he found the glasses. He filled one with cold water from the refrigerator and set it in front of her.

Richards said, "Phil, maybe you should check the car, see if dispatch is looking for us." He nodded toward the front door.

"You got it, boss."

"Take your time. Ms. Williams and I aren't going anywhere."

Summers left the house.

"Tell me about Jeffries' visit. What he said, how he said it, anything that might help us find your daughter. I've had my eye on him for a while. This might be our chance to put him where he belongs."

Williams blew her nose, then wiped her eyes with the back of her forefinger. "It was about a week and a half ago. No, that's not right. It was Sunday morning, a week ago. I remember because I was getting ready for church. The doorbell rang and when I opened the door, a man stood there. He introduced himself as a private detective. Said he was looking for Sammi."

She rubbed her eyes again. "I told him she wasn't here. She'd stayed the night with a friend. Like an idiot, I invited him in. I wanted to know why he was asking to see her. That's when he told me he had her—had her in a safe place where I'd never find her. He . . . ah . . . he said he wanted money, lots of money, and would give me a week to get it together." She shifted in her chair. "I told him I didn't have much, but what little I had, he could have if he just brought my Sammi back."

She dropped her head into her hands, sobs shaking her body. "I didn't know what to do. I was so scared. Sammi is all I have."

Richards placed his elbows on the table. "Did he give you any proof he had her?"

She looked up. "Proof? No . . . uh . . . I . . ."

"It's okay, Ms. Williams. You were probably too upset to think of something like that. What else did he say?"

"He told me not to call the police. He said . . . as long as it was between him and me, she'd be all right. But if I didn't do like he said . . ." She broke down again, her shoulders shaking. She cradled her head in her arms.

"I understand," Richards said. "I think we know where to find him. We'll make sure your daughter comes home."

She lifted her head. "Oh, thank you. I feel so much better now. I know you'll find her and bring her to me."

Richards leaned back. "I'd like to have an officer stop by so you can tell her all the details. In the meantime, try to remember anything you can. It might be a good idea to make notes if something comes to mind. And I *do* appreciate what you're going through. I have a daughter about Sammi's age. If she were kidnapped, I'd be going crazy."

Williams looked at him with doe eyes. "I hope you never feel what I'm feeling."

Richards pushed up from the table, took her hands in his, and gave them a gentle squeeze. "Rest assured we'll find Sammi."

When he walked outside, he found Summers leaning against the car. "Thanks," Richards said. "I felt like she'd be more comfortable if only one of us was there. She opened up after you left."

"So?"

"In a nutshell, she says Jeffries kidnapped the kid and is demanding money from the mother. Let's go find him."

"Huh? That's nuts, chief. I might not be thrilled with him, but that doesn't make sense."

"Why not? What is this thing you have for Jeffries? I told you from day one he can't be trusted. He's another sleazeball PI who'll do anything for a buck. He saw a single mom and took advantage. Nothing new about that. He's not the first, and he won't be the last to cross over to the dark side."

"When did all this happen?" Summers said. "We know he was looking for the girl most of last week. How do you explain that?"

"Maybe she broke free, I don't know. I just know I want him in the interrogation room. And your job is to bring him in. If you don't, I'll put out a BOLO and have him dragged in."

Summers went quiet for a moment. "So, you want me to head back to the station?"

"Yeah. I want one of our female detectives out here fast to take her statement. But I need to brief her first. How about Tobarth?"

"Good choice," Summers said. "She has a great way with people."

"That's who I'll assign then," Richards said, a note of finality in his voice. "Tell her this is her highest priority. Drop anything else. In fact, instruct her to call me as soon as she heads this way. That'll give me a chance to bring her up to date. In the meantime, I'm going to spend some quality time with my daughter."

"One more question, chief?"

Richards leaned against Summers' car. "Shoot."

"When did Jeffries grab the kid?"

"She didn't know for sure. Sammi was supposed to stay overnight with a friend. Jeffries showed up the next morning. She remembered specifically because it was Sunday morning."

"Sunday? You mean yesterday?"

"No. A week ago. She was getting dressed for church when—"

"But, chief. It wasn't until Tuesday of last week that Jeffries spoke with Gomez and got the address of the mother."

"You sure about that?" Richards looked perplexed.

"That's what Gomez said. Last Tuesday. So how could Jeffries have spoken to Ms. Williams before he knew she existed?"

Richards gave Summers a hard stare, his mind whirling between what Ms. Williams said and the disconnect Summers pointed out. After a moment, he said, "Yeah, something seems unbalanced. But I still want Jeffries brought in. It's time we heard his story—maybe he'll even tell us the truth for a change. And I still want Tobarth to take a statement from the Williams woman. If she's lying, we'll let her hang herself. If she's telling the truth, we'll help her hang Jeffries."

"But—"

"I'm tired of discussing it. Do what I asked you to do." He hesitated, then in a calmer voice said, "If it will make you feel better, I'll make sure you're in the interrogation room with Jeffries."

CHAPTER TWENTY-FOUR

Summers ushered Tom into an interrogation room where Richards awaited them. Furnishings consisted of three chairs and a table, two of the chairs on one side of the table and the third facing them.

Tom looked around, waved at the two-way mirror, then said, "I'm guessing the single chair is bolted down and mine, right?"

"That's the usual procedure," Richards said. "Have a seat."

Tom walked to the side of the table with two chairs and sat. "Fine. I'll take this one."

"You're a real wiseass, Jeffries. You know the routine. You're over there." Richards pointed across the table.

"Nope, but you *are* right. I *do* know the routine. Show me a warrant, and then . . . maybe. Otherwise, I'm staying here, not that this is such a great improvement. Haven't you guys heard of cushions?"

"Pansy," Richards said. "Summers, get another chair."

Summers ducked his head as he headed out the door, but not before Jeffries saw a grin flash across his face.

Once Summers returned, the three of them settled. Summers flipped up the cover on a digital recorder. "Okay if we record this?"

Jeffries glanced at Summers, then glared at Richards. "Okay if I call my lawyer first? I'm sure he'd like to know you guys are railroading me without benefit of an arrest warrant or explaining my Miranda rights. I remember him saying something about the fourth amendment."

Richards pinched the bridge of his nose. "You know, I could have been a sixth-grade teacher. But instead, I choose a profession where I deal with third-grade jokesters. Kill the recorder, Summers. I don't want our *guest* to feel any obligation to tell the truth."

He looked at Tom. "I *asked* you to come in because I have some conflicting information. I would *appreciate* it if you would help me sort out the truth. Phil *assured* me," he shot a look at Summers, "that as a good *citizen*, you'd be more than *happy* to do so."

"But, of course," Tom said. "What's the problem?"

Richards looked at Summers, back to Tom, then said, "I have reason to believe you know the whereabouts of one Samantha Renée Williams, a young female teenager. Is that true?"

"And what makes you think this?" Tom asked.

A look of frustration crossed Richard's face. "Do you ever play straight with anyone? No, don't bother to answer. I spoke with the girl's mother. She fingered you."

Tom bounced to his feet. "She what? You *have* to be kidding. The Manchurian-Candidate-mom fingered me? That woman should have been sewn shut at birth. She's the antithesis of the word mother. Just what the hell did she say?"

As Tom fumed, Richards laid out what Barbara Williams told him.

Finally, when he couldn't take any more, Tom interrupted. "Look, about the only truth in that fairy tale is that I did talk to her. I asked her if she knew where Renée was. Now, let me give you what she told me. It may not be an exact quote, but you can bet your sweet ass it's close. Write this down. 'If you find her, you can keep her.' That's what she thinks of her thirteen-year-old daughter." He crossed his arms and settled into his chair, clearly pissed off. "You gotta come up with something better, or I'm taking my butt out of here."

Richards massaged his temples. "Okay, okay, settle down. Even I'm not convinced she's on the level. And, of course, your patron saint, Phil Summers, is sure she lied. Even now, we have people discreetly checking on her. But, with the accusation she made—which still could be true—I had to ask. You're free to go."

Tom stood and stuck out his hand. "Now you know one of the many reasons I gave up my badge. You guys never catch a break."

Richards shook his hand, then held on. "Is there any chance you'll cooperate with us? You know, there *is* one girl dead and another *missing*. Also, a mother—if what you said is true—who should have her custody examined." He released his grip.

Tom stared at his hand, then glanced at Summers.

"Jeffries, you know how hamstrung we are," Summers said. "Do you want other young girls dead in this town? Do you want the gutter-scum that sells drugs to these kids winning? What about the teenage prostitutes that will go down on or with any man for the money to buy a fix? What about the young boys who fall prey to pedophiles and are brutalized?" Summers leaned back in his chair. "I don't think you want that. I think the only question is which path is best to stop it—work alone or work with us."

"Well said, Phil." Richards grinned. "Maybe I should let you speak more often. Now, Jeffries, those are solid questions. Any answers?"

Tom looked at the door, then at Summers, frozen in mid-step, his brow wrinkled. He smiled and settled into his chair. "Sit down, gentlemen. I have a story you want to hear." He started with rescuing Renée in the alley and finished with her story about Jeannie's abduction. He emphasized his two conversations with Renée's mother.

* * *

Mr. GG leaned forward and placed his elbows on his desk as Antoine entered his office. "My patience is running thin. Why haven't you found this man Jeffries yet?"

"I'm trying to do it without bringing the cops down on us. I've checked him out pretty good. He's a tough guy who won't come easy. If we try to grab him off the street, there's going to be blood, and some of it, maybe a lot of it, will be from my boys. Rumor has it he took out a whole gang, then went for a manicure because his only injury was a cracked fingernail. I have a plan for making him come to us. But, I need to find the right connection."

"Well, do it. He owes me money. He'll either pay, or he'll follow Mr. Future Star Miller into my ecology experiment as fish food." Mr. GG chuckled. "That damn Miller was so big, though, the fish might not be hungry for a while. Of course, I can always use him to please the alligators. They love fresh meat."

Mr. GG picked up a paper clip from his desk. "Who'd you put on Miller's route?"

"New guy I just signed on. Name is Lemon. I figured it's a good way to break him in. A bunch of old women shouldn't give him any problems."

"Yeah, that's what we thought about Miller. Put a tail on him. If he decides to rip me off, your job is to make sure he doesn't."

"Got him covered, boss. While we're keeping him honest, I'm hoping Jeffries will show up again. If he does, we'll make a grab."

Mr. GG leaned back in his chair. "Yeah. I like it—a nice quiet way to reel him in. That's why I keep you around, Antoine. You produce good results. Keep me informed."

* * *

Tom walked out of the police station, hoping he hadn't screwed up by letting Richards into the picture. But he needed help—official help—to prove Barbara Williams an unfit mother. If Richards did as he promised and turned the system loose to investigate her, it could simplify a transfer of custody to Renée's father—assuming he wanted her. Tom hoped he did. If he didn't, that left Department of Children and Families, and that was an option he didn't want to face, an option no child should have to face.

He popped the lock on his car and swung the door open, then slid in and started the engine. As the air conditioner blasted on high, he slipped the transmission into reverse. His phone rang. When he checked the caller ID, his face lit up in a smile—Abby. He pulled back into the space and put the car in park.

"Hey, Sunshine. You trying to brighten my day."

"Not really. Just need to hear your voice to boost my confidence."

"What's up?"

Abby's sigh echoed across the airways. "I'm beginning to worry, Tom. He was outside again this morning."

"He, who? I don't understand."

"Sorry. I need to take a deep breath."

There was a moment of silence, then Abby continued. "Angel Rodriguez, the husband of Maria Rodriguez. Remember her? The woman whose husband abused her and got away with it."

"Of course," Tom said, as memory flooded in of Abby's several instances of *bumping* into the husband since his acquittal. "Where did you see him?"

"He was leaning against the wall by the rear employee entrance. When I walked by, he said, 'Morning, Ms. Archer. I hope you enjoy this special day.'"

"That's all?" Tom asked. "Did he threaten you or insult you or . . ."

"No. And that's part of what makes it so frightening. He's just there. It seems like everywhere I turn, he's there. He's up to something. I know he is—and he's scaring me."

"So it's time for me to have a *Come to Jesus* moment with Mr. Rodriguez? Give me his address, and I'll pay him a visit."

"No. That's not . . . I mean . . . Tom, I don't know why I'm calling you. I don't want you going after him, but I don't know what to do. I need ideas, not violence."

"Ideas? Have you spoken to building security?"

"Yes. And to Wilbur, my boss, and to the police. Everyone tells me nothing can be done unless he makes some kind of overt move against me. Wishing me a good morning is not a crime, no matter who does it. Our security people say they'll watch for him, but unless he tries to force his way into the building or commits an illegal act on the premises, their hands are tied. It's so damn frustrating."

"Congratulations, Sunshine. You're feeling some of my frustration about the system. All benefit of doubt goes to the guilty. The innocent pay the price."

"That's not true, Tom. I refuse to believe it."

"Give me another explanation. I'll stay quiet while you put it together. However, if you don't convince me, get me Rodriguez' address. He's messing with the woman I love. He deserves a visit."

"You won't hurt him, will you?"

"Not unless he acts first. If he does, I'll defend myself."

"I'll think about it. There has to be a way within the system to resolve this."

"Abby. This man is a threat to you. No one does that to my fiancée. Either the police take care of him, or I will."

"Thank you, Tom. I knew talking to you would make me feel better. Now I have to worry about you taking matters into your own hands. See you tonight?" The words came out clipped, dripping with sarcasm.

Tom winced. *Oops, guess I pushed too hard.* "Of course, Sunshine. If you want my help though, bring his address when you come home."

"We'll see."

The line went dead. Tom sat for a moment, then put the car in reverse and backed out, his mind working. *There must be a way I can protect Abby without her stuffing me in the doghouse.*

A few blocks later, as he turned onto University Drive, his phone rang again. He smiled. *Abby changed her mind. No, Lonnie.* He hit his Uconnect Blue Tooth button. "Tom Jeffries here."

"Tom, it's Lonnie. Do you have a moment?"

"Sure. Nothing wrong with Renée, is there?"

"Oh, no. She's fine and a delight to have around. But she's why I'm calling. What would you think if we took a vacation? Went away for a couple of weeks?"

Tom stroked his cheek. "What do you have in mind? I'm not sure it's a great idea since her mother could decide she wants her back at any second."

"That's one of the reasons I thought of it. I broached the subject with Renée. She is adamant she won't go home, and if anyone makes her go, she says she'll run away the first chance she gets. Tom, we can't afford to have her on the street again. Who knows what might happen?"

Tom considered Lonnie's words, recognizing the truth in them. He had little doubt that Renée would run away again if taken back to her mother. Even more scary, she might go in a different direction the next time. With Jeannie's abduction fresh in her mind, she might be afraid to return to her previous area.

Tom sighed. "As you know, I have no control over what you do with Renée or what she does with you. However, I do appreciate your asking. What do you have in mind?"

"At first, I thought she might enjoy a cruise. There are some great tours of the Caribbean during the summer. But she would need a passport, so that's out of the question. Then, I thought about a tour of the country—well, part of it. Atlanta is a major hub, so we could fly there and catch a bus. Hit Memphis, Nashville, St. Louis on the way to the Grand Canyon. Then come back by way of Dallas, New Orleans, Tallahassee, whatever. I'm only guessing at the stops along the way, but I'm sure there are lots of historic cities we could visit. It would be a great educational trip for her. What do you think?"

"Sounds great. Is there such a tour? Heck, I might want to go with you. What does Renée think of the idea?"

"I haven't asked her yet. But we've discussed travel in general, and she loves the idea. I spent awhile on the Internet checking bus tours. Haven't nailed it down yet, but I'm pretty sure there is something we can do. Give me an opinion."

"I say go for it. Just stay in touch."

After disconnecting, Tom blew out a deep breath. *This is perfect. It'll give me a couple of weeks to find Renée's father, Jeannie's killer, and a way to wrest custody of Renée from her mother.* A picture of Abby popped into his head. *And take care of Señor Rodriguez.*

CHAPTER TWENTY-FIVE

The next morning, Tom rolled out of bed at five-thirty—not by accident but because of his screaming alarm clock. He clicked the off button, stretched, and walked into the kitchen where his trusty coffeemaker had once again performed its miracle. After filling his cup, he sipped as he headed for the shower.

His plan for the morning was simple. Abby arrived at her office about eight-thirty, so he would be in place by seven-thirty, watching to see if Rodriguez showed his face. If he did, Tom would take him aside and explain a few facts to him. The trick would be to do it without Abby finding out. If she did, he'd get a stern lecture about interfering in her professional life. That continued to be a major point of contention between them—her belief in the justice system and his disdain for it.

However, his love for her drove him to protect her even if it cost him that very love. Rodriguez *would* leave her alone.

At seven-fifteen, Tom pulled into a public lot five blocks from Abby's building. If he parked in the state facility, she might spot his car. If she did, he'd be in the doghouse forever.

He got out, walked to the rear of his car, and opened the trunk. He took out a zippered hoodie and a baseball cap, then opened a hatbox and placed his Western hat in it. He looked at the cap, grinned at its New York Yankees logo, then slipped it onto his head. Once he put the hoodie on, he figured no one would recognize him unless that person stood less than five feet away and stared straight into his face. And Abby would never expect him to show up dressed like he'd just dropped in from *the city*. Sometimes dressing like a Texan in Florida paid off.

He walked to the state parking lot where Abby had a reserved space and positioned himself in a shady spot so he could watch the entrance and the employee doorway to the building. When Abby drove in, he'd duck, but he didn't want to miss Rodriguez' arrival. Of course, he was at a disadvantage since he didn't know what Rodriguez looked like. However, according to Abby, he perched outside where he could ambush her. That's what Tom would look for—any man speaking to her. He figured her reaction would be his signal.

Eight o'clock rolled around and the area began to fill with cars. No one paid any attention to him—probably because the employees were accustomed to seeing the homeless rousing themselves from a night's sleep under the hedges that bordered the lot.

At eight-fifteen, a man attracted Tom's attention as he walked into the area, hesitated, looked around, and then headed toward the building entrance. He stopped about twenty-five feet from the doorway and sat under a palm tree. From his attire—jeans, dingy T-shirt, and sneakers—Tom surmised he was not a state worker, at least not a state office worker. Could be his man.

Promptly at eight-thirty, Abby rolled into the lot, parked in her assigned space, and got out of the car. Tom watched as the man rose and moved behind the tree where Abby couldn't see him. That had to be Rodriguez.

Abby walked toward the building, looking around. As she came abreast of the tree, the man stepped out and said something. Abby froze, then turned on him, her mouth working. He shrugged and walked away.

Abby started after him, then stopped, appeared to think, and turned toward the entrance.

Tom let out a sigh of relief, figuring Abby realized how foolish it would be to confront the man. The good news, though, was he had an identity for Rodriguez.

After studying him a moment, Tom pulled the cap low over his brow and began a path that would cause them to meet. He caught up with Rodriguez as they neared the street. "Mr. Rodriguez? Do you have a moment?"

Rodriguez turned. "Me? What do you want? How do you know me?"

"How is not important, but for you, it's important that I do. I'm here to save you a severe ass kicking, maybe even your life."

"What? What the hell do you mean?"

As Tom stepped up beside Rodriguez, he lowered his voice. "I know who you are. You're Angel Rodriguez, a wife beater. It's all over the area how you been harassing Ms. Archer. You think you're being cute, scaring her, making her wonder where you'll turn up next. But you haven't been half as smart as you think you've been."

"Yeah? How? What am I missing? That bitch tried to send me to prison. I got plans for her. But she's going to sweat first."

Tom clenched his fist, resisting the urge to smash Rodriguez. After a deep breath, he said, "See. That's what I mean. You don't have all the facts. I happen to know her fiancé. He is one mean son of a bitch. You don't want him on your ass."

"Quit beating around the bush and say what you came to say. I have to get to work."

Tom looked around. Satisfied he wouldn't be overheard, he said, "His name is Jeffries. He's ex-Army, Special Forces even. They say he won lots of medals for killing people all over the world. Then he became a cop in Dallas. Killed three robbers in a shootout—three shots, three dead men. Got a commendation for that. Yep, I'd sure hate to have him upset with me. He is one cold-blooded bastard—so they say."

"So. Big deal. Don't mean shit to me."

Pausing for a deep breath, Tom glanced around again, leaned toward Rodriguez, then continued, his voice softer. "I can tell you what else I heard. I heard that if you mess with his woman, he *will* kill you. And, he will do it the most painful way you can imagine." Tom placed his hand on Rodriguez' shoulder and squeezed in a friendly gesture. "Can you imagine being fed to an alligator, one part at a time?" He paused and looked around again. "That's all I have to say. Make your own decision whether you want to live . . . or die in a really nasty way." He walked away, leaving Rodriguez with his mouth hanging open.

Tom went about ten steps, then looked back toward Rodriguez who had not moved. "Consider yourself warned. I'm not kidding. He will *hunt you down.*"

There were worry lines on Rodriguez' face as Tom continued on his way. When he reached the corner, he turned onto a side street, stopped and waited for Rodriguez while taking off the hoodie and turning the baseball cap backwards. When Rodriguez passed, Tom followed at a discreet distance until Rodriguez reached his car, a late model Honda Accord sedan. Tom noted the license number, then hustled back to his car.

Tom pulled in behind the Honda when Rodriguez passed and tailed him to his work place. Once Rodriguez entered the building, Tom parked near him. He got out and moved toward Rodriguez' vehicle. As he walked, he checked for cameras and for anyone who might observe him. When he reached Rodriguez's car, he *keyed* it, leaving a deep scratch. Then he took out an ice pick and pierced all four tires. From his pocket, he retrieved the note he'd prepared before leaving home. *Messing with another man's woman can be bad for your health.* He stuck it under the windshield wiper, returned to his car, and drove away.

I don't think Mr. Rodriguez will be bothering Abby again, he thought. Now all I have to do is find Jeannie's killer and reunite Renée with her father. Yep, that will make life good again. Piece of cake.

* * *

"In my office," Richards said, tapping on the post to Summers' cubicle.

Summers looked up from the file he'd been studying. "Subject?"

"My choice." Richards continued down the hall.

Summers sighed. To no one in particular, he said, "He's been thinking again. Wonder if there's some way to keep him busy twenty-four seven? Maybe I should ask his wife to keep him more occupied at home."

He grabbed his notebook and headed toward Richards' office, wondering what had his boss in such a foul mood.

Richards slammed a file shut. "I'm not satisfied."

Summers shook his head as he settled into the visitor's chair in front of Richards' desk. "Am I supposed to understand this? We're talking about . . . breakfast? Your coffee? Your sex life—no, scratch that one. Not something I want to know."

"What subject seems to occupy more of our time than it should? Jeffries, of course." Richards shifted to the back of his chair.

"Okay, what did he do this time?"

Richards' chair rocked side to side. "I've given a lot of thought to that story he told us yesterday—the one about Sammi Williams' mother being unfit. I'm not convinced."

"Chief, what about the holes in her story? You could drive a full-sized SUV through them."

"Maybe. Have you considered they could be the product of a distraught mother? Her child is missing. Should we expect her memory to be perfect?"

"Not perfect, but reasonable would be nice. She didn't even know when her daughter ran away. Sorry, chief, but that's too much for me."

"I agree—up to a point. She may be the devil-mother of the year, but she is still Sammi's mother. Jeffries is not a mother, he's an untrustworthy private investigator."

Summers sighed. "Alright. What is it you want me to do?"

Richards leaned forward in his chair. "As I told you a few days ago, I want you to keep an eye on him. Don't let anything else slip, but when you have time—and I expect you to make time—know where he is and what he's doing."

Summers locked eyes with his boss. "And what about checking out Jeffries' allegations against her? Who's going to follow up on that?"

"Tobarth. I put her on it. We need someone who can view this from a woman's perspective—not someone enamored with PIs."

"Thanks a lot. So now I'm not capable of doing my job in an objective manner? Anytime you want my badge, I can always get a PI license."

Richards pinched the bridge of his nose. "Simmer down. You know I didn't mean that. I just mean you always find some reason to support Jeffries. I need fresh eyes on this. You're still the best in the squad room."

"So?"

"I want you on Jeffries. If he burps, I want to know." He hesitated. "Phil, it may be stupid, but there is something about Jeffries that raises my antenna. Humor me on this." He stood. "Now, maybe you'd better get to work. Slurping stationhouse coffee will not get the job done."

Summers rose to his feet. "Okay, chief, you make the call and I jump. But are you forgetting our Jane Doe, or Jeannie, as the object of your derision identified her?"

"Good point. Resolving that is still your number one assignment. Any questions? No? Get out of here and get to work." He sat and flipped the folder open.

Summers scratched the back of his head. "Chief, if I didn't love you so much, I'd really wonder." He threw up his hand. "I say that only in a figurative manner. Your wife need not feel threatened." He headed toward the door. "You don't have to see me out. I know the way."

CHAPTER TWENTY-SIX

The next several days passed with little of significance happening. Lonnie and Renée took off on their see-the-country bus trip. They flew to Atlanta to join a group they'd travel with through Tennessee, Arkansas, Oklahoma, the Panhandle of Texas, New Mexico, ending at the Grand Canyon. After five days at the rim, including a trek into the canyon, they'd grab another tour that would bring them home on a southern route through New Mexico, Texas, Louisiana, the tip of Mississippi, a touch of Alabama, and the Florida Panhandle before turning north to Atlanta where they would fly home. Lonnie said it was something she had always wanted to do. Renée was almost speechless. All she could say was it would be so much *fun.*

Tom took them to the airport and kissed them *bon voyage* with a smile, relieved they'd be on the road for a full month. If people were looking for Renée, they'd never catch up with her on a tour bus. Heck, not even Tom would know where they were unless they called. Seemed like a great solution, leaving him and the police time to track the people who'd killed Jeannie.

Each day, Tom wondered if Rodriguez was bothering Abby. Her silence on the subject drove him nuts. Finally, after a week passed without a word, he asked, "Have you seen any more of that Rodriguez character, the one you thought was stalking you?"

She said, "It's funny, but I haven't seen him since . . ." She stared at Tom.

Tom wanted to duck, knowing he should have kept his curiosity to himself. Her look said it all.

She continued, "Since I talked to you. What did you do to him?"

Tom tried to look shocked. "Me? Nothing. You asked me not to touch him, and I didn't."

"Did you threaten Rodriguez? Did you tell him to stay away from me, or else? Tom—"

"C'mon, Sunshine. You asked me to stay away. Would I do otherwise?"

She studied Tom, a frown crinkling her beautiful forehead. "I think you'd do anything you thought kept me safe—and I love you for it. But we've had this discussion before. You cannot go around beating on everyone who disagrees with me."

"Like I said, I never touched him. Don't you believe me?"

Abby ran her fingers through her hair. "I'll have to, I suppose . . . this time. But there had better not be any more coincidences like this. I can take care of myself. I don't need your interference. Are we clear on that?"

"Of course, Sunshine. I never thought otherwise. You're one tough lady."

She cupped his face in her hands and gave him a light kiss on the lips. "You best remember that. I'm tough enough to kick your butt—and I will if I need to."

Tom grinned and pulled her close. Relieved that Rodriguez was leaving her alone and that she hadn't trapped him into a confession, he let the subject drop.

* * *

Tom worked the area where the crimes against Jeannie occurred—her abduction and murder. No one admitted knowing anything. Either everyone wore blindfolds when the goons grabbed her, or there was a power behind it that had them cowed. Even Jumbo and Rocky clammed up, in spite of the money he waved in their faces. They salivated, but kept their secrets to themselves. The trail grew colder.

On Friday, Tom received a call from Ken Dotson, of Dotson and Nelson, the law firm from which Tom drew a retainer.

"Tom, I need your help again. Do you have time to take on an assignment?"

"Sure," Tom said. "What's up?"

"It's not new, but this time I'll put you on the books. The extortionist is back. He hit Mom's friend, Ellen, last night, demanding payment for protection."

"Did she pay?"

"Of course. He scared the hell out of her. She's seventy-seven years old. What choice does she have?"

"Best choice is same as before—call the police. Is she still afraid to bring them in?"

Ken sighed. "Yeah. She told Mom that would make it worse. The bum told her a story about a woman who didn't pay. According to him, she fell down a flight of steps, broke her hip and arm. She'll be laid up for the next six months—if she survives at all."

"Understand. Is it the same guy?"

"No. New guy. Tall and skinny with long greasy dreadlocks that stick out in all directions. Ellen told Mom he looks like a Halloween fright mask. Even more scary than the one who collected from her before you intervened."

"Uh-huh," Tom said. "What do you want me to do?"

There were several seconds of silence, then Ken said, "I want it stopped. You're the only person I know who might be able to do that. Are you willing to take it on? I don't need to know what you're doing, just that it's effective."

"Not smart, Ken. I *discouraged* the first thug, and a second took his place. If I neutralize this one, who's to say there won't be a third? The next one might be worse." Tom hesitated. "Look, I know a couple of detectives. Why don't I run this by them and see what they think? I'll keep it generic without identifying you, your mother, or Ms. Lowenstein. That okay with you?"

"Involving the police in any way worries me. Let's assume, for the sake of argument, the police arrest this guy. He'll be out on bail the next day and paying Mom's friend a visit to make sure she doesn't testify against him. Will the police protect her? No. They have neither the manpower nor the inclination. Therefore, I simply don't believe that's a viable solution."

Tom chuckled. "Damn, we tend to think alike, which means I can't disagree with you—even though I should. I'll look at it and

176

see what I can do." He paused, thinking through the situation. "Was the collection schedule the same?"

"Yes. Thursday night, eight o'clock."

"Let's keep this between us. Don't tell your mother or Ms. Lowenstein, but I'll be nearby next week when he visits. I don't want anyone to give me away, not even accidentally. I have to tell you, though, don't expect more than a brief respite. Even if I'm successful in shooing him away, there'll probably be another. She might want to consider finding another place to live."

"Thanks, Tom. Anything you can do will be appreciated. Like I said, you're on the books for this one. Submit your bills."

After hanging up, Tom considered the possibilities. With a second person taking over the route, it smelled of an organized effort. Someone had to be pulling the strings. How organized, he couldn't guess, but he could ask the new collector—and he would. At least he'd be on the law firm's payroll. That would help. Since getting involved with Renée, he'd accepted no paying jobs. His bank account could use the boost.

The old adage about *returning to the scene of the crime* came to mind. Was he setting himself up through repetition? He sighed. He wouldn't know until it was over. Might as well get started.

He drove to the Lowenstein condominium, parked, and walked around the parking lot and the grounds. He needed a plan, an approach different from the one he used before. Something that would take him to the taproot, the person or persons behind the scheme. An hour later, he left, hoping he had devised a scheme that would work—and not lead to disaster. He intended to return on Monday, Tuesday, and Wednesday evenings to see how much the environment changed.

* * *

As the day wore on, Tom's mind flitted between Renée and Ellen Lowenstein. The thought of scum preying on the elderly, the loneliest and most vulnerable of society, haunted him. He felt obligated to stop it. But he had to do it without becoming a victim, or running afoul of the justice system. If only the police could help.

In spite of Ken Dotson's reservations, Tom decided to call Phil Summers. If he worded his questions carefully, it couldn't hurt. He need not identify any of the players. He dug out Phil's card and dialed.

"Detective Phil Summers."

"Phil. This is Tom Jeffries. Remember? The PI your boss doesn't like very much?"

"Of course, Mr. Jeffries. What can I do for you? Want to confess to something that'll make my boss happy?" A disarming chuckle followed the question.

"To please him, it would have to be murder one, right?"

"No comment," Summers said. "What's up?"

"I have a hypothetical for you. Will you play the game?"

"You're not recording, are you?"

"Of course not."

"Okay, shoot. I'll be your sounding board. You did say this is hypothetical, didn't you?"

"Yes. Let's say you get a tip on a shakedown operation against elderly women. Suppose a description, day, and time when the shakedown artist would strike found its way into your hands, what would you do?"

There were a few seconds of silence punctuated by Summers' breathing. "First, I'd want to speak with one of the hypothetical ladies to verify the tip. If she supported the information I received, I'd lay a trap to capture the shakedown artist."

"And then?"

"I'd haul the punk to the station and book him into jail. Then I'd spend three-four hours filling out the paperwork to support my arrest." He paused. "Does that answer your question?"

"Not quite. Give me your best on what happens next."

Summers sighed. "The next day, no more than the day after, the perp would go before a judge. By then he'd be represented by an attorney of his choosing or the system would have appointed someone. The lawyer would lodge a wonderful bleeding heart plea for bail, swearing his client was innocent and no threat to anyone.

"The judge would consider everything, then set bail—probably a small one for a *minor* offense like you described. By noon, the perp would be on the street, free to do as he pleased. With luck, he'd show up for court at some time in the future, and I'd spend one of my days off sitting in the hall waiting to testify. If everything went perfect, he'd be found guilty and receive a slap on the wrist—that's assuming I could get one or more of the women he extorted to testify. Of course, if his attorney could impeach their testimony by confusing the elderly ladies, or find one T uncrossed, or one I undotted, he'd walk, and I'd have to face the Lieut. "That's how it would go down." He paused again.

After a moment, and a deep sigh, Summers said, "Of course, I speak hypothetically since we have no such crime. Does that respond to your hypothetical situation?"

"Pretty much," Tom said. "Another question. Would you or anyone in the system provide protection to those extorted by this scumbag, those who blew the whistle? Would you do anything to keep them safe and encourage them to testify against the shakedown artist?"

Summers chuckled. "I guess we reached your *gotcha* question. You know we don't have those kinds of assets. Hell, we can't even protect a victim of attempted murder after the alleged killer arranges bail. I'm sure you read the papers. Budgets are shrinking everywhere. Police are the first targets for cuts."

"Yeah, I get it. Once again, the guilty get everything the state can give. The victim is on his own."

"C'mon, Tom. You know that's not right. We do what we can."

"I know, Summers. Each officer does everything he can. It's the system that is broken, not the people inside it. If you guys could get a little support from the politicians, our society would be different. I respect you, but that doesn't mean I have to support the mess you're a part of."

After a few seconds, Summers said, "So, I gather your hypothetical is going to stay a hypothetical. You're not sharing anything else with me, right?"

"I was only musing—musing about our justice system and how it might react. It sucks to know I was right. Thanks for your help." Tom hit the off button.

He leaned back and rubbed his temples. "Wonder what it would be like to live in a society where the victim gets top billing."

CHAPTER TWENTY-SEVEN

Over coffee the next morning, Tom played with a plan for stopping the extortionist and whoever was behind him. It wasn't a situation where he could use a frontal assault, as he had before. A second time around had to be handled in a different way. It would require subterfuge, perhaps some kind of flanking movement. However, he lacked two critical factors every commander needed before launching an attack—intelligence on the enemy and his order of battle. Whoever was at the top of the operation would not be dependent on someone like Future Star Miller, aka Big. Miller's size and muscles were his stock in trade, not brains. Tom didn't expect Big's replacement to be much better.

There would be several layers between Big and the *boss*, each led by a trusted lieutenant. Tom needed to get through those tiers before he could cut off the head of the snake. It could be five people or fifty-five. In wartime, no commander would be foolish enough to move with so many unknowns. Unfortunately, he didn't have the luxury of such a commander. Nor did he have the support mechanism of an army at war. He had only himself.

After two hours of writing, doodling, and making guesses based less on fact than on hopeful wishing, he pushed his coffee cup away. "Time to prepare for combat. Everything has to be perfect, or I'll fail."

He went to his bedroom and dug into the back of the closet, searching behind the front row of boxes. The first one he opened held a Colt M1911 pistol, commonly called a Colt .45 during its years of military service. It was a recent acquisition. He lost the original the night Charlie died.

Next, he took out a Mossberg 590 pump-action shotgun, another new piece to him. The one he'd nurtured through so many operations had gone with his Colt .45. He smiled as he checked to make sure the Mossberg was unloaded, then held it up by the pistol grip and pulled the trigger. Its twenty-inch barrel made it easy enough to handle with one hand although the kick from the loads he fired mandated a two-handed operation.

He considered for a moment before reaching for another box. It held four speed loaders for his single-action, five shot mini-revolver, the weapon he wore on his left ankle inside his boot. Its two-inch barrel and nine-ounce weight made it an excellent carry, while its .22 magnum cartridges inflicted maximum punishment on whatever they hit. With the speed loaders, he could carry twenty-five rounds. If he needed more than that, the battle would already be lost. His next stop was the closet in the guest bedroom. From under a loose floorboard, he retrieved ammunition.

He spent the next hour cleaning and checking the weapons. When each met his exacting standards, he loaded them and laid them aside. He'd slip the ankle holster on later with its mini-revolver and put the .45 and the shotgun in his car in their special compartments. Until this was over, he would not go unarmed or unprepared.

Checking the clock, he saw it was almost noon. The morning had slipped away during his preparations. But prepared he was, or as close as he could get.

His cell phone rang. Looking at the caller ID, he smiled. "So Ace, what's up?"

"Are you sitting down?"

Tom dropped into a kitchen chair. "Sounds like an ah-shit. Give me the worst."

"No, my man, the best. We found your man. We found James Robert Williams—or I should say Kit found him. Ready to copy?"

"Oh, yeah," Tom said, pulling his note pad toward him. "Give me a number."

Ace read off a phone number. "Did you get that?"

Tom read it back to him.

"Good. He's expecting your call. Now, here's a gift I'm betting you didn't expect."

"You're being too mysterious. Let me have the bad news."

"Nope, try this one on for size. Here's his email address." Ace rattled it off. "Notice anything about the SRW0703?"

Tom repeated the address under his breath. "I don't get it. Should this mean—" He stopped, realization settling in. "SRW, Samantha Renée Williams. And her birthday is July third. Damn. It means—"

"Yep, it's a strong indication he loves his daughter. As soon as I mentioned her name, I had his absolute attention. Call him. He's waiting to hear from you."

Tom wiped his brow, finding it difficult to believe what he heard. "What did you tell him?"

"Well, that was a problem. He wasn't about to turn me loose without my giving him something. I told him she has some minor problems, and you're trying to help her through them. I assured him you'd be in touch before the end of the day. Don't let me down, or he may find me and stomp a mud hole in my ass. That's how fired up he was."

"You got it, my friend. Now, let me off the phone, and I'll call him right now. You're my salvation, Ace. I can't begin to thank you enough."

"Just keep me informed—and remember, you owe Kit and me a trip to Disneyland."

Tom rang off and placed his phone on the table, his hands trembling with excitement. His long shot had paid off. There not only was a James Robert Williams in the Dallas area, but he loved his daughter.

Tom wanted to call Abby, wanted to tell Lonnie. However, those calls should wait. He needed to speak with Williams, explain the situation, and hope Williams could break the legal stranglehold her mother had on Renée. He wondered if Williams had money, or at least enough to fight a legal battle across state lines. Only one way to find out. He dialed the number Ace gave him.

"Mr. Williams, my name is Tom Jeffries. I'm a private investigator in Florida and—"

"Yes, yes, I know who you are. What's happening with my daughter? What kind of trouble is she in? I called her mother, and she wouldn't tell me anything."

Tom took a deep breath, hoping he could make the father understand. "No trouble, Mr. Williams. But she does need something, she needs *you*." Leaving out as little as possible, Tom explained his association with Renée, especially his conversations with Barbara Williams. There were no interruptions.

When he finished, the line was quiet. After about five seconds, Williams said, "Don't take my silence wrong, Mr. Jeffries. I'm trying not to let what I feel come out. This kind of rage should stay bottled. My first impulse is to fly to Florida and strangle the bitch. Allow me another moment, then we can talk." His words were clipped, angry, filled with emotion.

Again, Tom heard only a slight crackling across space. Then there was a deep sigh.

"I want my daughter—full custody, no maternal visitations. She has paid the price of my foolishness, and I'll carry that to the grave. I thought feeding Barbara's greed would be enough to make her a responsible mother to Renée. You see, I come from a background that says a daughter is better off with her mother. Looking back, I know I was fooling myself then and have fooled myself every day since. Your news reinforces that knowledge. You can't—no one can—imagine how bad I feel."

"So," Tom said, "what can you do about it?"

"I can do what I should have done ten years ago. I can fight for my daughter. I need you to provide the ammunition required to defeat her in court. Can you do it? Can I hire you to deliver the goods?"

"Whoa. Slow down. I want you to win, but this could get really, really nasty. You have a mother who—my opinion only—will do whatever it takes to keep custody. Her interview with the police proves she has no scruples. Renée is her meal ticket. Lawyers will rush to represent the poor woman whose motherhood is threatened. The media will vilify you as they paint a portrait of the new Joan of Arc. Second, you have Florida versus Texas. You'll have to fight her here, her home state. You're from out of state. Not good, you *damn cowboy*. Third, she's had custody for ten years while you walked away. What I'm trying to tell you, Mr. Williams, is you'd better have the best attorneys money can buy, and that will cost dollars—lots of dollars. Can you afford it?"

Williams chuckled. "Obviously, you know nothing about me or the oil industry. The name J. R. Williams sits in the top ten of Texas oilmen. At the risk of sounding pompous, I can buy Florida—well, maybe not the Keys. I have so damn much money, I have no clue what to do with it. Right now, I'm in Alaska closing a drilling deal that should produce a few more millions. In short, I have whatever it takes to gain custody of my daughter—everything except patience. I ran out of that ten minutes ago—as soon as you started talking."

He paused. When he spoke again, his voice was softer, more sincere. "But this isn't just about beating Barbara in court. I was a bitter man when she and I divorced. No more weddings for me. Barbara had turned me off marriage for the rest of my life. Oh, I went out with women, but not with any idea of a forming any kind of permanent relationship. I needed someone with me on social occasions, and that's how I saw them—eye candy for a swinging bachelor. However, seven years ago, I met a special person who put the lie to everything Barbara stood for and every feeling she left me with. Her name is Debbi, and we've been married for five years. If there is a more perfect woman in the world, I don't want to know. Debbi is the only one I need. We have two children—a boy, three, and a girl, one.

"Almost from the time we began dating, Debbi has wanted me to bring Renée to Texas to live with us. I hemmed, hawed, and ducked the issue. I'm telling you this because I want you to know I'm won't be acting alone, purely for revenge. My wife will be with me every inch of the way. We want Renée as part of our family."

Tom pulled on his earlobe. Either Williams was a master bullshit artist, or he was speaking from the heart. "Okay, as long as you know the odds. You'll need a set of Florida lawyers. Do you have any?"

"No, but I'm sure my people in Dallas can scare some up. After all, don't lawyers work for those who can afford them? I'll turn my Texas law firm loose on it."

"Maybe I can help with that. I know a local firm who might take you on. Their weakness is they're highly ethical. If they find out you're not what you say you are, they'll walk away. Want I should talk to them?"

"Sure. Sounds like the kind of people I need on my team. Or better yet, give me their ID and, if my people concur, they'll be contacted soonest."

Tom gave him the particulars on Dotson and Nelson. "I'll let them know to expect a call."

"One more thing, though, before we disconnect. I'm afraid to face Barbara. Not because of her, but because of what I might do to her. I'd prefer not to meet her in court, and doubt I'll need to. Her weakness is greed. I can afford to buy her off, and that is my preference. Renée doesn't need to see her birth parents in a go-for-the-jugular courtroom setting."

"That's something for the attorneys to work out. However, before this goes too far, we are overlooking the most important thing."

"That is?"

Tom hesitated, then said, "Renée. I will help you only if she agrees to live with you."

"Understood. I won't try to contact her until you give me the okay. Is that fair?"

"Yes. I don't have anything else, do you?"

"One more. What about you?" Williams said. "Are you on the payroll?"

Tom chuckled. "Can I back-bill you for the last two weeks—if Renée approves?"

"Account for all your time and expenses. I'll take care of them. Oh, by the way, I'll be sending Ace Edwards and Kit Levitt healthy checks, too. If not for you three, I'd have never known. I can't begin to thank you enough. And I'm not the kind who forgets an obligation."

Tom clicked off, a smile growing on his face. He called Abby, then Lonnie. Both were overjoyed with the news. He asked Lonnie to feel Renée out on living with her father and get back to him as soon as she could. His last call was to Dotson and Nelson. Ken Dotson thanked him for the referral and said he'd be waiting to hear from Texas.

CHAPTER TWENTY-EIGHT

The next week zipped by as Tom collaborated with his boss at the law firm, Ken Dotson, on how to best approach Barbara Williams, Renée's mother. Dotson reported he'd discreetly checked out James Robert Williams and discovered he was the real thing. Dotson's words were, "From the reports I received, he can't count high enough to know how much money he has—and he finished in the upper ten percent of his class at the University of Texas. In the last few years, his investments have paid beyond anyone's expectations."

Williams preferred they make a cash offer to his ex-wife before filing court papers, and his offer sailed into the upper six figures. If she balked, he'd do whatever it took to strip custody from her.

Tom checked in with Detective Summers, but learned little. The police had inquiries out on Barbara Williams, but nothing concrete had come in. Lt. Richards' investigator of choice, Detective Tobarth, refused to deliver an opinion until she checked every source. However, Summers shared with Tom that her daily reports were less than complimentary.

Rodriguez, the wife beater, stayed away from Abby—or Abby didn't tell Tom about it. When Tom asked, she changed the subject. Tom's inclination was to surveil Rodriguez, but he knew that could wreck his relationship with Abby. He had to let things play out. He'd done all he dared. But if Rodriguez harmed Abby in any way . . .

In the evenings, Tom observed the parking lot of the condominium where Ellen Lowenstein, the friend of Dotson's mother, lived. He studied those who came and went, memorizing faces when he could see them, mannerisms when he couldn't. It was important Tom be able to spot the extortionist when he made his round on Thursday evening. He might be smarter than his predecessor and attempt to blend in. Tom had to know who belonged and who didn't. During his quiet surveillance, he saw that most of the people who entered between seven and eight were elderly. They parked in assigned spaces, entered the building, and didn't show themselves again. Residents, Tom assumed.

The few departures he saw appeared to consist of medical aides and younger people, probably relatives. By eight o'clock, the lot was quiet, almost no cars arriving or leaving. With that insight, Tom was confident he could spot the man who chose to rip off the old ladies.

He also hoped to establish a presence in the community. With luck, his red convertible would become accepted as belonging there. If things went south, he didn't want people describing him to the police as a suspect.

* * *

At seven on Thursday evening, Tom pulled into the parking area in the front of Ms. Lowenstein's condominium. He drove to a dark corner and parked in a visitor's space. After fifteen minutes of checking the area, he concluded nothing appeared out of order and exited his car.

On previous trips, he had picked a spot where he could hover and observe the building entry without being too obvious. He moved there and leaned against a stone pillar, placing himself in shadow. He wore navy slacks, a black T-shirt, and a navy zippered hoodie, none of them in good shape. A New York Yankees baseball cap sat on his head. Not his first choice in clothing, but dark enough to help him blend into the shadows. On the other hand, he anyone seeing him might consider him another homeless person and not a member of the local burglars' guild. In nights past, he had noticed the area attracted a large number of those who lived on the street.

He settled onto the ground and began his vigil. As in the other evenings, nurses, medical aides, and a few young people exited the building, got into cars, and left. A half-dozen vehicles or so entered, parked in numbered spaces, and the occupants entered the building. All older, some using walkers. Probably coming in from dinner.

The minutes ticked by and the mosquitoes came out of hiding. Tom's Special Forces training and common sense had prepared him for the bloodsuckers. He had sprayed all exposed skin with an unscented anti-bug spray. He could hear them zing as they flew past his ears, but none took a nibble.

At ten minutes before eight, he rose and did an abbreviated stretching routine. When the extortionist showed up, Tom wanted to be ready to move. A cramp was the last thing he needed. He reached into a Publix plastic bag he carried and pressed the start button on an item inside.

The clocked ticked on, burning five more minutes before an older car came into the parking lot. It clearly did not fit with the newer, upscale models the building occupants drove. Tom watched as it parked in a handicapped space beside the entrance. A tall, thin man with dreadlocks got out, consulted a piece of paper, then entered the building.

Tom smiled. That had to be his man. He was about as far from the profile of building occupants as he could get.

With no apparent haste, but wasting no time, Tom assumed his homeless stance and shuffled across the lot, passing close to the end of the vehicle. As he came abreast of the rear quarter panel, the bag fell from his hand, spilling its contents. Tom knelt and began collecting the items. As he reached under the car to retrieve one of his possessions, he slapped a magnetic GPS tracking device into the rear wheel well. After another moment of finding his stuff, he stood and walked toward his convertible, a smile playing on his lips.

Upon reaching his car, he opened the door, threw the baseball cap and hoodie into the backseat, then got in and slipped on his western hat. He checked his receiver and saw a strong signal from the tracking device. *Nice. Go where you please, Mr. Punk. I'll be right behind you.*

He backed out of the space, left the parking lot, and drove to a strip mall he'd scouted a block down the street. He settled in to wait until the extortionist finished his business.

Fifteen minutes later, his quarry began to move, and Tom tucked in behind him, a few cars between them. They visited several more condominiums before the extortionist headed out of the area. Tom smiled. *Maybe he's on his way to meet his boss.*

They worked their way westward, past the cheap strip malls and the more upscale covered malls. The four-lane street passed fewer gated communities and entered an area of single-family homes. After another few miles, the houses grew larger, then into mini-ranches surrounded by fences.

His curiosity grew, wondering just where this lowlife was leading him. Could someone in this upscale area be extorting little old ladies? Stranger things had happened in Florida, so it was quite possible.

They turned onto a two-lane street where each estate seemed larger than the one previous. Tom and his rabbit were the only two cars moving. Tom turned his headlights off and slowed, allowing additional space to develop between them. They had to be getting close.

The thug slowed and pulled into a driveway leading to a closed gate a few yards off the street. A wall joined the gate from both directions. Bright lights illuminated the entryway.

Tom crowded the curbing, then stopped a few hundred yards behind, left his engine idling, and watched.

The driver got out and walked to a box mounted on the edge of the gate. He appeared to speak into the box, then returned to his car. The entryway swung open, and he drove through.

Tom drove past the gate and attempted to see in. He glimpsed a large, well-landscaped yard with a curving driveway splitting it. At the rear, a three-story mansion loomed. It was a brief look, telling Tom little.

He continued past more gated mansions before turning back. About fifty yards from the edge of the property, he pulled over and killed the engine. Only one way to find out what was behind that wall. He got out and studied the sky. Heavy clouds, promising rain, covered the moon. That part was good. However, Tom knew the weather could change from downpour to clear sky in a matter of minutes. Monsoon season in South Florida produced some strange results. If caught in the open when the clouds moved, he'd be visible to anyone looking out a window. Couldn't be helped. He had to go inside—that's where the truth lay.

He took the Mossburg shotgun from its compartment and checked its load. After a moment's hesitation, he put it back. *Too cumbersome for climbing fences and sneaking around.* The .45 went into a shoulder holster. Touching his calf and his boot, he assured himself his knife and ankle pistol were at the ready. He was as prepared as he'd ever be.

Everything in Tom's training told him he was being foolish. Scaling a fence into unknown territory with no intelligence and no pre-planning was plain stupid. Yet, he couldn't think of a better plan. If the extortion was to be stopped, he had to do it, and he had to do it tonight. Waiting would only allow the evidence to disappear, Dreadlocks to become a welcome visitor. The answer lay behind the wall, and Tom had to uncover it.

He thought of Abby and how much he loved her. Was he being fair to her? If things went south inside that compound, would she forgive him? How about Renée? He should . . . No, he'd taken that as far as he could. Whatever happened was a matter for her, her father, and the law to decide.

Tom shook his head, realizing his ruminations were nothing more than procrastination. Being a civilian had softened him. Tonight, he needed his hard Special Forces edge—the training that had allowed him to return from so many dangerous missions. Soft was for times with Abby.

He walked to the wall, figuring it measured about eight feet tall, and appeared to be stucco over concrete blocks. He checked to make sure his .45 was tied down in its holster, then reached to the top of the fence. Expending little effort, he pulled himself up until he could look over. As he'd glanced through the gate, there was little to see—landscaped lawn leading up a hill to a lighted house.

He pulled himself onto the top of the wall and lay prone, listening for any noise that did not fit the quietness of the night, while his eyes adjusted to the darkness ahead of him.

A car's lights reflected on the street. He made himself as small as possible and squeezed his eyes shut lest he lose the precious little night vision he'd gained. Once the vehicle passed, he gazed again into the interior of the compound.

The moon chose to find a hole in the clouds, illuminating the yard behind the wall—and threatening to spotlight Tom. He swung off the wall, landing in a fighter's stance, all senses alert, ready to bolt or attack like a feral cat. His Special Forces training was not lost. It had kicked in the moment his feet touched the ground.

When nothing appeared to threaten him, he scuttled down the fence about twenty yards, then dropped to the ground, studying in all directions. He used his peripheral vision to watch for changes in shadows, any kind of unnatural movement. In such darkness, it was more dependable that direct vision. Everything seemed still, then the moon hid again, dropping his environment back into blackness.

He waited, wondering what type of security he faced. There had to be something, of that he had no doubt. Motion detectors, infrared cameras, CCTV, roving patrols, guard dogs? He hoped not the last. A couple of well-trained dogs, even if he survived their attack, would leave him wounded and pouring blood. Plus, the barks, growls, and screams of the dying dogs would undoubtedly bring more bad news.

From a careful crouch, he studied the house and the large area in front, wishing he had night vision goggles. However, he didn't so there was nothing to do but wait for a transition in his eyes. The brightness of the house didn't help. It was three-stories, illumination flooding from each floor. Spotlights made the front and the side look like high noon at the OK Corral. The good news was he saw no guards circling within that huge cone of light.

But that was for later. He had about fifty yards to negotiate before reaching the light. He pulled his eyes away and stared into the darkness. Slower than a crippled snail, his sight sharpened and he began to make out bushes, trees, and a walkway on his left. The path connected to a pedestrian gate. *Damn. There may be a guard. Even if he hasn't seen and reported me, he won't miss when I start toward the house.*

Pushing against the wall, Tom inched leftward in a semi-crouch. He made a silent plea that the lawn service kept twigs and other noisemakers picked up. In that silence, a broken twig would sound like a rifle shot.

As he closed on the gate, he saw the silhouette of a man leaning against the wall. It was too dark to make out anything about his clothing, except he wore a baseball cap, but the utility belt around his waist, especially the holster, stood out. Tom hoped he was looking at a thug hired by the owner, not some retiree trying to supplement his income by playing late night rent-a-cop.

Tom continued his relentless stalking of the guard, moving a couple of steps, then freezing. Move, freeze, move freeze. He relaxed when he was within five feet, knowing he could launch an attack if necessary.

Hiding in the moon shadow of a bush, he studied the guard again—male, short-sleeved shirt, long pants, apparently some kind of uniform. He saw cuffs dangling from the rear of the utility belt, a holster on the man's right side, and other pouches scattered around his waist. He probably carried pepper spray or some other kind of chemical to incapacitate.

Tom had to neutralize him. However, not knowing what else waited in the darkness, he would have to do it without any sound. That meant one attempt and one only. There would be no time for a second.

He returned his gun to its shoulder holster and switched his knife to his right hand. Another two steps, and he reached out and tapped the guard on the shoulder.

"Uh, wha—"

That was as far as he got as Tom's fist smashed into the side of his jaw, using the haft of the knife in his fist like a roll of quarters.

The guard dropped, unconscious, Tom catching and easing him to the ground.

Tom searched him, noting with satisfaction he was not a retiree. Instead, he appeared to be in his twenties, a hard-body. Definitely not a candidate for an anti-obesity program. Instead, his workout habits were obvious because of the muscles straining the seams of his clothing. Tom felt blessed the man had a glass jaw.

After using the guard's cuffs to secure his hands behind him, Tom searched the pouches. He smiled when he found plastic ties, allowing him to bind the man's ankles, then by linking two ties together, drawing his legs up behind him, and connecting them to the cuffs. His right rear pocket held a handkerchief, which Tom used to gag him. He took off the man's shoes, sturdy leather, steel-toed brogans, and his socks. He tied the socks together and used them as a blindfold.

Tom pulled him away from the gate and placed him under a bush, hogtied, and out of action. He couldn't see, couldn't call for help, and couldn't move. That should hold him.

Last, Tom took the small radio that rode the guard's epaulette, noting with a smile that it had an earplug. At least he'd know if and when he was spotted.

Taking the guard's gun and shoes with him, he retreated about twenty yards from the gate. After hiding the footwear in the middle of a hedge, Tom settled in to watch the night.

CHAPTER TWENTY-NINE

Detective Summers rubbed his chin as he stared into the darkness. Something was going down, of that he was sure. Yet, the badge he carried prevented him from investigating. Charging onto a citizen's personal property without a warrant was a quick way to the unemployment line. As far as he could tell, the vehicle gate was unmanned. Apparently, it was kept locked and controlled from the house. He shrugged. *Guess I'd better let the boss know what's happening.*

Summers took out his cell phone and punched in Lt. Richards' number.

"And to what do I owe this interruption?" Richards said as an answer to the ring.

"I work. You work. It's simple, boss."

"You said you had a date tonight. What happened? She stand you up?"

"Of course not. Women don't stand me up. That would be absurd. She texted to break the date, said her mother was in the hospital."

"Oh, sure. And you believe it, so you're calling because you're lonely—on one of the few evenings I get to spend with my family? Tell me I'm wrong."

"Sorry to spoil your temper tantrum, but I'm following your orders."

"How so?"

"Well, after my latest Miss Perfect lost her shot at euphoria, I went for a drive. And, what do you think I saw—a red Chrysler convertible driven by a man wearing a cowboy hat. It pulled into a strip mall and parked. Ring any bells?"

"Your cuteness is only exceeded by my growing irritation. Get to the point."

"Jeffries. It was Tom Jeffries, your favorite PI to not-trust."

"You don't say. A strip mall, you say? Who would have ever thought he'd visit such an exotic location?"

"Oh, boss. Do I detect a bit of sarcasm? You really should leave that to me. I do it so much better."

"So, move on already."

"As I said, I saw Jeffries so I decided to latch onto him. Pulling my invisibility cloak over both my car and myself, I followed him into the parking lot. He pulled into a space and . . ."

After Summers gave him a moment of silence, Richards said, "Okay, I'll bite. What?"

"That's just it. Nothing. He sat in his car. Ten-fifteen minutes passed with nothing happening. Then, he cranked up and headed out. Naturally, I followed."

"Naturally," Richards said, his impatience showing.

"We drove about a mile, then he pulled into a parking space and repeated his *sitting-in-the-car* routine. By then, I was getting pretty curious, and—"

"Perfectly understandable. Is there a moral to this story? Hell, is there an end to this story?"

"Hang with me, boss. It gets better. He pulled the park-and-wait bit three more times, then started west. And when I say west, I mean west, west where the big money is. After doing a U-turn, he got out of his car and scaled the wall of a huge estate. He's been in there close to an hour. What do you want me to do?"

"Any shots? Any noise that makes you think something's going on that shouldn't be?"

"Nope and nope."

"Any strange lights, UFO's buzzing the place?"

"C'mon, boss. I'm worried about him. He sure didn't scale that wall because he lost his key."

"Okay. Give me the address, and I'll find out who Jeffries is spooking on. This might be our chance to get him out of our hair. If he's far enough afield, we can get his license revoked."

"Sorry, chief. That's not exactly what I was thinking. My bet is this somehow ties in with the runaway girl and the Jeannie we found in the dumpster. I suspect Jeffries might be in front of us on this."

"If he is, more power to him. Let me off the phone so I can do my homework. In the meantime, you sit tight. If Jeffries comes out of there, or all hell breaks loose, let me know."

* * *

Tom stared into the darkness, his night vision gradually sharpening. Every few minutes, he closed one eye and took a quick look into the lighted area between him and the house—just long enough to see if anyone was in view. Nothing. No movement.

So, hotshot, he thought, how do you plan to get inside. No way to cross that yard without being seen. Well, there's always the military way—hi diddle, diddle, straight up the middle.

He worked himself to the edge of the light, letting the last bush in his path conceal him. He slipped out of his shoulder holster and placed it with the .45 inside under the greenery. If he got lucky, he might retrieve it. If not . . . well, in the afterlife he'd earned, it wouldn't do him any good anyway. With a deep breath, he rose and walked toward the front door, wondering how far he'd get before someone confronted him.

He'd gone about twenty feet when he heard, "Stop where you are. You are trespassing on private property. Do not move."

Tom looked around, but saw no one. Apparently, a loud speaker. He wondered if it was a real person or a recording.

"Alright, you, hit the ground. Face down and spread-eagled."

This time, Tom saw the man. He was big, black, well over six feet, with well-proportioned weight to match. But that was the good part. The bad part was the Uzi he held, pointed in Tom's direction. A noise behind Tom made him turn in that direction. He saw dreadlocks approaching, the punk he'd followed. He, too, carried an Uzi. Time to obey instructions.

"Search him," the big man said.

197

Dreadlocks stuck his Uzi in the back of his baggy jeans and gave Tom a pat down. When he found the knife, he studied it, his eyes large. "That's all," he said, handing the knife to his partner.

"Alright, let's get him inside."

They hustled Tom around the side to the back of the house. As they approached, a door swung open.

"Bring him in here. I'll talk to him first. If he passes that, the boss wants to see him." He motioned toward a chair. "Over there, tie him down, then leave us alone."

The two walked Tom to the chair and plopped him into it. After several turns with white rope, probably nylon, they had Tom secured.

Dreadlocks spoke to the third man. "Are you sure you want us to leave? I ain't never seen nothing like that knife he had. Bet he's a mean sonnavabitch."

The third man chuckled. "Oh, I think I can handle him. Besides, he promises to behave himself. You two can wait in the next room. Close the door."

As they exited, he dropped into an easy chair. "You're not going to disappoint me, are you, Mr. Jeffries?"

Tom looked at his bindings. "Oh, I probably won't run—not far with this chair tied to my butt. Do I know you?"

"Not exactly, but you will. Yes, you certainly will. I have to tell you, though, it'll probably be a short friendship. I have to give you credit. You're either ballsy or dumber than roadkill. I saw you come over the wall and wondered what you'd do. You made it tough to follow at times, the way you blended into the shadows. Good thing our cameras are supplemented with infrared lens. You did a fine job of handling Snowcone. One punch and it was lights out. All I saw you swing was your arm. Did you use brass knuckles?"

"Your boys didn't find any, did they? I'll have to remember a set the next time I visit."

"Sure you will. I'll make you a deal though. If you cooperate with me, I'll keep Snowcone away from you. Last I saw of him, he was not happy with the way you bound him."

"Where is he?"

"Right where you left him. You gave him a lesson in staying alert. I'll let him stew for a while so it will have ample time to sink in. I doubt anyone will slip up on him in the future."

"You sound like a tough man to work for. Send back my résumé. I'm glad to know he's okay, though," Tom said. flexing his fists. "He sure has a hard head. I could have hurt myself."

"Nice line. I'll have to remember it. Enough of the chitchat. My name is Antoine. Yours is Tom Jeffries. You have become a nuisance to my boss, and that's a problem. He's not a forgiving man. Why are you on his property?"

Tom considered his options. "I suppose telling you it's none of your business is not an acceptable answer."

Antoine nodded. "You're making progress. You're recognizing what not to do. That's a step in the right direction. Back to my question."

Tom chuckled. "It's almost too funny to tell. It's dreadlocks in there. He owes me money. I spotted him earlier tonight, but he drove away before I could ask him for it. I followed him. He led me here, and I came over the fence. Pretty simple, isn't it?"

Antoine glanced toward the door to the next room. "That's almost believable. If you said Lemon owed everyone in this town, it wouldn't surprise me much. I didn't hire him for his credit rating."

"Why did you hire him?"

"Basically, because I scare the hell out of him. He'd rather crap his pants than cross me. But, that's not important. What is important is you didn't tell me the truth." He sighed. "Mr. Jeffries, there are several ways we can do this. One, you and I can have a civilized conversation. Two, I can bring my two friends in here, and we can have an uncivilized conversation. Three, I can tell the boss you refuse to cooperate, and he'll introduce you to the most uncivilized conversation you can imagine. After that, it'll be fish food city. Which will it be?"

"Interesting use of words—fish food city? Care to explain?"

"Not really. Trust me, you don't want to know. Which way should we go? You want to level with me, or . . ."

Tom tugged at his bonds as he stared at the door to the other room. He could hear faint conversation coming from there. "One of dreadlocks, uh, you called him Lemon, didn't you? Anyway, one of Lemon's customers is under my protection. He took money from her. I'm going to get it back—with interest. Very simple."

Antoine threw his head back and laughed. "You're a funny man, Mr. Jeffries. A very funny man. Yet, I believe you. You took Big down, didn't you? I thought he was bullshitting us, but you took his stash and sent him home without a dime. I wish I could have seen it. He was twice your size and mean as hell. He should have taken you with one hand."

"Yes, but he didn't. You said was and could have. Does that mean I won't be meeting him tonight?"

"That's right. You probably haven't heard. He had an accident, turned himself into fish food."

"Oh."

"Yeah, the boss don't like it when his collection agents come in empty-handed."

Tom stared around the room. "What now? You asked. I answered. Is this when you drag Lemon out here so I can collect?"

"You're good, Mr. Jeffries," Antoine said through a smile. "In another situation, we could share a beer. But no, this is when I talk to the boss to find out what he wants to do with you. I'll have Lemon and Howard sit with you." He rose from the easy chair. "Don't leave before I return."

He walked to the door and opened it. "Come in here. Keep Mr. Jeffries comfortable. I'll be back in a few."

Tom watched as the guards changed places with Antoine. Lemon looked like he'd live up to his name, not much of a threat. But Howard was the opposite. Not only did he have the size, but a nasty scar along the right side of his face pulling at his eye made him look Halloweenish.

Lemon's gun might be a problem, but Howard would have to be accounted for first. He wondered how much time he had before Antoine returned.

Okay, Tom thought, it's now or never. Let's drive a wedge. "Good to see you again, Lemon. I might have known the Lemon Drop Kid would find a nice cushy setup like this."

"Huh? What you mean?" Lemon said.

"Oh, c'mon. Am I supposed to act like I don't know you? I didn't recognize you at first, but you're definitely the Lemon Drop Kid. You've done something with your dreadlocks, haven't you? The tips used to be blond, kind of a bright yellow like a lemon. Guess you let them grow out."

"You know this guy?" Howard said, pointing at Tom.

"Of course, he does," Tom said. "Or maybe I should say he knows my money. He's one of my best snitches. I paid him, oh I don't know, hundreds for info. I can always depend on him to give me the straight stuff."

"Is that true, Lemon?"

"No. I never seen him befo'. He lyin'."

Tom watched as Howard stared at Lemon, then at him, clearly confused. Time to add another layer.

"Are you still in touch with that cop you fed info to?" Tom pretended to think. "What was his name? Roberts? No, that's not right. He was a high roller in homicide, lieutenant, maybe captain. C'mon, Lemon, you know who I'm talking about."

"No, I don't. I swear I don't." He looked at Howard, his face in agony. "I don' know no policeman."

"Richards. Lieutenant Richards. That's the guy," Tom said. "He had a lot of respect for you. He'd probably be disappointed to find out you were shaking down little old ladies."

Howard bounced to his feet. "That's enough of this crap. One of you bastards is blowin' smoke. I'm gettin' Antoine. He'll sort you two out." He took a few steps away and spoke into a two-way radio. "We need you in here. There's some funny crap goin' on."

Ten minutes later, Antoine came through the door. Howard met him, and they whispered for a couple of minutes.

Tom smiled as he watched Lemon sweat and the scowls on Howard's and Antoine's faces grow. Things were going well.

Antoine faced Tom. "Listen, Jeffries, you're on a one-way road to hell if you're messing with my people. Howard says Lemon snitched for you. Is that right?"

"If I'd known everyone would get so upset, I'd have kept my mouth shut. In fact, that's just what I think I'll do. I'll close the subject by saying I've never seen him before. Does that make you happy?"

Antoine chuckled. "Too bad you have to die. You're an interesting person. Howard, cut our guest loose, cuff his hands behind him, then you and Lemon take him to the basement. It's time he met the boss." He stared at Lemon. "Just when I thought you might be worth training. Howard, make sure Lemon doesn't do anything stupid."

CHAPTER THIRTY

Howard snipped the plastic ties securing Tom's hands as Lemon trained his gun on him. Before Tom could comment, handcuffs snapped around his wrists. "Let's go, pretty boy. You heard what th' man said."

Uh-oh, this is not good. Need to make a move soon, or it'll be too late. "Hey, easy with the cuffs. You're cutting circulation."

"Tough. Move in front of me, into the hall to the elevator." He gave Tom a push.

Tom walked in front of Howard, following instructions, but his mind swirled as he looked for an advantage—any advantage. They went to an elevator, got in, and Howard pushed the down button. *What the hell? A basement in Florida?* They descended two floors. *A sub-basement? Damn. What kind of building is this?*

"Does the city know about these basements?" Tom asked.

Howard rolled his eyes.

The door swished open, and Tom found himself in another world. He blinked as he looked from one object to another, wondering if this was how an accused felt when facing the Spanish Inquisition.

"Very interesting," Tom said. "Someone has a strange sense of humor." *If someone told me about this, I'd be slow to believe him.*

"I thought you'd be impressed," Howard said. "Forget humor, though. There ain't no laughter here—only screams of pain for them who don't cooperate. I trust you will."

Tom's stomach bounced like a small boat in a hurricane, but he forced a smile. "Time will tell. I told Antoine why I'm here. Don't know how much more I have to say."

Howard nudged him toward a polished metal chair and shoved him onto it.

"Easy, my man. I'm not very comfortable with my hands behind me," Tom said. "Want to take off these cuffs?"

"Nope," Howard said, securing Tom's legs, "I saw what you did to Snowcone. We'll wait."

Howard walked about ten feet away and sat in a cushioned chair.

Tom squirmed on the hard seat and examined the room. Directly across from him was what looked like an upright casket, but not a rectangular one. It had more of a human shape, wide at the shoulders and tapering toward the feet. The head area was also narrow and transparent, covered with what appeared to be clear plastic. It looked like something he'd seen in a museum, a mummy's casket—except for the faceplate. What had he stumbled into? This was more than a simple extortion plot. He continued scanning, his stomach continuing to flip.

Howard interrupted. "Your eyes tell me you're looking for the escape hatch. Save your energy. There ain't none. Many tried, nobody made it."

"Just admiring the furnishings." Tom forced a chuckle. "But, don't count me out. There's a first for everything."

"Not this time. You're—"

"Aha, so this is the formidable Tom Jeffries, inscrutable private investigator."

Tom twisted toward the door and saw a new person entering. His clothing screamed expensive, black silk shirt and wool slacks with a crease sharp enough to cut a tough steak. But what caught Tom's eyes were the boots peeking out from the legs of the pants. "Yeah. That's who I am. Who are you?"

"Your host. Are you comfortable?"

"Not exactly, but things have been worse."

"Oh, my. Howard, are his hands handcuffed behind him? That's terrible. Undo them, please. Never treat a guest like that. Strap him to the chair arms. Antoine will make sure Mr. Jeffries tries nothing stupid. Won't you, Antoine?"

"My pleasure, boss."

Tom heard the sound of a round being chambered and turned to see Antoine holding a pump action shotgun. He chuckled. "If you use that, Howard will catch part of the load, too."

"True," Antoine said, deadpan. "But you'll never know who got the worst of it."

"Your argument is very persuasive. Howard, I promise to keep both of us safe."

Howard grunted and reached behind Tom. After a moment, the cuffs clicked open and Tom brought his arms around. Before he could rub his wrists, Howard had the right strapped to the arm of the chair. The left soon followed.

"Perhaps," the boss said, "you should use the safety belt. Mr. Jeffries might appreciate a demonstration of the chair."

"Before we do that," Tom said, "maybe you'll tell me about your boots. Are those caiman tail? They look great."

The man laughed. "Not hardly. I never settle for second rate." He pulled his pants leg up and showed off the boot. "These are American alligator, the best money can have made. Oh, I'm sure you think I'm exaggerating, but I assure you I'm not. Behind here, I have my own lake and enough alligators to supply South Florida. But I harvest only what I need. I enjoy feasting on the tails, and my boot maker works wonders with the hides." He paused and smiled. "The rest of the gators have other purposes, if you get my drift."

"I hope I don't," Tom said, suppressing a shudder.

"But, enough chitchat. The demonstration, Howard. Have you forgotten already?"

"No sir." A smile creased Howard's face as he fitted a strap around Tom's waist. "Yeah, boss. This should be fun. I was hopin' you'd show him."

"Now, Mr. Jeffries, an example of my ingenuity. I designed this chair and oversaw its construction. The legs, Howard."

Howard knelt, and Tom felt the rear of the chair rising, causing him to slip forward. He tried to stop his slide by forcing his arms down, but the chair arms slid with him. The belt stopped him with a bump.

"Now, as you felt, Mr. Jeffries, you have little control over your position. You go with the tilt."

"Sure, I get that," Tom said. "Interesting, but I fail to see what you accomplished. Is that it?"

The boss laughed. "Howard, the next step. Satisfy Mr. Jeffries' curiosity."

"Just what I wanted to do, Mr. GG."

Tom thought, Mr. GG? Strange name. The belt tightened around his waist, then yanked him to the back of the chair. Once there, it relaxed and he slid forward, only to be jerked back again. The cycle repeated—slip-jerk, slip-jerk, slip-jerk.

"This is great fun," Tom stuttered, the motion affecting his speech. "What's it for?"

"Give him another couple of minutes, Howard, then stop it," Mr. GG said. "If he doesn't understand by then, we'll give him a longer demonstration." Slip-jerk. Slip-jerk. Slip-jerk for what seemed an eternity.

When Tom was sitting on a flat surface again, Mr. GG continued, "It's for my enjoyment—and to encourage others to cooperate with me. When people cross me, this is the first step toward ensuring they do not do it again. It has also proven itself as an excellent lie detector and, when necessary, truth extractor."

Tom sucked in his gut, trying to ease the pain. "Want to explain all that?"

Mr. GG chuckled. "Let's say I had an employee who didn't perform to my expectations. For the sake of simplicity, we'll call him Big. As you might have noticed, I like nicknames. Anyway, we'll assume Big did not garner my satisfaction. In fact, there also might have been some doubt about his veracity. I'm a fair man, though, so I would give this imaginary employee a second chance.

"I might send him on a simple errand to capture and deliver a young girl who interests me because of her association with a man I want to find. It could be I put the girl in my chair and discover Big failed me again. Maybe he picked up the wrong person." Mr. GG hesitated and rubbed his chin. "I ask you, Mr. Jeffries, what would you have done? The chair performed flawlessly, convincing the girl to reveal her true identity, proving again that Big was untrustworthy. I was quite disappointed in him."

"Oh, I bet you were," Tom said, swallowing the words he wanted to say. "What happened next?"

"What do you think? Am I so inhuman I would keep a young girl when there was no reason for it? Of course not. I instructed Big to drop her off where he found her. I encouraged her not to tell anyone about our visit, though. They left here together, both in good health. Later, I learned Big killed that poor, defenseless child." He shook his head, his face a portrait of sadness and disappointment.

Jeannie. So Big killed her. Tom stared at GG. *I doubt he acted alone.* "If I had a free hand, I could offer you my handkerchief for those crocodile tears," Tom said. "It's a sad story, all right. So, where is Big? Did you terminate his employment?"

Howard laughed. "That's a good 'un, boss. Terminate, I mean. Yeah, I'd sure say you terminated his employment."

Mr. GG turned on Howard. "Do not speak lightly of the dead. Whatever he was in life is finished. We have much to respect him for. You forget, he was so big, he fed our fish for several days. More fish means more ducks. More ducks mean more alligators, which means more food and hides for us. Nature's food chain is a miraculous cycle and we, its beneficiaries."

CHAPTER THIRTY-ONE

Tom frowned. *I hope I misunderstood.* "You fed him to the fish? Do you have a fish tank? I'd like to see it."

"Tank? No," Mr. GG said. "I have a grinder and a lake." He chuckled. "And you may very well get to see it." An ugly look crossed his face.

"Okay, let's say you appropriately impressed me. Why'd you bring me down here?"

"You have interfered with my business, and you owe me money."

"How—and how?"

"You took three-thousand dollars from my employee. That was the interference because it was my money. I do not tolerate those who interfere or those who allow the interference."

"You mean Big? The one you say fed the fishes?"

"I have a low tolerance for incompetence, and any of my employees who allow an outsider to meddle in my business is incompetent. Big made that mistake, then compounded it. However, you're shifting the subject. We're not here to discuss Big. Your actions are what bother me. Tonight, you followed Lemon here, again intruding on my operations. As I'm sure you'll agree, I cannot allow that."

"Yeah, I see the problem. What's your solution?"

"First, you're going to pay me the ten-thousand you owe me. Then, you're going to forget you ever met me."

"Hmm. One question. You said I took three-thousand. Where'd the figure ten come from?"

Mr. GG smiled. "Interest. You do believe in capitalism, don't you?"

Is this guy for real? "In that case, perfectly understandable. Get me out of this contraption, and I'll go after the money. I left my checkbook home."

Mr. GG's smile never flickered as he stared at Tom. "While I'm sure your check would be honored, I *do* prefer cash. It has such a nice, crisp feel to it. However, we can take care of that trifle later. First, I'd like to show you a couple of my toys, each of them designed by me. Antoine, set up the truth table."

Tom glanced at Antoine, whose face lit up in an evil smile. "I could wait until another day."

Mr. GG's laugh echoed through the room. "We have all the time in the world. Right, Antoine? Besides, I don't think you're in any kind of hurry, Mr. Jeffries."

Antoine walked to a steel table approximately six-feet long. The ends had what appeared to be tie-down straps.

Tom frowned, thinking it didn't look quite like any table he'd ever seen before.

When Antoine shifted a lever, the ends extended about twelve-inches each. "Is that enough?"

"We'll see. Lemon, join Antoine. Since you've never seen this either, you'll be our demonstrator."

Lemon looked at Mr. GG, the table, and Antoine. "Uh, I druther not—if you don't mind."

"I do mind. I expect you to obey me. As I said, join Antoine. He'll show you what to do."

Lemon shuffled to the table.

"Lay down," Antoine said.

Lemon climbed up and stretched out.

Antoine walked to Lemon's feet and secured each foot with a wide Velcro strap. Then he switched ends. "Stretch your hands over your head and grasp the bar at the end of the table."

Lemon did as instructed and Antoine used more Velcro straps to tie the wrists down. Finally, he applied ties around Antoine's upper arms and thighs, leaving some slack.

"Very good," Mr. GG said. "Are you comfortable, Lemon?"

209

"No sir. Kin I git up now?"

"Stay with us. It'll only take a moment. Continue, Antoine."

Antoine moved another lever and the table rose to a height of about five feet. "Want me to turn him?"

"Yes. First to his feet. Mr. Jeffries, keep a sharp watch. This is where my innovations come into play."

Antoine pulled and held another lever and the table began to tilt. When Lemon was upright, feet down, Antoine released the lever.

Mr. GG turned toward Tom. "We can leave him in that position, hanging from his hands. After a few minutes, it gets rather uncomfortable, especially if we leave him overnight." He swiveled back toward Antoine. "The other way."

Antoine pushed the lever and the platform reversed itself, elevating Lemon's feet into the air. When it reached vertical, he released the lever.

"This works better than the first position. You can see he is hanging from his ankles with the blood rushing to his head. After an hour or so of this, most people plead to cooperate—if they haven't passed out."

Tom grunted. "What do you do if they go unconscious?"

"Bring the table down, wake them up, and try again. Simple pain or a medical situation doesn't change anything. Truth needs to be aired."

"Oh." Tom rolled his eyes. "Is that it? That's what you wanted to show me?"

"There's more. Give him a spin, Antoine. Face first."

Antoine hit a button and the platform began to move toward level. However, it did not stop in the horizontal position, but kept moving, then did not stop at vertical. Soon, Lemon was spinning faster and faster. His moans grew with the speed of the machine.

"Now backwards," Mr. GG said.

Antoine pushed another button and the rotations slowed and stopped. Then the table began moving in the reverse direction so that Lemon revolved backward. His moans turned to pleas as the RPM increased.

"So, what do you think of my toy?" Mr. GG asked.

"Very impressive," Tom said. "You said you designed it?"

"Yes, but you still haven't seen all its functions. Okay, Antoine, stop it, and let's give him a stretch. Not much though. He's quite tall enough. Just nudge him so Mr. Jeffries can see how it works."

As Antoine manipulated the machine, Mr. GG said, "I'm sure you're familiar with the rack as it was used during medieval times. It was an unsophisticated device, but it did the job. Mine does the same, but in a much more efficient way. Watch."

When the table had returned to horizontal, Mr. GG nodded, and Antoine pushed another button. There was the soft hiss of pistons activating.

The straps on Lemon's ankles and wrists tightened.

"No," Lemon cried. "It's pu . . . pulling on me. It's—"

"Shut up, Lemon," Antoine said. "I haven't done anything much, just a few pounds of pull. If you don't be quiet, I'll rip your arms out."

"He could do it, too," Mr. GG said. "And pull his legs off. It's a marvelous machine. I am so proud of it."

Lemon was now sobbing. "Please, Mr. GG. *Please*."

Tom stared, not believing what he saw.

"That's enough of a demonstration. Let him free, Antoine."

Another button and the machine resumed its original position. Antoine undid the straps and helped Lemon sit up. "That's what happens to people who cross Mr. GG. Make sure you always turn in every dollar you collect. Do you understand?"

Lemon nodded so hard, Tom was afraid he might scramble what little brain he had.

"That was interesting," Tom said. "Can I go now?" *This guy is beyond nuts.*

"Banks aren't open at night," Mr. GG said. "Besides, I have another device I want you to see. Antoine, escort Lemon to the maiden."

Lemon's eyes grew large, threatening to bug out as he stared at the upright mummy's coffin. "I ain't going in there. Please, Mr. GG, don't make me go in there. I's scared of tight places."

Antoine shoved him. "Quit whining, or we visit the lake."

Lemon inched himself forward, looking like he'd rather be anywhere else.

A moment later, Lemon stood beside the case as Antoine undid the latches. The clicks echoed through the room. The fear leaping off Lemon was almost tangible.

"Perfect, Antoine," Mr. GG said. "Stand by." He turned to Tom. "You have presented me with a problem, Mr. Jeffries. You accused Lemon of being a snitch, both for you and for the police. Obviously, I cannot have someone like that on the payroll—if you were telling the truth. Lemon says it's untrue. Perhaps we should discover who is lying. Any questions?"

"Nope. Let's get on with it. But, before we do, how about letting me out of this chair. My butt is killing me on this hard seat. You've got enough firepower here to make sure I don't do anything hostile."

Mr. GG looked at Antoine, who picked up his shotgun.

When Mr. GG looked at Howard, he nodded, pointing his Uzi at Tom.

"Remember, Mr. Jeffries. Misbehave and die, which would make me so unhappy. I'd be out ten-thousand dollars."

"Trust me, I'd be even more disappointed than you," Tom said.

Mr. GG released the straps securing Tom to the chair.

CHAPTER THIRTY-TWO

Tom stood, flexing his shoulder and back muscles. His eyes danced around the room, looking for anything he could use to cause a distraction. Lemon's sloppy search had missed his boot gun, but with an Uzi and a shotgun pointed at him, retrieving it was another matter. He'd find something. He had to—or die trying.

Mr. GG nudged him on the arm. "I like a man who's always thinking, but I suggest you give it up, or you're back in the chair."

Tom stared at him. "Understood. What's with Lemon and the casket?"

"The correct term is iron maiden, or more accurately for my invention, aluminum maiden. As you may know, the original had sharp spikes inside. When the door closed, they pierced the occupant. Death was painful, but quick. Mine is far more sophisticated. It, too, has spikes, but they're built to collapse within themselves. I control them with the simple push of a button. The level of penetration is my decision—anything from a simple pinprick to death. Walk over here and take a look."

He guided Tom to the maiden and opened it. The inside walls appeared dimpled, but there were no sharp points protruding. "Now, here's how it works. Rest your hand on the inside surface."

After glancing at Antoine and his shotgun, Tom did as instructed.

"Give him level one," Mr. GG said.

Antoine punched a button without taking his eyes off Tom.

Sharp points leaped out a half-inch, causing Tom to jerk his hand away. "Ouch. That was a surprise." He sucked on his palm. "Damned sharp. It drew blood." *Playing to his ego can't hurt.*

Mr. GG grinned. "Level six."

Antoine pressed and Tom gasped as numerous eight-inch spikes protruded from the front and back of the maiden. A person locked inside would be pierced like a tough steak under a meat tenderizer.

"As you can see, Mr. Jeffries, it is an efficient machine."

"You got my attention. Have you ever used it?"

"Let's just say the maiden is not a virgin." He chuckled. "In fact, one of your acquaintances proved its worth."

"Big?"

"Yes. Future Star Miller, or as he called himself, Big. He wasn't the first, but he was the largest specimen I've run through. After he failed me the second time, I couldn't keep him around any longer."

"I thought it was three times."

"Of course, you're correct. First, when he let you take my money. The second was when he identified the wrong girl and brought her here." Mr. GG shook his head as if recalling the event. "She was a tough cookie, though. Took a couple of hours in my special chair to break her. When I learned she was not who Big said she was, I sent her home. Then, as you counted, his third mistake. He killed her. I had to get rid of him. Not only untrustworthy, but irresponsible."

That explains what happened to Jeannie. "I see. So I'm to believe you had nothing to do with her death?"

"Believe whatever you please, Mr. Jeffries. The triggerman is gone."

"What happened to the body?"

"You can see the maiden stands over a grate in the floor. The process gets rather messy, but the blood drains through the grill into a catch-tank below. There, it is mixed with fresh water, then pumped into the lake. The creatures enjoy the nutrients. After that, it's simply a matter of washing out the maiden, readying it for the next visitor."

Shuddering, Tom wondered what kind of monster he stood beside. "Yeah, I'd say that's effective to get rid of the blood. What do you do with the rest?"

Howard laughed. "Fish food. Alligator food. Ain't that right, Mr. GG?"

Mr. GG glared at Howard. "He is a bit crude, but he's right. I have a grinder and pelletizer in another room. It reduces the remains to usable content for my friends who occupy my small lake. It's very effective, Mr. Jeffries. But enough chitchat. Lemon, step into the machine, please."

"No sir. I ain't going in there."

CHAPTER THIRTY-THREE

In a calm voice, Mr. GG said, "Lemon, your choices are limited. If you don't go in, you will die. If you go in and have told me the truth, you will live. So you see, the only reason you have to fear the maiden is if you have lied to me. What's your decision?"

"I don't go, you gonna kill me?"

"Yes."

"If I do go, you ain't gonna put them big nails through me, are you?"

"Of course not. I simply have a few questions for you."

Lemon swallowed, his large Adam's apple bobbing like a vertical metronome. "Yes, sir, I do it then."

Mr. GG nodded at Antoine, and he pushed a button. The spikes retracted. Lemon stepped inside, and Antoine closed the maiden around him. He secured each latch with a loud snap. Lemon's face could be seen through the plastic window.

Tom watched, fascinated, hoping Lemon wouldn't have to pay because of him—but hoping harder for a distraction.

"Okay, Lemon, I want you to relax," Mr. GG said. "Nothing bad will happen unless you lie. Were you a snitch for Mr. Jeffries and the police?"

"No sir. I ain't never done that."

"What do you think, Antoine? Did you hear sincerity in his voice? I'm not sure. Level one, please."

Antoine pushed a button, his attention on the maiden.

Lemon's scream was loud enough to rival a fire engine's siren. Mr. GG, Howard, and Antoine appeared fascinated by it, their attention riveted on Lemon.

216

Tom shoved Mr. GG as hard as he could, then went to his boot. As he came up with the .22, he saw Antoine swinging the shotgun toward him. Tom snapped off two shots, both scoring, center of mass. The shotgun fell from Antoine's hands as he collapsed over the maiden's control panel.

Lemon's screams increased in intensity.

Diving to his left, Tom hit the floor in a roll as the clatter of an Uzi filled the space he vacated. He saw that Howard had the Uzi on full automatic, and it forced his arm upward as bullets continue to spew out.

Fool, Tom thought. He put two rounds into Howard's chest, watching him fold into himself. Howard's finger stayed on the trigger sending bullets ricocheting around the room. Tom rolled under the *truth table*, then scanned the room for Mr. GG. He was not there. The door to the hallway hung open. Howard released the gun as his body hit the floor.

"Damn," Tom said, then remembered Lemon. When he stared at the maiden, his stomach rolled. Blood flowed out of the bottom, running through the grate in the floor. Lemon's face was locked into a permanent scream.

Tom studied Antoine's position where he lay over the control panel, realizing he must have hit button six when he collapsed. "One hell of a way to die," Tom muttered, his conscience forcing him to stare into Lemon's enlarged eyes. Then he twisted away. "Okay, time to flush out GG and avenge Jeannie—and Lemon."

He stood and inched his way toward the doorway, expecting a burst of gunfire in his direction at any moment. When he reached the opening, he peaked around the frame. No one in view. Then he gazed at the elevator. The floor indicator pointed at the number one. Apparently, GG had grabbed a ride to the first floor.

Taking a deep breath, Tom stepped into the hallway, trying to see in all directions at once. He hoped his guess about the elevator was right, and GG was on the first floor, not waiting to ambush him. He saw no one, no movement. He exhaled and looked for the stairwell, knowing riding the elevator would be foolish.

He saw a door at the end of the short hall and headed that way. When he arrived, he turned the knob, jerked the door open, and stepped to the side, all in one motion. A burst of gunfire erupted.

Tom fired a quick round, then held his position beside the opening, hoping he was ready for GG's next move. He heard steps on the stairs, going up. Another retreat to set another ambush? Probably.

Tom gazed at his boot pistol. "Not exactly what I need to counter his firepower." He flipped out the cylinder. Empty. "Time to borrow a gun—or two." He worked his way into the torture room, knowing Antoine's shotgun and Howard's Uzi were there.

He picked up the shotgun, then put it down. Too long at over three feet. He needed something he could bring to bear quickly, something like Howard's Uzi. The question was, had he emptied the magazine in his firing frenzy?

Kneeling beside Howard's body, Tom examined the weapon. It was a Micro Uzi, no stock, more like a standard pistol, only larger—and more lethal. He examined the chamber and discovered it empty, as he'd feared. He mumbled, "Damn fool should have had it on semi-automatic. A three-shot burst is far more effective than bullets flying everywhere with no guidance." He patted Howard's jacket and found what he hoped—a full magazine. *Idiots like him think thirty-two rounds are never enough.* He slipped the new load into the Uzi and flipped the control switch to semi-automatic. "Okay, Mr. GG, now we're on a more even footing. Let the best man win." He stood. "That's me."

Tom went into the hallway and looked at the elevator, then the stairwell. If he took the elevator, he could expect GG to be waiting for him when the doors opened. One solid chance for GG to take him out. On the other hand, every stair he climbed gave GG a chance to fire down at him. "If I have to go, I may as well take the less strenuous way." He pushed the call button and stood to the side.

The elevator arrived and Tom waited, out of view of the inside. If GG was there, Tom didn't want to give him an open shot. The doors closed. Tom watched the indicator. Nothing happened.

With a deep sigh, and a silent prayer, Tom pushed the call button again and, when the doors opened, jumped inside. Empty. So far, so good.

He stared at the control panel. It contained buttons for floors one, two, three, and basements of one and two. Perhaps he could create a bit of confusion. He pushed the three button and squeezed himself into the front corner. If someone decided to shoot through as he passed the first or second floors, he didn't intend to be in their field of fire.

When the elevator reached the third floor, the doors opened and Tom peeked out. A luxurious bedroom. The lights were on, perhaps triggered by the arrival of the elevator. Depressing the open button, he examined the area. It looked like a man's room, nothing feminine in sight. A king-sized bed, heavy mahogany furniture, and lots of space.

It appeared GG entertained because there was a wet bar and a conversation niche. Tom wondered what kind of women would spend time with a fiend like GG. Then again, maybe they didn't know about the basement. He hoped not. Everything Tom saw said GG was a bachelor. Good. That meant he wouldn't leave a widow. Scum like GG didn't matter, but bringing pain to innocents needed to be avoided whenever possible. Tom knew because he had suffered when his sister died, and he remembered Lonnie's anguish when Charlie died.

Pulling back into the elevator, Tom pushed buttons two and one. If GG waited for him, he'd have to guess where Tom exited.

On floor two, Tom saw what appeared to be a business complex. There were soft chairs along the wall and a desk in front of a door opening into another area. Could be GG's office behind the door with his secretary, or bodyguard, occupying the guardian position. Visitors, or more of his bodyguards, could occupy the chairs. Everything was empty and quiet now.

The elevator doors closed, and Tom was on his way to the first floor. Showdown time was coming fast. If he hadn't fooled GG into thinking he'd gotten off at one of the upper floors, Tom could expect a *hot lead* welcome.

CHAPTER THIRTY-FOUR

The elevator stopped, and Tom pinned himself into the front corner near the controls. His finger hovered over the door-close button, ready to punch it if he didn't like the scene in front of him. The panels slid open with a gentle whoosh. As they reached maximum width, Tom heard a shotgun and pellets slamming into the back wall. Hoping it was another pump-action, he dived to the floor and snapped off a three-round burst, walking the barrel from left to right. He kept the shots low, assuming the shooter would be in a defensive crouch. He glimpsed a silhouette with a long gun as he hit the floor and fired three more shots. The figure went down.

"Oh, my leg," someone screamed. "Oh, damn, that hurts."

Tom saw a man writhing on the floor, holding his leg, a shotgun near him. Tom sprang to his feet, dashed out of the elevator, kicking the gun away as he did. He dropped to his knee, checking in all directions for another shooter. He saw no one.

Looking back at the man, Tom was surprised to see it was someone new. "Who the hell are you? Where's GG?"

"My knee. You took out my knee. Call nine-one-one. I need a doctor."

Tom rose and stood over a black man with snow-white hair. He was dressed in what appeared to be a guard's uniform and wore a utility belt around his waist. The holster was empty.

He remembered Antoine or GG saying something about someone named Snowcone—the man Tom immobilized at the pedestrian gate. Could this be him? It didn't matter. "Where's GG?"

"Please, man. Help me. You shot out my knee."

Tom kicked him in the side. "Answer my damn question, or I'll take out the other one. Either that or I'll punt you up and down the hall like a football. Your choice." He kicked him again.

"I don't know, man. He ran out the back. Told me to take care of you. But you shot my knee."

Tom looked down the hall, first left, then right. Doors at both ends. The stairwell was to his left, so the right must open outside. "What kind of gun is he carrying?"

"I don't know. When you work for Mr. GG, you learn not to look too close at him."

Tom kicked him again. "Try again. I'm not buying that crap. Shotgun or Uzi."

"Alright, alright. Uzi. Like the one you shot me with. Now, call an ambulance."

Tom wiped his mouth, sorting his options. He knelt beside Snowcone. "Move your hand." He examined the wound. Snowcone was right, the bullet went through the knee cap. Not much blood, but he'd need a knee replacement. "You'll live. Stop whining like a baby. Here's what we're going to do."

Grabbing the thug's uniform shirt by the back of the collar, Tom dragged him into the stairwell, ignoring the screams that he was dying and Tom had to help him. He took Snowcone's belt from his pants and secured his hands to the banister. "Stay there until I get back. Then I'll get you some medical attention—if I'm in the mood."

Snowcone cried, tears rolling. "No, man, don't leave me. Get me a doctor. I help you. I do anything. Please, man."

"Funny how you punks are. Take away your big guns, and you're just sniveling assholes. Now shut your face or I'll give you lots to blubber about." To punctuate his words, he kicked him in the side again. "Either I'll be back, or you can explain to GG how you missed me."

Tom returned to the hallway, securing the stairwell door behind him. Even with it closed, he could hear Snowcone blubbering. He headed toward what he thought was the back door of the house. *Here I go again. Heading into another ambush situation. Damn, I can be stupid.*

221

Tom stopped at the door and looked around. This had to be the opening onto the area behind the house. He took a deep breath and turned the knob, anticipating a burst of gunfire. Inching the door open, he peered through, expecting darkness. Instead, a lighted area greeted him. A quick look told him why. Poles were scattered around a lake, each bearing a flood lamp in full glow. It wasn't high noon, but it was a nice twilight-like illumination.

Tom stared into the night, hoping to spot GG. Not there. Maybe in the other direction, which meant Tom had to show himself, at least his head. The door would no longer conceal him.

When he checked, he saw a man about thirty yards away, quickstepping along the edge of the lake. "GG. Stop where you are. Your game is over."

GG spun and unleashed a burst of automatic weapons fire. Fortunately for Tom, GG knew as much about an Uzi as Howard. The barrel kicked right and up, taking out one of the pole lights.

Tom fired a three-round burst over GG's head, then pulled back behind the door. "Put the weapon down. Don't make me kill you."

"No way, you bastard. I don't know how you got through, but my guys will be at your back any moment. You're dead, Jeffries." He shot again, smashing a couple of windows in the upper floors. Broken glass tinkled to the lawn.

Tom peered around the door at GG, realizing he was learning how to handle the weapon as he fired. Tom needed to end things before GG got lucky. Tom preferred not to wound him. An Uzi slug could kill, no matter where it struck. He sighed and unleashed another three-round burst, kicking up grass beside GG. "Next time, I won't shoot to miss."

"What's wrong? No guts? Step into the light. We can do it *old west* style."

"No. Put the weapon down. Your thugs are dead. They won't be coming to your rescue. Lemon died in your maiden. I took out Antoine, Howard, and Snowcone. You're all alone."

"Picture me laughing, Jeffries. I don't know what happened, but you're not that good."

Tom squinted. Had he seen movement behind GG? Something low and slow moving along the bank. He couldn't be sure because if there was something there, it was in GG's shadow. "C'mon, GG. You know you can't outgun me. I had more training in one week than you've had in your whole life." He saw what could have been more movement. What was it? Or were his eyes playing tricks on him in the dim light?

"Step out and we'll find—" GG spun and screamed. "No. Get away, get away." He fired, his finger locked on the trigger. Grass exploded, then the sky filled with rounds. GG turned and tried to run, but went down hard, face first, his legs jerked from under him.

Tom stared. It couldn't be. Could it? He dashed toward GG, trying to get a clear shot at what he believed to be a huge alligator dragging GG toward the water.

GG's screams pierced the air and Tom's ears. GG clawed, his fingers digging grooves in the lawn, right up to the pond's edge. His sounds turned to gurgles as his body slid underwater. The lake exploded as the alligator spun, moving out of the shallows.

Tom tried to get off a shot, but there was no viable target. He couldn't tell the difference between the alligator and GG in the frothing water colored with mud. Tom continued to run, hoping to get alongside the commotion before GG was gone.

Out of the corner of his eye, he saw a movement to his left. Another gator? Then more movements as two more slipped onto the shore.

"What the hell? Damn." Tom backed away, blasting three-round bursts into the creatures. A fourth showed, and Tom shot him. Whether his shots were lethal or not, Tom didn't know or care, but the beasts backed off. That was good enough for him.

As soon as possible, he looked to where GG had disappeared. The surface was relatively calm, ripples moving out in concentric circles, the only evidence anything had happened. Keeping one eye on the edge for more alligators, he resumed his way toward the spot he last saw GG. Another alligator showed, and Tom shot him. He eyed where GG had been, torn up sod marking the area. There were drag marks leading into the water. Without relaxing his vigil, Tom squatted, wishing he'd killed GG. That would have been more merciful. No one deserved to be taken down by a gator, no matter how despicable he was.

"This is the police. Put down your weapon and back away from it, hands on your head."

A spotlight flooded Tom. He put his hands straight up into the air, his Uzi in his right hand. He backed away from the water's edge. Over his shoulder, he shouted, "This lake is filled with hungry gators. I'm not dropping my weapon until I'm safely out of their range."

"Back out of there. If you turn, one of my sharpshooters will bring you down. And don't bullshit me. That's not a joking matter." There was a pause. "Is that you, Jeffries?"

"Yeah, it's me. Tom Jeffries. Who are you? Have one of your men throw a flood on the shoreline. I'm betting you won't be disappointed."

Light speared the lake. "Damn," Tom heard. "That son-of-a-bitch has to go ten feet."

"Keep backing out of there, Tom. We're covering you."

An alligator came out of the water, headed toward Tom, and the night erupted in gunfire, none of it from Tom—or at Tom.

Tom kept backpedaling, swinging his head in all directions. Finally, he felt someone take his Uzi. "Take it easy. It's me. Phil Summers. My people will take over from here. You come with me. You have a lot of explaining to do."

"I can do better than that. I can show you things you won't believe." He looked toward the lake. "Justice has been served, though. There's an alligator out there with a full belly." Tom rubbed his hand over his face. "Not something I'll soon forget." He looked at the house. "Do you know whose place this is?"

"Yeah, a guy named Lester Goodrich-Green. I checked after I saw you go over the fence. He's been suspected of a lot of things, but convicted of none."

Tom nodded. "It fits. He called himself Mr. GG, short for Goodrich-Green, I suppose. Oh, I forgot. There's one alive inside. He's tied up in the first floor stairwell. Needs a doctor."

"Is the house secure?" Summers asked.

"As far as I know. The wounded guy was the last of the gang—well, the last I met. I don't think he could get loose."

"Okay, you stay with me while we find him." He spoke to one of the uniforms. "Get the medics over here. Have them ready to go in as soon as we secure the premises. Let's go, Tom."

Tom led Summers and two of his men into the house. Snowcone had not moved.

"Hey, man. You come back." Snowcone looked at Summers. "Is you the police? You need to 'rest this man. He shot me, then he tied me to this banister. He a evil man."

"Could be," Summers said, studying the thug. "Cool it while the medics check you out. I'd hate for you to die on me."

The EMTs soon had Snowcone's leg stabilized and him out the door headed to the hospital. Summers assigned two uniforms to accompany them and insure the prisoner did not escape.

"That was interesting," Summers said. "Not as interesting as the alligators, but pretty good. What's chapter three?"

"Downstairs. Before we go, though, I need to prepare you. It's not something—"

"Downstairs?" Summers said. "We're on the first floor already."

"This is not a typical Florida mansion. There's a basement and a sub-basement below us. The lower holds things like you've never seen before. It also holds the bodies of three people, two of whom I dispatched."

"The third?"

"You'll have to see it to believe it."

Summers gave Tom a skeptical look. "Are you bullshitting me—or, better yet, stalling? Why? What's going on?"

"You'll see." Tom led the way to the elevator and punched the B2 button.

Tom led Summers into the torture room. Nothing had changed since Tom left. Antoine was still draped over the control panel, Howard lay in the floor amidst a pool of blood, and the head of the maiden still showed Lemon's face of agony.

Summers rushed into a corner and threw up.

CHAPTER THIRTY-FIVE

Summers posted a uniform outside the door to the sub-basement, telling him not to go in or let anyone in until the M.E. and the CSI people arrived. He and Tom returned to the first floor and entered what appeared to be a den. Heavy, leather furniture in a room decorated for a man.

Once they were settled, Summers said, "What the hell *is* that . . . downstairs? I've never . . . I mean, how could anyone . . ." He quit talking, his face a mask of disbelief.

"I wish I knew. I've seen some nasty things in some really nasty areas of the world, but those machines go beyond anything I've ever encountered. And the truly disgusting part is that man, that GG, was proud of them. He bragged about it. He talked about people he'd used those machines on. One was a thug named Future Star Miller. He went by the street name of *Big.* If you're looking for him for any crimes, you can close the cases. Food for his wildlife, GG called him."

Summers ran his hand over his face. "Hard to believe there are people with that much evil in them." He squared his shoulders and shook off his look of despair.

"We can agree on that."

They sat silent for a moment, then Tom said, "How'd you know I was here? What caused you to come barging in like an avenging . . . Hmm, I would say angel, but you don't fit the bill."

"Forgive me for not laughing, but this is no time for humor. I was on your tail and saw you go over the fence. I'm bound by the law so all I could do was standby. What happened after that?"

"So, what changed your mind?"

"Gunfire. Once I heard the chatter of Uzis, I called for backup and rushed in. You might say I felt the need to rescue you."

Tom gave him a look, but decided to let the subject drop. Might be one of those times when ignorance was better than knowledge. It could open up a course of conversation Tom did not wish to pursue. Instead, he gave Summers an abbreviated version of the night, including GG's disappearance into the lake in the jaws of a huge alligator. He finished by saying, "Look, Summers. it's been a tough night. I don't mind going into detail on everything that happened here, but can we bring in a steno? Or a recorder? I'd prefer not to go over it more than a dozen times or so. To be honest with you, I'm bushed. My adrenaline flow is at zero. If we keep going, I might forget a key fact."

"I get your point." Summers hesitated, appearing to think. "Look, Lt. Richards will be here soon with a full team. Judging from the mess downstairs, it's going to be a long, a very long, night. I suggest you get out of here and get some sleep before he arrives. I'm sure the boss will have lots of questions for you, but I think they can wait until tomorrow—probably sometime in the afternoon. Of course, he'll take ten pounds off my ass for not holding you, but I don't have the energy either. I promise you though, if you run on me, I'll track you to hell and fire the pit myself."

"Sounds like a winner. Can I catch a ride to my car?"

"Walk. The exercise will keep you awake. Just don't climb the wall again." Summers grinned, stood, and left the den, a slump of fatigue in his shoulders.

* * *

Driving home, Tom considered calling Abby, then decided against it. She would grill him with questions, and he was in no mood to relive the experience. Tomorrow would be soon enough to give her a sanitized version. It would have to be sanitized. No way could he recount the horror he'd witnessed that night.

Sleep seemed out of the question so he collapsed in his recliner, fully clothed, with a Killian's. When his mind finally closed down and sleep came, horrific dreams of iron maidens, alligators, and Uzis spraying rounds in every direction filled it. Tom dodged and jumped, but bullets slammed into him and alligators dragged him toward a lake. He awoke, sweat streaming and the morning light filling his eyes, the sun forcing the nightmares to his subconscious.

He rose, stretched, and rolled his head, trying to loosen the muscles of his neck. Six empty beer bottles sat on the side table, which explained how he'd slept through the dreams. A small headache nudged him, whether from a hangover, his sleeping position, or the events of the previous night he didn't know.

After making coffee, he headed for the shower, intent on washing away the last twelve hours. As he'd done so many times during his time in Special Forces, he reviewed each moment while the hot water pounded on him. He analyzed his actions, probing for weaknesses, looking for things he could have done differently to force a different outcome. He found nothing that would have changed things. When he stepped from the shower, he had filed GG, Antoine, Howard, Snowcone, Lemon, and the alligators away in a special compartment, ready to talk to Lt. Richards about them. After that, he would lock that compartment, and they wouldn't bother him again.

He dialed Abby's cell and was relieved when it went to the message box. "Hi, Sunshine. It's Tom. Just thought I'd check in with you. Sorry I missed you last night, but it turned into a long one. How about dinner out tonight? Call me. Love you." He clicked off, believing he'd be more able to face her in public. She'd be less likely to explain in detail how stupid he was.

Next, he called Ken Dotson at his law firm. He assured him the extortions were finished, but expressed regret he'd been unable to recover the money Ms. Lowenstein paid. Ken didn't ask questions, just accepted Tom's words, and told him to file his expense reports.

Tom thought about that. A few gallons of gas about covered it. He had recovered his .45 when he walked to his car, and Lemon had left his knife on a table where Tom found it. The rest was GG's expense—a magazine of Uzi rounds.

He thought a moment, then decided a *to-do* list was in order.
1. Call Abby. Done
2. Call Ken Dotson re extortions. Done
2a. Prepare billing for hours and expenses

3. Call Lt. Richards (rather not)
4. Visit with Richards. (no way around it)
5. Call Ken Dotson re Renée's custody progress
6. Call Lonnie, if there's anything positive to report

He stared at the list. Procrastination would be nice, but would hurt his case. Although Summers might back Tom to a certain extent, Richards would be the alligator in the pond. He shuddered at the last thought. Shouldn't have gone there. Best to get it over with. Look on the bright side, he thought. If he throws me in jail, I won't have to pay for Abby's dinner. He forced a smile.

He picked up the phone again and dialed.

* * *

Tom, Jim Richards, and Phil Summers sat in Richards' office. The chairs weren't comfortable, but were better than those in the *interview* room. Plus, the smell was better—not great, but better.

"I'm on your dime," Tom said. "What do you want to know?"

"Let's keep it simple," Richards said. "Give me your version of what happened last night."

"Do I get read my rights first?"

"No. That way, nothing you say can be used against you. Work for you?"

"Fine." Tom sighed and launched into his story beginning with his going over the fence. He didn't mention Dotson's part in the events.

Jim Richards quit tapping the pencil he'd been drumming on a stack of papers. "Interesting—to say the least." He pointed. "I have here preliminary reports from last night—the uniforms, the CSI geeks, the M.E., and, never to be ignored, my assistant's glorified report of the heroism of one private investigator." He paused, while flicking the edges of the papers. "It's times like this I wish I were an author. I could write a best seller about a PI climbing a wall and uncovering evil that only the most ginormous imagination would believe. That's not all. This PI would overcome obstacles not known in modern history to destroy this den of iniquity. Bodies are left strewn about as if a hurricane descended unexpectedly. But, and this is important, as those who are appointed to protect society show up, the final evidence is swallowed by alligators in a

229

domestic pond, leaving our hero as the sole survivor to tell the tale."

Lt. Richards looked from Tom to Summers, back to Tom. "Would you buy my book?"

Tom rubbed his chin. "You spin a good yarn, even though you omitted one important fact. Snowcone is alive and can corroborate my story—well part of it anyway. Of course, that assumes you're good enough to extract the truth from him. But, to answer your question, yes, I would buy your book—if you labeled it non-fiction. I can think of two adages that apply. The first is universal, *truth is stranger than fiction.* The second is local, *it's South Florida.*

Tom kept his eyes locked on Richards, but heard what sounded like a snicker from Summers.

Richards stared at Tom, then grinned and stood. "One of these days, you'll step far enough outside the law to give me good reason to bring you down. However, this is not that day." He stuck his hand out. "Today, I want to thank you for your help. Lester Goodrich-Green has been on our radar for some time, but we could never close the loop. From what you told Phil, he won't be bothering us anymore."

Tom grimaced as a picture of GG's torturous path to a watery meal for a hungry alligator filled his mind. For a moment, he heard the screams, then the gurgles as water silenced them. "Mr. GG may cause indigestion, but he'll never punish anyone again."

Tom stood and shook Richards' hand. "Believe it or not, we're on the same side. It's just that we follow different approaches to problem solving. I wish yours wasn't so tied up in bureaucratic P.C. crap, but as long as it is, I'll do what I do." He walked from the room, mentally ticking another item off his *to-do* list.

CHAPTER THIRTY-SIX

Tom pulled out of the police department parking lot feeling much better than when he arrived. He was well aware Lt. Richards could have found plenty of things to make him miserable. And, if Richards took him into a courtroom, there was no telling what a judge or a jury might do. But, knock wood, Richards apparently had decided not to pursue any actions against Tom.

Next on his *to-do* list was to catch up with Renée's situation. He dialed Ken Dotson, and when he came to the phone, asked, "What's happening with Mr. Williams and the custody issue?"

"Things are moving nicely. You should know these type cases take time. I have to make sure every legal I is dotted and every T is crossed. Then, I have to go back and add many more pages of legalese to justify my fee."

Tom chuckled. "An honest lawyer. What is this world coming to?"

"To give you a better answer, Renée's mother has hired an attorney to represent her. We've had three or four conversations. As you surmised, it's not a question of maintaining custody, it's a matter of how high the bidding will go. Mr. Williams is ready to write a seven-figure check. I'm trying to discourage that. Her greed will cause her to cave for less. Even her lawyer isn't talking that high, and I'm convinced he's using a padded figure."

"Yeah, but—"

"Don't but me, Tom. I don't nitpick your investigations, don't nitpick my legal manipulations. Trust me. I know what I'm doing. When will Renée arrive home?"

"Probably another week."

231

"Good. Has she agreed to live with her father?"

"The pig in the parlor. I don't know. I asked Lonnie to feel her out about it, and I haven't heard back. It's been a few days, though. Could mean bad news. I have my fingers crossed, but that's about all I can do. My gut says Renée will warm to her father fast as long as he's sincere and honest with her. Right now, she's cynical about adults in general. Perfectly understandable based on her experience with her *mother.* Lonnie won her with love. He'll have to do the same thing."

"Let's worst-case it and say Renée refuses to go with her father. Could she stay with Lonnie until he wins her over? Or . . . better yet, would Lonnie make a temporary move to Texas to be with Renée while she adapts to her new life?"

Tom hesitated, letting the idea roll around in his head. "That's a tough call, Ken. We'd be setting Lonnie up for major heartache. I already worry about how close she's gotten to Renée. If she goes with her, then has to turn her loose . . . The last thing Lonnie needs is another loss in her life."

"Okay, I'll soft peddle that idea. But let's not ignore it. It could solve a couple of problems. Mr. Williams gets his daughter back. Lonnie gets to stay with her longer. Renée gets an aunt and an adult confidant she's never had. Not all bad."

"We'll see. That's the best I can say. In the meantime, I'll get in touch with Lonnie and find out their schedule and Renée's reaction to the news about her father."

"If the opportunity should arise, consider asking Lonnie about my idea."

"No promises on that one."

"Understand."

They rung off, agreeing to talk when either had fresh news.

Tom drove toward US 441 so he could head toward Palm Beach County and Abby's house. If he had a chilled Scotch and water waiting for her, she might let him off with only a few digging questions. Probably not, but that didn't lessen the value of the drink.

After turning north, he passed one of the many strip malls and an idea hit him. Roses. What woman could resist the magnetism of

232

red roses? He pulled in and stopped in front of a florist. A few minutes later, he walked out with three-dozen long-stemmed, red roses, lighter in the credit card, but leaving a happy clerk behind. He knew Abby would accuse him of having done something wrong for which he needed forgiveness, but she'd only do it in a half-joking way. A liquor store beckoned, so he went in and bought a bottle of The Famous Grouse, Abby's favorite, and a twelve-pack of Killian's.

When he arrived at Abby's house, he pulled three vases from the cabinet and put a dozen roses in each. One went on a table in the foyer, the second on the washing machine, and the third in the living room. If she parked in the garage, she'd enter through the laundry room. If she parked in the driveway, she'd use the front door. Either way, he was ready for her. He wondered if he should split the roses into six containers, but gave up when he couldn't find more vases.

He put the beer and the Scotch in the refrigerator and settled in to wait, resisting the temptation to open a Killian's. He'd make a Scotch and water a few minutes before her normal arrival time and put it in the freezer. She liked her drinks cold. Slivers of floating ice pleased her.

After calling for restaurant reservations, he remembered his *to-do* list and dialed Lonnie's cell number. It went to voice mail. "Hey, it's Tom. Call when you can. I'm lonely without you. And Abby wants to hear about your trip."

He leaned back in the recliner and considered how much he had to tell Abby about last night. She'd probably pick up rumors from the police and their subsequent investigation. Certainly, when Snowcone was charged, she'd find out much of what happened. Of course, if Snowcone were smart, he'd deny any knowledge of the basement and its use. Tom decided to gamble on that angle and wait until he knew what facts she had before providing more than generalities.

* * *

A car horn tooted, causing Tom to put down the book he'd been reading and stand. Abby. He listened for the garage door and smiled when he heard it opening. Hustling into the kitchen, he pulled Abby's drink out of the freezer and opened a Killian's for himself. He raced into the laundry room, placed the glass beside the vase of roses, then retreated into the hallway where he couldn't be seen when she entered.

"Tom. You're up to something. What is it? Or, better yet, what have you done?"

Tom stepped into the laundry room and swept Abby into his arms. "Making things perfect for the woman I love."

"Yeah, right," she said, then kissed him hard and long. "I've been looking forward to that all day—almost as much as I was looking forward to this drink." She took a long sip. "Both are perfect, and the roses add just the right touch. But don't think you're off the hook. I know you're hiding something. Have you threatened Angel Rodriguez? I haven't seen him in quite a while."

"Not me. My conscience is clear on that."

"So, what is it?"

"Nothing, Sunshine. Nothing but my undying love for you."

"Uh-huh. You'll tell me. It might take all night, but you'll tell me. Now, grab the flowers, and let's find a more romantic place to enjoy them."

"My thoughts exactly," Tom said, waggling his eyebrows.

"Not until you feed me. You promised dinner out, and I plan to collect. After that, I'm sure you'll want to tell me where you were last night."

"Of course," Tom said, knowing she wouldn't turn it loose until he satisfied her curiosity. One of the things that made her such a good Assistant State Attorney.

The second dozen roses brought a squeal of delight and more suspicion. The third convinced Tom he'd overdone it. Next time, he'd stop at one dozen no matter what the occasion—or what he needed absolution from.

Dinner was perfect. Tom was content to stare at his beautiful fiancée while listening to her talk about her day. It seemed there were no uneventful days in her office. The crush of crimes in Coral Lakes and the efficiency of the police guaranteed a plethora of new cases coming in daily. Tom could only wonder how she kept them straight. Then, a picture of GG as he'd last seen him popped into his mind causing him to smile with the realization that was one thug's expensive mouthpiece she'd never have to face. In this case, justice might be blind, but the alligator wasn't.

Later, as they cuddled in bed, Tom told Abby about Ken Dotson hiring him to stop the extortions, and how he'd followed Lemon to GG's headquarters. He skipped the more macabre details, only saying there had been a shootout and the police arrived. When he added that the leader of the gang, a Lester Goodrich-Green had also been responsible for Jeannie's death and the hunt for Renée, Abby squeezed him and kissed him on the cheek. Tom finished with, "That's it. Another normal day in the life of Tom Jeffries, Super PI."

"Okay," Abby said, "I want to be sure I understand. Ken Dotson hired you to stop an extortion, which led you to Jeannie's killer and Renée's hunter. It ended in a shoot-out, and the police rescued you. Is that it?"

"Pretty much," Tom said.

"Well, it just so happens I've heard of this Goodrich-Green character, also known as Mr. GG. He surrounds himself with a gang of gunmen, and the police have never been able to bring him in—even though we knew he was dirty. So now I'm to believe you simply walked in and wiped out his whole operation?"

"I'm good, aren't I?"

"Right." She paused, as if thinking. "Okay, if you're so damn good, make love to me."

Tom's cell phone rang.

CHAPTER THIRTY-SEVEN

Tom picked up his phone and looked at the caller ID. "Lonnie. Should I answer?"

"Of course, you idiot. I'm dying to hear about her trip."

"Not what you were saying a moment ago."

The phone rang again.

"Later. Answer now."

Tom hit the on button. "Hello, tourist. How goes your travels?"

"Wonderful. Is this a good time? I just got your voice message. Renée and I went to a museum this afternoon, then dinner. I turned off my phone and forget to turn it back on until now."

"We're good. If I said otherwise, Abby would disembowel me. She wants to hear all about your trip. But first, have you talked to Renée about her father?"

"Yes. After we left the museum today, I brought it up. I waited because I wanted her in a more receptive mood. This trip has worked a miracle on her. Each day, I've seen more of what I believe is the real Renée. Hard to describe, but . . . more relaxed, more accommodating, more trusting. Like she's begun to accept me not just as a friendly adult, but as a friend. Today was the best yet." Lonnie paused.

"So?"

"She's ambivalent. On one side, she thinks it's wonderful that she has a father who wants her. On the other, he's another adult who could disappoint her. Her mood appeared to swing up, then down, then up, etc. I told her she didn't have to make a decision right now. She has time to think it over. Nothing will be done until we get home."

"Hmm, not good, but not unexpected. That's asking an awful lot of a thirteen-year-old to make a quick decision on something like this. She—"

"Fourteen."

"Huh?"

"She's fourteen. Today is her birthday."

"Uh-oh, I forgot. Wish her a happy birthday from Abby and me. Tell her we have a special surprise for her when she gets back here."

"Really?"

"Tell her what I said. Abby will come up with something before you get home." He raised his eyebrows at Abby who shook her fist at him, then grinned.

"Lonnie," Tom heard through the phone. "Oh, "I'm sorry. I didn't know you were busy."

"It's okay, Renée," Lonnie said. "I'm talking to Tom and Abby. Would you like to say hello?"

"Hello," Renée said into the phone. "We're having a wonderful time. I wish you had come with us."

"Happy birthday," Tom said as Abby wrestled the phone from him.

Tom picked up his book from the nightstand, knowing Abby, Lonnie, and Renée would talk for at least thirty minutes. *May as well read a couple of chapters.*

Twenty minutes later, Abby hit the off button and handed the phone to Tom.

"You hung up?"

"Lonnie said Renée has something to discuss with her. Could be about her father. She'll call back."

"Great. I guess you won't be in the mood again until after that?"

"Maybe not even then. You might have missed your chance." She kissed him on the cheek as she picked up her book.

* * *

Forty-five minutes later, Tom's phone rang again. Tom hit on, then turned on the speaker. "Hey, Lonnie. It's been a long time since we talked."

"Yeah. Sorry to be calling so late. I just remembered we're two hours behind you."

"No problem. Abby and I have our books, reading before calling it a night. So, what was the big confab?"

"Renée threw me a curve, something I never expected. She asked if I'd move to Texas with her. She wants me to live with her and her father."

"She what? What would he think of that, not to mention his wife?

"Be serious. Tom, I don't know. Even if they approve, it's such a big jump. Renée means the world to me. I'm afraid," her voice caught, "I'm afraid of getting hurt again. Yet, I want to help her, and that would be one way to do it—wouldn't it?"

"Yeah, I suppose. But it's such a big step—a complete life change. I'm glad it's not me having to make the decision. Think it through, then do what you think is best."

"No. I want your advice. Don't skate on me. Abby, are you there? What would you do?"

Abby leaned toward Tom who held the phone out. "Every once in a while, my man comes up with the right thing. It doesn't happen very often, but when he's right, he's right. This is one of those occasions. All we can do is tell you we'll support you and Renée no matter what you decide. We love both of you."

Lonnie laughed. "You've been around a certain hardheaded Special Forces NCO too long. But I know you wouldn't butt in, and I appreciate it—really, I do. I have to make the decision on my own—well, mine and Renée's. I'll call you tomorrow maybe, or when I make up my mind."

The phone went dead, and Tom and Abby stared at one another.

* * *

Two days later, Lonnie called with her decision.

"I'm going to give it a try, Tom. That is, if Mr. Williams agrees. On one side, Renée is thrilled with the idea of living with her father, and on the other, she's scared to death. She says she won't go without me."

"Is she serious?"

"I can only take her at her word. She's young and vulnerable, eager to face the world, but afraid of the curves it will throw her. I mean, she hasn't exactly been wrapped in family love all these years."

"Lonnie, what you're offering Renée goes way beyond any experiences I've ever had. I only want what's best for you and for her. If you've made your decision, know that you have my support . . . and Abby's, one hundred percent."

"Thank you, Tom. That's what I decided. It won't be a permanent move. As soon as Renée is comfortable with her father, I'll come home."

"You're an angel, Lonnie."

After the call, Tom frowned, hoping things would work for the best, but proud of Lonnie for her decision. Then he sighed in relief and called Ken Dotson with the news, expecting Dotson to give him a pat on the back for his powers of persuasion. Instead, he heard, "That's wonderful. Proves one more time that coincidence is stranger than fiction."

"Okay, I'll bite," Tom said. "What are you talking about?"

"Thirty minutes ago, we closed the deal. Dear Ms. Barbara Louise Williams agreed to sell . . . oops, shouldn't use that word, should I? She reluctantly and with many crocodile tears agreed to relinquish custody to Renée's father. Of course, the size of the check helped assuage her grief. She is one major league bitch."

"For sure," Tom said. "Lonnie and Renée will be home in two days. Suggest to Mr. Williams that he be here when they roll in."

"Will do."

Tom hung up, a huge smile splitting his face. After a moment of reflection, he called Lt. Richards and brought him up to date.

Richards said, "I'm glad the girl and her father are reuniting. Hopefully, it will work and both will be happy. Not to worry though, I haven't finished with her mother. There may yet be something I can charge her with. The neighbors and folks from the school are opening up, and my investigator is hearing some interesting stories."

"Well, she'll have enough money to afford a top attorney. It would be ironic justice if she had to spend it all defending herself."

"True. The system sometimes gets it right."
* * *

A month later, outside the security queues at Fort Lauderdale International Airport, Tom shook Jim Williams' hand, hugged his wife, Debbi, then turned to Renée and Lonnie. "I want the two of you back here soon. You to visit, Renée, and you to stay, Lonnie. I am so fortunate to have you in my life. And Abby agrees with me. She had court today, or she'd be here mewling like a kitten."

"Don't go all squishy on me," Lonnie said. "You'll have me bawling like a *'cruit* in basic training." She engulfed him in a long squeeze and whispered in his ear. "Renée has been practicing what she wants to say to you. Let her speak. Don't interrupt."

Tom nodded as Lonnie stepped away.

"He's all yours, Renée. Don't let his ugly mug scare you. He's just a big teddy bear."

"Mr. Jeffries," Renée said in a tentative voice. "I . . . I can't think of any words to say how much I love you and Abby. If it hadn't been for you . . ." She looked at Lonnie, then her dad and Debbie, "I'd have never . . . never." She stopped and threw herself into Tom's arms, tears flooding from her eyes. "Thank you. Oh, thank you for giving me . . . giving me everything."

Tom held her for a moment, then pushed her out to arm's length and stared into her eyes. "As you grow older, you'll discover there is no giving without receiving. You may think you received, but you'll never know how much you gave Abby and me. Since I've known you, my whole outlook on life has changed. You're very special to me. All I ask is you have a wonderful life."

He turned Renée loose and gave Williams a mock glare. "If you don't take care of both of them, I'll find you." He broke the stare with a smile, which may or may not have been real. Tom wasn't sure which.

"Don't worry. I *will* take care of her . . . and of Lonnie. Debbi feels the same. I can never thank you enough for bringing my daughter home to me. Money is a poor measuring stick, but I've arranged for a transfer into your account. I'm doing the same for Ace and Kit. Without you three . . ." He turned his head, swiping a finger under his eye.

240

"Thank you, Tom," Debbi said. "You'll never fully understand what you've done." She rose on her toes and kissed him on the cheek. "You're my hero."

"Aw, pshaw, ma'am. 'Twarn't nothin'," Tom said with fake modesty. "Now, you guys better get in that line, or you'll miss your flight." He watched as Jim herded his brood into the queue, then stood by as they worked their way through security. A last wave when they cleared the scanners, and Tom walked away, feeling better than he had in a long time.

He drove to Abby's house in Palm Beach County and let himself inside. For some reason he couldn't finger, his mood had begun to sag. He went into the kitchen and removed two steaks from the freezer, figuring he'd throw them on the grill for dinner while Abby worked up a salad.

His cell phone rang. The caller ID brought a smile and a lift in his feelings. "Hey, Sunshine. How long till you'll be home?"

"I wish I'd let you beat the hell out of that son-of-a-bitch. He deserves that and so much more. If you'd killed him, I'd be celebrating." A sob interrupted her speech.

"Whoa. What? I'm not with you. Who are you talking about?"

"Rodriguez. The aptly misnamed *Angel* Rodriguez. That's who I mean. That rotten—"

"Slow it down and tell me what happened."

There was a moment of silence while Tom pictured Abby struggling to get herself under control. Then she said in a calmer voice, "The police just brought him in. He killed his wife. Beat her to death with a hammer."

THE END

Author Comment

Thank you for reading my THE RUNAWAY. If you enjoyed Tom's adventure, please watch for further adventures as he and Abby, each in his/her own way, battle crime in South Florida.

And, if you like South Florida adventures, read a sample of my Beth Bowman series and her zany group of cohorts.

I'd love to hear from you at RandyRawls@att.net. And, if you feel like posting a review on Amazon, I'd greatly appreciate it.

Happy reading.

Randy

www.ingramcontent.com/pod-product-compliance
Lightning Source LLC
Chambersburg PA
CBHW022004170626
46808CB00001B/283